CRIME CLASSICS

The Python Project

Also in the Crime Classics series:

CRIME CLASSICS

The Python Project

A REX CARVER MYSTERY

VICTOR CANNING

ABOUT THE AUTHOR

Victor Canning (1911-1986) was one of the most prolific thriller writers of the 1950s, 1960s and 1970s. Despite his output, his writing standards were very high and his books were enjoyed as much by critics as the wider reading public, garnering rave reviews. Among his most successful novels were those featuring wisecracking private investigator, Rex Carver. *The Python Project* is the third book in the series.

This edition published in the UK by Arcturus Publishing Limited
26/27 Bickels Yard, 151–153 Bermondsey Street, London SE1 3HA

Design and layout copyright © 2012 Arcturus Publishing Limited
Text copyright © Charles Collingwood, The Estate of Victor Canning, 1967

Cover artwork by Steve Beaumont, coloured by Adam Beaumont
Typesetting by Couper Street Type Co.

AD002456EN

Printed in the UK

ONE

Sunshine in a Shady Place

His name was Hawkins and I knew him very well. I'd worked for him – or his company, rather – on and off for the last five years. He was always embarrassed when he had a dubious client – as though it reflected somehow on the good name of his company, though I couldn't think why, because since they had been first established in 1870 they must have been gypped, swindled, and cheated hundreds of times. After all, that's what most people think insurance companies are there for.

'I'm not saying there's anything wrong about her,' he said, 'but I just get a feeling. If she'd been an old customer I wouldn't be so sensitive, but she only switched her insurance to us about six months ago. Yes, I've a very definite feeling about her.'

Usually when he had that sort of feeling he was right, and he always came to me. It was handy to have someone do your dirty work for you.

He slid a glossy photograph across the desk to me and it skidded fast and fell to the floor. I reached down and retrieved it and felt my arm muscles stiff from my last session with Miggs. The bastard had enjoyed himself for half an hour teaching me new arm-holds and throwing me all over the gym. You couldn't see more than a yard ahead for the dust from the mats when he had finished.

I looked at the photograph without interest.

'I don't want a job. I've made some big money lately and it's put me off work.' It always did. Besides, outside in Northumberland Avenue it was spring, the cock pigeons chasing the hens around, the cab drivers watching the miniskirts go by, and an icy wind coming up the street canyon from the river. I thought of golden sands, golden girls, golden nights in casinos, and wondered if they would do anything for the tired feeling I had in the mornings or whether just a bottle of the old tonic from the doctor up the road from my flat wouldn't be cheaper and more effective. Cheaper, certainly.

'What I want,' I said, watching Hawkins' moist, pebble-grey eyes on me, 'is a real lift. Salt in the blood. A different beat in the pulse. A sense of discovering a new man inside this weary old frame. Something you can't get from Ovaltine or Metatone but maybe from the Mediter- ranean. Certainly not from work. Not from chasing around trying to find out if some woman is trying to cheat your company over a jewellery claim. The odds are high that she is.'

I tapped the photograph.

'This is the most ghastly bit of Oriental bazaar work I've seen for some time.'

'It's Indian, seventeenth century, and it's worth about five thousand pounds. The eyes are diamonds, somewhere around fifty carats each, and each coil is studded along the whole length with emeralds. And the body-work is pure gold.'

'I still think it's vulgar. I don't want work. I want rejuvenation.' I slid the photograph back to him.

He fielded it with one hand, neatly, and flipped another photograph across with the other. For a moment there was the suggestion of a twinkle in his watery eyes.

'That's the owner,' he said. ' I brought it along because Wilkins said it was going to be difficult to get you off the ground. She's worried about you.'

'She always is. There's no pleasing her. Hard up or well off, she worries.'

I let the second photograph rest where it had skidded off the desk to the ground.

'You're lucky to have Wilkins,' he said. 'I'd give her a job any day at twice the salary you pay. I've written all the details of the owner on the back of that photograph. Incidentally, she's a widow and worth about a quarter of a million – and she's only twenty-seven.'

Just for a moment I felt a flicker of interest. But it died quickly. I just didn't have the blood count to boost my imagination into orbit.

Wilkins was right. Something was wrong with me and it was going to be difficult to get me off the ground. Wilkins was my secretary – and also a partner in Carver & Wilkins. She was thirty-five, spinster, and lived in Greenwich with her father, a retired ship's steward. She had red hair, blue eyes, no dress sense, and mostly thought nothing of me. She was zero to look at and I don't know what I would have done without her. She had a fiancé, a Swede who was a Suez Canal pilot, and saw him about once a year. I didn't think he represented any threat.

Hawkins said, 'Have a look at it. Or haven't you got the strength to pick it up?'

'Just,' I said. I reached down for the photograph. It was face down, the back covered with Hawkins' notes. The chair tipped a bit and I nearly went over. I came back to a level keel with the photograph, the right way round, a foot from my nose.

I didn't say anything. But somewhere inside me the motor turned over, fired, missed a few cycles, and then steadied to a quiet tick-over. I stared at the photograph, not hypnotized, but quietly, almost happily, absorbed. Somewhere inside me a thin trickle of adrenalin began to seep into the blood stream.

'This,' I said, 'is not a woman of twenty-seven.'

'Taken when she was nineteen. The year before she married. She used to do that kind of thing, professionally.'

'Judging by this, she did it very well. Where did you get it?'

'Sources. Interested?'

He stood up, which I thought was taking a lot for granted. He buttoned his overcoat and adjusted his neck-scarf, which was red with little white horses all over it.

'Could be,' I said.

'Good. Usual terms. I've left the company file outside with Wilkins.'

'Any particular line?'

He put the photograph of the Indian piece of jewellery on the desk. 'I think it was stolen, but not the way she describes it. Have a word with her. I'm sure you'll feel better when you have.' He nodded at the photograph in my hand. 'It's things like that which cheer up a dull world.'

'Personally, on a freezing day like this, it just makes me feel colder.' It wasn't true of course, but I didn't see why I should admit that his tactics had paid off. Since there isn't much dignity in my profession I had to cling to the little I could muster.

He looked at me, decided not to wink, and went out. Wilkins was in ten seconds later, carrying the company file. I was still holding the photograph in my hand.

She put the file on my desk, sniffed hard to keep abreast of the cold she had picked up three months before, and said, nodding at the photograph, 'Disgusting.'

'Absolutely. But maybe what I need.'

'For a reasonably nice person,' she said, 'you respond to the coarsest stimuli. Sex, alcohol, and gambling.'

'Thanks.'

She turned away, but when she got to the door she paused and cocked her head back at me. I knew all about that pause and half-turn of the head and waited for one hand to go up and touch her hair. Something was coming.

'Mrs Burtenshaw, my sister, will take over next Monday.'

'Christ!' It was out before I could stop it. At least some reflexes were working properly.

She gave me a chilly look.

'Sorry. Why is she coming?'

'Because I am going to Cairo, to be with Olaf. It's my annual visit.'

Olaf was the Suez Canal pilot. His other name was Bornjstrom, or something like that. I'd met him once and kept a very clear impression of a blond giant, about eight feet tall and three feet wide, who made the ground shake beneath him as he walked. Any ship he went aboard was in danger of capsizing unless he kept dead centre on the bridge. Whenever Wilkins made her annual visit her sister came and did for me. And there is no more accurate description. She was three times tougher and more efficient than Wilkins and I couldn't get into the office if there was the faintest whiff of beer on my breath. In my present low state of health she was all that was needed for my sister in Honiton to be able to collect my death insurance money.

'Think he'll pop the question this time?' I asked.

Wilkins changed the chilly to her basilisk look, and said, 'I suggest you read the file before you visit Mrs Stankowski.'

'That can't be her name.'

'Her late husband was a Pole who made a fortune from scrap-metal dealing. He had a thrombosis almost two years ago.'

'Couldn't stand the pace.' I looked at the photograph. The subject was clearly death to anyone with a weak heart.

'Before her marriage she was a Miss Freeman. Gloria Freeman.'

Eyes still on the photograph, I said, 'Gloria. It's just the name I would have chosen.'

'I find it, myself, rather common. Are you going to see her today?'

'If I can find the strength.'

Wilkins looked at her watch. 'That shouldn't be difficult. They've just opened.'

I went across Northumberland Avenue and into the public bar of the Sherlock Holmes.

Although it had only been open ten minutes, Dimble was there. Half an hour later and I would have had to go to the Chandos Arms. Dimble had a strict routine for the lunchtime session. Everyone who knew him, professionally, that is, knew it. At any time of the day during licensing hours it was possible to say exactly where Dimble would be, or be between being. He was doing the quick crossword in the *Daily Mail*, using a stump of pencil half an inch long. Dimble got the maximum use out of everything he possessed. When he struck a match he transferred the spent number into another box, saved the boxes and burnt them on his fire at night. He was a dedicated miser, about fifty, and never got crowded on a bus or the tube because he applied his miserly principles even to the matter of personal hygiene.

I bought a couple of Guinnesses and sat down two feet from him. I reached over and put one of the Guinnesses in front of him.

' 'Lo, Mr Carver,' he said.

' 'Morning, Dimble.' I raised my glass and drank to him. He looked at his and decided to save it for a while.

I put my glass down and passed him a photograph. Dimble's profession included knowing every fence worth knowing in London and having an unrivalled knowledge of the movement of stolen tomfoolery. Quite a big slice of my work was recovery and Dimble had worked for me often.

I nodded at the photograph. 'If you've seen that anywhere around lately I'm willing to pay for its return.'

He looked at the photograph without touching it and his face stiffened in Presbyterian disapproval. Then he edged it away from him with the tip of one finger and said, 'Contrary to most, Mr Carver – I have a higher opinion of you than that.'

I saw that I had given him the wrong photograph. Hastily I corrected the mistake. You'd be surprised how many people in Dimble's world have very old-fashioned ideas about women.

'Sorry,' I said. 'I meant this.'

Dimble picked up the other photograph and examined it. It showed the piece of Indian antique jewellery, an arm bracelet in the form of a coiled python. Stretched out straight, I suppose, it would have been about two feet long. Personally I don't go for snakes or for the snake motif in jewellery. I think both can bring you bad luck. Thinking that then, of course, I didn't know that I was casting my own horoscope for the weeks ahead.

'Haven't seen it around,' said Dimble. 'Leastways, not up until the day before yesterday. I'll ask and give you a ring.'

'Thanks.' I took back the photograph.

'Where would it have come from?'

I gave him Mrs Stankowski's address and he fished out a cheap notebook and wrote it down. He picked up his glass and drank carefully, timing himself for his departure for the Chandos Arms.

'How's Miss Wilkins?'

'Blooming.'

'Heart of gold that girl's got. Always sends me a Christmas card.'

'Once you're on the list, only death gets you off.' I stood up to go.

He cocked his head up at me and said, 'You didn't ought to carry that other photo round with you. Say you got knocked down and they went through your pockets? Look bad. I mean, at the hospital, and so on.'

I walked through the passageway under Charing Cross Station and got a taxi in Villiers Street. The cabby told me there was a sharp nip in the air and I gave him Mrs Stankowski's address.

I didn't believe in making appointments. That always gave people an hour or so to think about what they would say or not say. If she were not at home I could always call again. And again, and again, I decided, as I sat in the back of the taxi and studied her photograph. It was neither disgusting, as Wilkins had said, nor calculated to shock any doctor or nurse, as Dimble had suggested. It was just a reasonably modest study of a naked girl richly endowed by Mother Nature.

The cabby slid back the glass partition and from the corner of his mouth said, 'What you think of this business in China then? Old Mao and the Red Guards and seven hundred million of the little yellow bastards all trying to make up their kinky little minds which way to go. Some situation, eh? That's if you're interested in international affairs. Worry you stiff really, international affairs, I mean, if you thought about it.'

I always got the chatty ones. Always. Years ago I had decided that it was some sort of punishment settled on me by the gods and only they knew for what.

I said, 'The only thing worrying me at the moment is that you're going a long way round to get to my destination. That makes you a deviationist.'

He closed the glass partition and frowned at me in the driving mirror. I put Mrs Stankowski away and smiled back at him. Suddenly I realized that I was feeling better, only a little, but better.

Upper Grosvenor Street it was; a fourth-floor flat in a place called Eaton House. The door was opened by a maid, about thirty-odd, with a strong Scots accent and an unfriendly glint in her eye. I gave her my card and asked if Mrs Stankowski would be kind enough to see me about her recent jewel robbery. She said she would find out, not letting any hope slip into her voice, and shut the door on me. I stood in the narrow hallway that served the three or four flats on that floor and waited. A plump woman, cuddling a miniature poodle inside her mink coat, came out of one of the other flats and I reached out and punched the lift button for her. The poodle yapped bad-temperedly at me. The woman nodded bleakly at me, then kissed the beast on its muzzle and stepped into the lift. I felt unwanted. What was I doing here anyway, I asked myself? At the moment I had plenty of money, which was unusual for me; although I admit that you can't really have too much of the stuff or fuss overmuch about the way you get it. But the last thing I wanted at this moment was a job.

The flat door opened and the James Barrie character said something like, 'Will ye cum in the noo.'

I did, wiping my feet without being told.

I didn't pay much attention to the hall, which was about the size of a large pantry, except for a semicircular, marble-topped table with ormolu-crusted legs. I stumbled against this as a rug slipped under my feet and had to make a quick grab to stop a heavy eight-branched silver candelabra from going over. The Highland number frowned, not sure whether I was drunk or about to make a quick snatch-and-run.

The main lounge was very big, overheated, the air faintly laced with scent. The maid announced me and I looked around and made a quick inventory of the main features. Either side of the fireplace, on small tables, were a couple of porcelain lemon trees, the soft light gilding the yellow fruit. In a corner was a television set with the biggest screen I had ever seen. Next to it was a bar alcove, hard stuff on the lower shelf, a bottle of Chivas Regal rubbing shoulders with a Glenlivet, and the shelf above holding the biggest private collection of liqueurs and aperitifs I'd seen in a long time. The Slivovitz was half empty and the Strega Alberti unopened. The whole alcove was backed with mirrors and flooded with concealed pink lighting. I felt thirsty. The carpet was ivory and I could feel myself slowly sinking in it. Just off centre of the room was a low walnut table with some coffee-table books on it, and a centrepiece in silver of a benign Buddha holding one hand on his navel and looking as though he wanted, or had just taken, a dose of bicarbonate. At an angle to the window wall was a black-and-ivory-striped settee big enough to hold about six people and ensure that each had complete privacy. Sitting on this, her legs curled under her, and wedged up on either side with black-and-white silk cushions, was Mrs Stankowski. I had saved her until last, which was just as well, otherwise I would never have noticed any of the other things.

She was wearing a little jacket, collar high at the neck, which tipped her chin up slightly, and lounge trousers, the whole suit made of some silvery material. It was a perfect fit and looked as though it had been sprayed on to her. Her figure had matured a little over the last eight years but not to an extent that would prompt anyone to shout 'objection' to the stewards. She had red hair which made Wilkins' look like rust chippings from some old tanker, and it was short and curly and full of bright lights and must have cost her a packet every few days at somewhere like Vidal Sassoon's. She had blue eyes, cornflower blue; and it's not my fault if that's corny, because that's exactly what they were. In addition they weren't very friendly, but I wasn't worrying about that. It was just a challenge, and I realized there and then that that was what had been missing from my life for quite a while . . . challenge. Somewhere the adrenalin tap was turned on a bit more. She was the most gorgeous – no, glorious – thing I'd seen for at least two months. I gave her a warm smile and I could see that she thought nothing of it.

'Sit down, Mr Carver, and state your business quickly.' She pointed with a long ebony stick that had rested across her knees, to a small gilt chair by the fireplace.

I sat down, knowing the chair would stick to me when I got up.

I said, 'I've been employed by the London Fraternal Insurance Society to try and recover the gold python arm bracelet which was stolen from you.'

'I thought the police did that kind of thing?' She had a nice voice, a faint little gaspiness in it as though she suffered from a weak chest, though you would not have thought so looking at it. Somewhere, too, there was the echo of an accent, though I couldn't place it.

'The police rate of recovery is so low it hardly comes on to the graph. As you know, because you've been through it, they're very sympathetic, take down all the particulars and then – as you probably don't know – they go back to the police canteen for a quick one and forget all about it. So, insurance companies prefer people like me.'

'Why?'

'Because I get paid for the job and a commission on all recoveries. A sergeant-detective could recover the Cullinan diamond and still get only his pay packet and go on worrying about his hire-purchase payments.'

'The Cullinan diamond doesn't exist. It was cut up into one hundred and five separate stones.'

'It was a figure of speech.' But I was impressed, and followed it up. 'You know about diamonds?'

'A little.' The pale, creamy pink lips moved to something like a smile.

'Tell me,' I said, 'something about the Tennant Diamond.'

'It is a perfect yellow African stone measuring an inch by one and one-eighth inches. Sixty-six carats. But I'm not in the mood for quiz games. What do you want from me that I haven't already told the police?'

'With the greatest respect, the London Fraternal Insurance Society finds it hard to believe – though they would never say so, they leave that kind of thing to me – that while you and your maid were out someone entered this flat, using a key, walked off with a python bracelet from your dressing table, and took nothing else.'

'It might have been someone who specialized in Indian antiques. Just like these art robberies. They select what they want.'

'True. But why did they leave old Buddha there?' I nodded at the coffee table. 'He's antique enough. And Indian.'

'He's from the Tanjore district. Seventeenth century. But don't ask me why he was left, or other things. I'm not interested in the psychology of the thief. My bracelet was insured. I've made a claim for the loss. Just tell the company to pay me. The thing is perfectly straightforward. You don't think I'm lying to you, do you? Yes, or no?'

I'd had that kind of question before – mostly from women, too. Believe me, it's harder to answer than 'have you stopped beating your wife yet?'

Of course, there was no doubt in my mind that she was lying. The police weren't happy with her story, and neither was Hawkins of the LFIS. And having seen this place, I wasn't happy with it. There was a gold cigarette box on the side-table close to me, and plenty of other stuff around the room that any villain with an eye for tomfoolery would never have passed up.

'Well?' she said.

I stood up. Of course, the damned chair came with me. I prised it off and gave her a look full of confidence.

'I'm absolutely certain you're not,' I said.

'That's a very nice thing to say.' She was smiling.

'It took no effort.'

'But you only did it out of politeness.'

'*Noblesse oblige.*'

'Crap.' The underlying accent was stronger. I'm no Professor Henry Higgins, but I thought I could hear something North Country or Midlands in it. She raised her ebony stick and gave one of the cushions a whack. 'I only like people who tell the truth.'

I said, taking a chance, 'With looks like yours and a quarter of a million pounds, it can't happen often. You'll only hear what people think you want to hear.'

She gave me a long look, and said, 'Let's try again. Am I lying?'

'If I can recover the bracelet it won't matter either way.'

'Don't spare my feelings, Mr Carver.' She picked up my card which lay on a cushion at her side. 'Mr Rex Carver. Where the hell did you pick up a name like Rex?'

'I was told there was a two-week argument between my father and mother. He won. I've never forgiven him. I go round thinking I should have been a golden labrador. How come Gloria?'

'It's Gloriana, really. My father. He had a thing for Spenser. *Faerie Queene.*'

'Educated man.'

'Self-educated. He was an iron-puddler in a steel works at Scunthorpe. I think it was a puddler, anyway. He was a strict disciplinarian. Every Saturday night when he got back from the pub he used to beat my mother, me, and my brother.'

'Made for a quiet Sunday, no doubt. And coming back to the main point – yes, I do think you're being less than honest about the bracelet. Maybe it was stolen, but not the way you tell it.'

I began to move towards the door. If she could whack cushions with a wrist movement that Arnold Palmer would have admired, she could also throw things.

'Thank you.'

'Nothing to it.'

I put a hand on the door knob. It was a glass job with fancy brass filigree over it.

'Do you do anything else except recovery work for insurance companies?'

'Pay me the rate for the job and I do anything – except baby-sitting, unless they're above the age of consent

'Funny man.'

'Humour is the oil that—'

'Stuff it.' The accent was strong this time.

'As you say.'

'I do.'

'Goodbye, Mrs Stankowski – and thank you for sparing me the time.'

'It's the only thing I give away . . . usually.'

I inclined my head a few degrees, butler fashion, opened the door, and went out. I couldn't make out whether she liked me or not. Anyway, it wasn't a problem I was going to go to a psychiatrist about.

Outside the door, granite-faced 'Will-ye-cum-in-the-noo' was hovering. She steered me carefully past the semicircular marble hall table and opened the flat door.

I said, 'What's her problem? Thinking that nobody will love her, except for her money?'

She said, 'Ken this well, keep your gab steeket in guid company and gie your ain fish-guts to your ain seamaws.' At least, it sounded like that.

'You're dead right,' I said.

Dimble phoned just before five and said that nobody in the regular trade was handling a gold python arm bracelet at the moment. He would keep his eyes open and call at the end of the week for his money. I rang Hawkins and said that as far as I could tell – tell him, that was – Mrs Stankowski's story of the arm bracelet was on the level. He said what level? Knowing where that would lead, I pretended that the connexion was bad and rang off. Then I sat and thought a bit about Gloriana. Stankowski came too hard off the tongue. Her old iron-puddler of a father might have been a self-educated man, but so was I, having been to a Devon grammar school. '*Her angel's face as the great eye of Heaven shyned bright, and made a sunshine in the shadie place . . .*' Spenser. Well. I had an idea – which meant I was feeling better – that there were quite a few shady places about. If you were going to pick up a little cash or excitement there were no better spots than shady places. Cash, at the moment, didn't too much interest me – though that would come naturally if everything else was right – but excitement did. It was better than strychnine glycerophosphate (0.0025 gr) in the blood.

When I said goodnight to Wilkins she said, 'Try to be nice to my sister when she's here. She makes a great sacrifice to come.'

I said, 'Is she bringing that basset hound with her?'

'She has to, since there's no one to leave it with at home.'

I went on thinking about the long, mournful streak of dog. I'd be tripping over it six times a day and, since it favoured my desk chair, sitting on it even more often. I will say this for it, though – no matter what the indignity, it never bit. Just looked at me with sad, reproachful, blood-rimmed eyes.

I had a couple of whiskies in Miggs' office with him, on the way home. Behind his garage he had a small gymnasium. He had been a sergeant in the Commandos and for a couple of guineas a half-hour session gave workouts to a mixed clientele, and taught some of them how to kill a man with bare hands – twenty different ways – in twelve sessions.

'Manston,' he said, 'was in for a refresher today.'

'I hope he dusted the floor with you.'

'He did. He asked after you, health, finances, and sex life.'

'Tell him to keep away from me.'

Manston was an old friend of mine, though the friendship was usually in a bad state of strain. He worked in the same line of business, but in a much higher bracket. His monthly cheque came fat and regularly through the Treasury. He also knew thirty different ways of killing a man with his bare hands.

I took the Central Line home; home being a flat in a small street near the Tate Gallery.

Parked outside the house was a 1930 Phantom Two Rolls-Royce. It was ivory coloured and immaculate. There was a chauffeur, looking as though he were carved out of wood, behind the wheel. He wore a black uniform with tiny lines of white piping on collar and cuffs.

Mrs Meld, next door to me, and a great friend of mine, was leaning on her gate waiting for Mr Meld to come back with the supper Guinness in time to catch 'Coronation Street'. 'Gives a bit of tone to the place, eh?' she said.

'One of your rich relations?'

'The only one with money in our family is my brother Albert. He keeps a whelk stall at Southend and drives a Ford Consul. No, it's a visitor for you, Mr Carver. I let her in your place.' She winked at me. 'Don't do anything I wouldn't do. Not with a red-headed type. Otherwise you might be biffed over the nut with a bottle. She was carryin' one.'

TWO

Something Large and Bulky Fell Out

The flat consisted of a bedroom, a sitting room, a bathroom, and kitchen. From time to time, when I had had it, I had spent a lot of money on it. Mrs Meld came in and did for me in the mornings but somehow the place always looked untidy. From the sitting-room window, by risking a cricked neck, I could get a fair glimpse of the river.

When I went in there was no sign of Gloriana, except a new bottle of Vat 69 on the sitting-room table. I got two glasses and a soda siphon, and opened the bottle.

She came through from the bedroom, obviously the end of her tour of inspection, and said, 'Why on earth do you need such an enormous bed?'

'I sleep diagonally.'

I poured whisky into the two glasses.

'Water, not soda,' she said.

I went through into the kitchen for water and called back, 'Thanks for the present.'

'You seem to take it very much for granted.'

I came back with the water.

'It's happened before. People who change their minds sometimes bring a peace-offering.'

I fixed her drink and sat her in my best armchair with it. She looked good against the brown leather; red hair, a green tailor-made with mink collar and cuffs, and crocodile shoes. She smiled at me and then lowered the whisky in her glass in a way which would have made her old father proud of his daughter.

She said, 'How do you know I've changed my mind?'

I said, 'Where did you get the Phantom Two?'

'It was my late husband's. Jan was very fond of it and I've never liked to get rid of it.'

I said, 'Is it really a quarter of a million? It's important, you know, when it comes to fixing my fee.'

'Nearer a million.'

'Good. Now tell me about the bracelet.'

'You're a presuming bastard, aren't you?'

'I've been in this business a long time. I can read the signs like a Master Magi.'

'Magus. Singular. By the way, is the girl at your office always so cagey about giving your home address?'

'She can't get it out of her head that I'm now grown up and don't have to be protected. She's seen this, too.' I handed her the art photograph.

'Lord, those old things.' She reached down for the crocodile bag at the side of the chair and slipped the photograph in.

'Now, what about the bracelet?'

'It was taken, stolen, by my brother. So, naturally, I didn't want to tell the police that.'

'How did he manage it?'

'My maid – the silly old haggis – let him in when I wasn't there. She dotes on him. He took the bracelet and five thousand pounds in cash from my safe.'

I shook my glass to get the soda bubbles working again. 'He makes a habit of this kind of thing?'

'When he gets the chance. But usually only small things like the bracelet. Normally he writes within a week, sending the pawn ticket and apologizing.'

'And you get them out of hock and forgive?'

'Normally.'

'That's a lot of money to keep around the flat.'

'My husband said one should always have a substantial cash float, just in case. Jan was—'

'I get it. You fond of your brother?'

'Very.'

'Why should he steal from you, then? Why not just give him a handout occasionally? You could afford it.'

'I did. Sometimes a hundred, maybe five hundred, once or twice a thousand. But in the end I got fed up.'

'Tell me about him.'

'He's a dreamer. Not poetic. Big-business dreams, big schemes for making money. It always seemed unfair to him that I had so much from just marrying.'

I stood up, took our two glasses and began to refill them. 'Well, you're not going to miss five thousand or the bracelet. Equally clearly, this isn't one of the times when you are prepared to forgive – otherwise you wouldn't be here.'

'That's so.'

'Why?'

'All this happened two weeks ago. I haven't heard from him. I don't know where he is, and I'm worried about him.'

'Maybe for a bracelet and five thousand he reckons he should wait three weeks, perhaps a month?'

I handed her a drink and sat on the stool. She uncrossed and re-crossed her legs for comfort two feet from my nose. I had a controllable desire to reach out and run a finger over the right patella and tibia.

'But he's always been very punctilious.'

'It's a good word. But you wouldn't be here, bearing gilts, and with a touch of *Femme* by Marcel Rochas behind each ear, over a matter of punctilio.'

'I said I was worried. He's left his job and they don't know where he is.'

'Who are they?'

'He was a foreign correspondent for Intercontinental News Services.'

'Didn't he give them any reason?'

'They had a letter of resignation from him. It was written on Excelsior Hotel notepaper – that's Florence.'

'Was he based there?'

'No.'

'Well five thousand's a good reason for chucking a job. When it runs out he can get another. I don't think there's anything to worry about.'

'But there is. I'm absolutely sure that something has happened to him.'

'Sure is a very strong word.'

'That's why I used it. He's missed my birthday. That was four days ago. Ever since we both left home, no matter where he's been in the world he's always sent me a cable.'

'A man of fixed habits.'

'In some things.'

'You want me to find him for you?'

'Yes.'

'I'm expensive – particularly when it comes to foreign travel.'

She stood up. 'He's my brother. I don't care how much it costs.'

I stood up, slopping whisky over one trouser knee.

'I'll think it over and give you a ring in the morning. The cost, I mean. What's his name? Freeman?'

'Martin, yes.'

'Where did he hang out in this country?'

'He had a room in a Dorset Square hotel. The Mountjoy. I phoned them. He gave it up the day after he took the bracelet and the money.'

I cuddled my left palm under her right elbow and led her to the door. For a moment I thought of asking her to stay for dinner, poached eggs on toast, with a thin smear of Marmite on the toast, delicious, and a bottle of Spanish chablis. Then I remembered her flat and the ivory Rolls and decided against it. She'd think I was after her money with some homespun approach.

Her blue eyes frankly on me, her lips slightly parted, the length of her body slightly hipped out in a *Vogue* pose, she said, 'You will do your very best?'

I said, 'Yes – if you'll tell me what it really was that made you decide to come to me between the time I left your flat today and now. And no malarky.'

For a moment she said nothing. Then with a smile she said, 'I knew I was right about you. I have an instinct about people.'

'Come to the point.'

'Half an hour after you left I had an anonymous phone call from some man telling me not to worry about my brother.'

'Then why worry?'

'Because the last time it happened – an anonymous phone call, I mean – he got mixed up in some awful currency affair in France and only Jan's influence put it right for him. Jan was very fond of him. They got on well together.'

'Thank you for being frank with me. How many times has he been in jail?'

It took her ten seconds flat to decide not to give me a backhander, and then she said, 'Once – when he was twenty-five. He did two years for some . . . well, it was something to do with the City and share promotion. I told you. He's a dreamer, always after big money, big schemes. The trouble is he's hopelessly incompetent, really.' The smile flashed on. 'You will help me, won't you?'

'Absolutely. No matter how much it costs you.' I gave her my little butler bow and ushered her out.

I thought about her, all through the poached eggs and cheap chablis. And then I thought about brother Martin. Well, it all seemed straight-forward enough. I just had to find him. That should be simple enough. How simple can you get? Here was a case, I thought, which I could take just for health reasons; no escalation to the dangerous heights of the Secret Service world of Mansion and Sutcliffe, no excessive excitements – just find Martin Freeman. Somewhere – God damn it – somebody must have laughed at my innocence, knowing I was going to end up looking for another man, far more important than Freeman, a man who had been kidnapped – and for reasons which were to bring Manston and Sutcliffe down on me like a pair of hawks on a corn-fat dove.

Intercontinental News Services were around the corner from Fleet Street in Whitefriars Street. The weather had relented a bit and there were occasional strip-teasing gleams of spring sunshine. Walking the few yards from the taxi to the office, I thought I detected a suggestion of a new lift in my steps, something that in time might almost develop into briskness.

After a lot of delay and little cooperation I saw a Mr Addle who was the Office Manager. He lived in an office about the size of a big packing case. As I sat opposite him my knees almost touched his under the desk. His long grey face looked as though it had been moulded out of wet paper pulp and allowed to set hard. He had an absent look in his eyes and a rambling way of talking which suited me. All I had to do was nudge him now and again. I explained how Mrs Stankowski was worried about her brother and wanted me to trace him. Had he any views about the resignation?

His eyes wobbled, trying to focus on a point somewhere above my head, and he said, 'Not the first time he's resigned. Always comes back. Restless man, certain charm, though. Knew how to make friends and use people. Good at his job . . . well, good as most. Always trouble over his expenses, of course, but there always is trouble over expenses with all of them.'

'Did he specialize in anything, any particular field of news?'

'No. Anything he could pick up. Oh, well, maybe European political affairs more than most.'

'He'd been in trouble once, hadn't he?'

'Before he came to us. Impulsive, easily led. Always had some wildcat scheme for making a fortune. But then a lot of people have. You know, being Office Manager and responsible for staff . . . makes me a bit like a Father Confessor. Everyone comes to you with their stupid little confidences and problems. Particularly the secretaries and typists.' His eyes managed to focus briefly on me. 'Miss Lonelyhearts, that's me. Thank God I've only got another year to do. Got a bungalow down at Seaford. You can sit at the window and look out to twenty or thirty miles of nothing but sea.' His eyes wavered up to the wall a foot behind my head. 'Distance . . . lovely thing.'

'How was he on women?'

'Terrible, I'm told. But not here. I saw to that. Anyway, he wasn't here often. You should tell Mrs Stankowski he'll turn up. He's that kind. The turning-up kind.'

'Where was he based in Europe?'

'Paris, usually. Sometimes Rome. Beirut, too, for a while. Look, I can't tell you anything that'll help you trace him. He's just gone off.'

From Fleet Street I went round to the Mountjoy Hotel in Dorset Square. It was a quiet, modest place which could have done with a repaint job inside and out. Behind a little counter-fronted alcove which was the hotel desk sat a brunette of about thirty-odd, good-looking and pleasant, and with time on her hands. She was drinking coffee and reading a week-old *Observer* colour supplement. She looked up and gave me a bright, flashing smile full of false promises. Returning it in kind, so that we immediately became old and intimate friends, I said, 'My name's Addle. I'm the Office Manager of the Intercontinental News Services. And I want to make some inquiries about one of our correspondents – Martin Freeman – who used to live here.'

She nodded sympathetically and said. 'I'm Mary McCarthy, American novelist – but, of course, you know that – and I've taken this job to get material for a new book I'm writing. You don't have to go out of the door and come back and start all over again. You can do it from where you're standing.'

'You know Mr Addle?'

'He's been in Room Twelve for the last ten years. Martin Freeman came here on his recommendation. My real name is Jane Judd – yes, I know it sounds like a strip-cartoon character, but I'm stuck with it. Actually I *am* writing a book and it's called *Why I Sometimes Don't Like Men*. Subtitle – *Homo Hoteliens*. They think every chambermaid is a whore, or should be, and every woman receptionist is longing for escape to an illicit weekend. You're lucky I'm in one of my chatty moods. Yesterday you'd have found me glum and dumb.'

'Today's model suits me.' I dropped my card in front of her.

She glanced at it and said, 'I read about you once. In an old copy of *London Life* – a symposium on private-detective agencies in London.

All the magazines I read are old, left behind in their rooms by transients and regulars. What's that bastard Martin been up to and why has he left us?'

'Is your heart broken?'

'Chipped on one corner. I suppose he's been pinching from that sister of his again.' She held up a hand. 'This ring belonged to her once. Still does, I suppose.' It was a dress ring, a thin gold band with an oval-shaped piece of jade.

'She's cross with him this time. And he's given up his job. She wants me to find him. Any ideas? For instance' – I nodded at the small switch-board behind her – 'what about a list of phone numbers that he used to call?'

'We don't keep a record.'

Probably they didn't.

'Well, anything that could help me.'

'Maybe – if you could help me. Summer's just round the corner. I was looking at some super beachwear in Harrods the other day . . . I don't mean all the way, of course. But perhaps a contribution.'

I put two five-pound notes under the blotter on the counter. She stirred her coffee, looked up at me and I saw that she had gone glum. No smile. I slipped another fiver under the blotter. The smile came back.

'Martin Freeman,' she said, 'is a charming man, but potentially as crooked as Hampton Court maze. He never gave it any publicity, and certainly Mr Addle doesn't know about it, but he has a small place in the country.' She picked up a pencil and began to scribble on a tear-off pad. 'Don't run away with the idea of anything worth writing home about when I say "place". It's a crumby little cottage. Oil lamps and a chemical closet. Those were the things that put me off after two visits.'

She tore off the sheet and handed it to me.

'Thanks.' I gave her a genuine smile. 'One of these days I might get a small place of my own in the country.'

'Let me know sometime.'

'How long ago were you last at the cottage?'

She retrieved the fivers from under the blotter and began to put them in her handbag. 'Relations between Martin and myself have been very correct for the last year. I'm engaged to a PR man from Shell-Mex, but it doesn't inhibit either of us.'

'Thank you for your cooperation.'

'You *should* thank me. I refused it a couple of days ago to another man. He said he was from a hire-purchase company . . . something about a car Martin had bought. I didn't care for his manner. And anyway, Martin hasn't owned a car for all the years I've known him.'

'What did this man look like?'

'I kept on thinking of a well-beaten spaniel. Fifty-odd, shabby grey suit, mackintosh, and well-rubbed suede shoes. Brown eyes, thin wispy brownish hair, London-Scottish regimental tie, white silk shirt with the collar frayed, and his heart not really in his job, whatever it was.'

'You should have been in this business.'

'Let me know if you ever have a vacancy.'

I went out, thinking about the London-Scottish, beaten-spaniel type. Given a change of tie there were a lot of them about, and one of their characteristics was that they would never get anywhere unless they really believed that it was important to girls like Jane Judd that summer was just around the corner and Harrods was full of super beachwear.

The address on the sheet of paper read:

Ash Cottage, Crundale, near Wye, Kent.
Key under foot-scraper at back door.
Fire smokes when wind in north-east.
Drinks in cupboard under stairs.

Jane Judd was a girl after my own heart. There should be more of them around.

I phoned Mrs Stankowski and told her that I was doing some preliminary work on her brother and would call and see her the next day. She wanted to know what I had been doing, and what I still had in mind, so I pretended the line was bad and finally rang off. No matter how you get a quarter of a million, or a million, one of the things it does for you is to make you think that all your questions should be answered instanter. And let's face it, they usually are.

I called in at the office and had a ten-minute but not unreasonably acrimonious chat with Wilkins to put her in the picture. As I was going out to get some lunch she said, 'Well, at least this looks like a reasonably straightforward job.'

I said, 'In this business there is no such thing. Otherwise there wouldn't be any business. What about the chap with the London-Scottish tie? Debt-collector, or a divorce creep? Freeman been playing around? Or something really sinister?'

'I know which you would prefer.'

'Sinister? Why not? In my present condition any doctor would recommend it. Salt in the blood—'

'Don't start that.'

I had lunch in a pub, then went round to Miggs' place and borrowed a Mini-Cooper. An hour later I was in the green leaf and bare hop-poles of springtime Kent, going like a bat out of hell around the Maidstone by-pass, and convinced that it was better to hire a car and charge it up to expenses than to own one and spend daily misery in worrying over London parking places. I found Wye all right, but Crundale was more elusive because I was three times given explicitly wrong directions. It was half past four and a strong slanting rain, with a lick of sleet in it, was coming down when I got to Ash Cottage. At least, as near as I could get with the car. It was in a little valley, served by a dirt road that ended at a field gate. At the side of the gate was a wooden arrow stuck on top of a pole with the name – Ash Cottage – on the arrow and pointing up a low hill towards a beech wood. The cottage sat just in the lee of the wood. Coat collar turned up against the rain, I went up a muddy footpath for two hundred yards to the cottage. It was red tiled, wooden framed, with black timbers against white plaster, and had small diamond-lozenge window glass. A crack of thunder heralded my arrival. Behind me the footpath was becoming a coffee-coloured torrent. I took the key from under the foot-scraper, didn't dally to scrape my muddy shoes, and went in.

I found myself in the kitchen. Well, everyone says it's the most important room of the house, so why not enter through it? It was dark inside and I flicked on my torch and had a pleasant surprise. By the far door that led into the main part of the cottage was an electric light switch. I pressed it down and a light came on. Martin Freeman had had electricity installed since Jane Judd's last visit. I remembered then that there were poles all the way up alongside the dirt road.

Apart from being as crooked as Hampton Court maze, Martin Freeman was also untidy. The sitting room was large and comfortable, but there were old newspapers crumpled on the settee, and dirty glasses and an empty *vin rosé* bottle on a side-table. The open fireplace was a foot high with old wood ash and was decorated on one side with a pair of gum boots and on the other by an old cavalry sword which had been used as a poker. Against the window that looked up the hill to the beech wood was a dining table with a cloth half over it and, on the cloth, the remains of a breakfast set-up, yellow egg-spill congealed hard on a plate, and a paperbacked thriller propped against a Worcestershire sauce bottle. An open stairway ran up to the bedrooms. Round the newel post hung a pair of nylon stockings. Halfway up the stairs was an empty beer bottle with a faded red carnation stuck in it. I began to get a confused idea of Martin Freeman.

The main bedroom had a large double bed, unmade, covers flung back, the pillows crumpled. Over an armchair had been tossed a dressing gown, black with a white lightning-stripe motif all over it, and a red pyjama jacket. I found the trousers in the bathroom next door later. Just at this moment I was interested in a pile of letters, opened, that lay on the floor at the side of the bed. It was easy to tell that Freeman went down for his mail in the morning and came back to bed to read it. His procedure was clear. He opened an envelope, read the letter or contents, stuck it back in the envelope, and dropped it on the floor.

I sat on the floor and began to go methodically through the pile. The bottom one dated the accumulation as being four months old. Most of the stuff was bills – and all of the envelopes had been addressed to Freeman, care of Lloyds Bank Ltd, 50 High Street, Canterbury, and then redirected to the cottage from there. A January bank statement showed that he was £45. 11. 6 overdrawn. Sorting out what I hoped might be the wheat from the chaff, I was left with:

1. A New Year's card – postmark Firenze – inscribed '*Buon Natale e Felice Anno Nuovo.*' Signed: *Leon Pelegrina.* The message and name on the card had been printed and the name Pelegrina was struck through in ink just to leave Leon. Obviously Leon was a friend. The printed address in one corner read: 23 Piazza Santo Spirito, Firenze. Freeman's letter of resignation had been written from Florence.

2. A letter, only a few lines, from someone called Bill Dawson. It was on hotel stationery and in an hotel envelope – the Libya Palace Hotel, Tripoli, Libya. It was a month old, and read: '*Long time no see or hear. Tour out here extended another three months. What about it? Find some excuse. We could make Sabratha this time. And you could have your revenge on the Wheelus course. Additional incentive (?) the charmer is due in Uaddan next month sometime.*'

Well, if Freeman had taken off, it might be to Tripoli. Sabratha and Wheelus meant nothing to me. Charmer could be guessed at.

3. A statement of account rendered for £105. 7. *2* from a shipping and travel agency – Phs Van Ommeren, 118 Park Lane, London, W.1. I might be able to check with them whether Freeman had gone to Libya.

These were the only things that seemed to me might be of significance. There was plenty of other stuff – mostly from women – that no man of discretion would have left kicking about on the floor. However, it was clear – from the bank redirecting – that Freeman hadn't let any except very close friends – apart from Jane Judd – know about the cottage. I did a quick tour of the bathroom and the other bedroom and then went down to the sitting room. It was still raining outside and getting dark. I found the cupboard under the stairs. There was half a bottle of whisky there and a couple of bottles of soda water. I got a clean glass from the kitchen and fixed myself a drink. I sat down in an armchair and put the drink on a side-table. The ashtray on it was full of golf tee pegs, and lying face down by it was a small framed photograph. Tidy-minded, I stood it up. It was worth bringing out into the light. It was a photograph of a girl of about. . . well, not far off thirty . . . not that I was concerned with her age. She wore baggy Arabian Nights harem trousers, too diaphanous ever to keep out a cold desert wind, and two heavily sequined plaques over her breasts. On her head was a tiny turban with a large jewel at the front from which sprang a whisk of stiff horse-hair. She was slim, good-looking, and would have made the Sultan Schahriah's eyes pop. Scribbled in violet ink across the foot of the photograph was the inscription: For Martin – Paris 1966. Apart from being good-looking, she had a good face, interesting, intelligent, and something about the set of her lips, even in the posed smile, that said she was clearly on the ball. I couldn't make a guess at her nationality, but she was certainly not Arab.

I took a drink of my whisky, felt in my pockets – among the letters and stuff I'd taken from the bedroom – for my cigarettes, and had them out when a voice said from the direction of the kitchen door behind me, 'All right then, let us be very civilized about our behaviour.'

Before I turned I knew that he was not English. The French accent was as thick and meaty as *pâté de campagne*. When I did turn I found myself looking at the business end of what, later, I learned was a 9 mm Browning pistol, manufactured under licence in Belgium, at Herstal, by the Fabrique Nationale d'Armes de Guerre.

I said, 'Considering that thing you're holding, I think that remark applies to you more than to me.'

'I don't trust anyone.'

'It's a good rule-of-thumb procedure, but it still doesn't make you civilized. I hope you've got that damned thing on "safe"?'

'Naturally, Monsieur Freeman.'

For a moment my instinct was to disillusion him. Then I decided to play it for a while. He might say things to Monsieur Freeman that he would never say to Monsieur Carver. And when he did get the name I knew that he was going to pronounce it *Carvay*.

I said, 'I'm not going to give you any trouble. There's some whisky and a bottle of soda left. Get yourself a glass.'

He hesitated quite a while and then decided to accept the invitation. He put the pistol handy on a chair near the stair cupboard and began to help himself, managing most of the time to keep an eye on me.

He was a biggish man, about fifty, and with most of his weight around the middle. He had a nose in the de Gaulle class and rather close-set, worried little green-brown eyes. Fiddling with his drink, he made flappy, almost womanly, flutterings with his hands and kept on humming to himself as though to keep up his confidence. He was all wrapped up, untidily, in cellophane, or that's what it looked like, until I realized that he was wearing one of those transparent lightweight raincoats and a sou'wester kind of hat over his own cloth cap. Rolled up, the whole weather-protection outfit could be tucked away in a tobacco pouch. His drink prepared, he stood behind the chair on which his pistol rested and took a sip from his glass and, because of the way his eyes were, eyed me narrowly from above it.

I said, 'Why don't you take your wrappings off and sit down. You look as though you are collecting for the National Lifeboat Institution or something.'

He considered this, then put his glass down on the chair and began to slip his things off.

'Don't make any mistake, Monsieur Freeman. I am here on very serious business.'

He transferred his glass and pistol to the edge of the table and sat down on the chair.

'You'd better say what it is.'

'I'm from Monsieur Robert Duchêne.'

He waited for me to show surprise, but I didn't.

'Of Paris,' he said.

'You're French too, aren't you?'

'François Paulet. I'm surprised you are so phlegmatic, monsieur.'

'It must be the weather. And why are you from Monsieur Robert Duchêne, armed with a gun and dressed against all weathers?'

'Flippant, uh? It is an English characteristic, no? Oh, I know all about the English when I learn the language here many years ago. I was wine waiter, you know, at many restaurants. However, let us not bother with my history, considerable though it has been. From you I want what you have taken from Monsieur Duchêne. I have this' – he touched the pistol with a fingertip – 'because of the delicacy of the matter. My client cannot call in the police because, as you know, the things you have taken were not all legitimately acquired by him in the first place. Notwithstanding, it is my duty to recover them.'

'By force?'

'If necessary. And do not be misled by my docile appearance.'

'Perhaps you'd better tell me what I have to hand over.'

'Certainly.' He smiled, and it was quite a warm, genuine smile, touching and appealing. 'It is good that so far we talk amicably. All business should be like that. Everyone would finish more quickly and get more money.' He fished in his jacket pocket and pulled out a sheet of paper and slid it across to me.

I reached for the paper and unfolded it. It was a quarto sheet, typewritten, and read :

> Ancient Greek coins, the property of
> Monsieur Robert Duchêne, 2 bis Rue du Bac,
> Paris.
>
> Item – one Electrum stater of Lydia.
> Item – one Electrum stater of Ephesus.
> Item – one gold stater of Croesus.
> Item – one Daric of Persia.
> Item – alliance of Siris and Pyxus, two.

Item – Knossos with Minotaur and Labyrinth, two.
Item – stater of Thasos, two.

There were quite a few more items, twenty-two in all, finishing with:

Item – one, gold 100 litrae of Syracuse.

I said, 'These have been stolen?'

He said, 'You know they have, Monsieur Freeman. By you. And it was, if I may say so, a great abuse of hospitality. No doubt you thought that since Monsieur Duchêne had acquired them for his collection in ... a devious way ... that you would not be pressed to return them. Legally, I mean. But Monsieur Duchêne has employed me to recover them for him without the help of the law. I may say I am an expert at such matters. A large part of my business is the recovery of stolen goods.'

I said, 'Monsieur Paulet, take a good look at me. I'm in the same business. The name is Carver, Rex Carver, and I'm after Monsieur Freeman too, to get back stolen goods.'

He looked at me blankly for a moment or two.

Then he said, 'You are not Monsieur Martin Freeman?'

'No.' I took out one of my cards and flipped it to him.

He looked at it and his face fell.

'Carvay,' he said.

'That's right.'

'Not Freeman?'

'No.'

'*Merde!*' he said. 'Why do I always get things cocked up?' I really felt sorry for him. In disappointment he had a warm, collapsed human appeal.

'It was a natural mistake,' I said. 'I am in Freeman's cottage, drinking his whisky. I could have made the same mistake. Tell me – when did Freeman pinch these coins?'

'About two weeks ago. No, a little less.' He smiled suddenly and leaned forward and held out a big hand across the table to me. 'Monsieur,' he said as I took it, 'it is a pleasure to meet someone of my own profession on this side of the Channel. *Enchanté*. And what was it he has stolen from your client?'

He had a grip like a vice. I rescued my hand and shook it to ease the numbness. 'He lifted five thousand pounds and a piece of jewellery from his sister. You understand, I tell you this in confidence.' I could feel the old Gallic protocol taking over in me too.

'But naturally, monsieur.'

'How,' I asked, 'did you trace this cottage? Freeman never advertised it.'

'Haaaaaa!' It was a great gust of a knowing sigh and then he did something I hadn't seen done for years. He laid the index finger on his right hand against the side of his big nose and winked. I knew better than to probe a professional man further. Then he stood up and said, 'You have found many clues in this place?'

I waved my hand around and said, 'You're welcome to what there is. I'll have another drink while you look round.'

'*Merci*, monsieur.'

Ignoring me, he took a leisurely look around the room and then disappeared upstairs. I lit a cigarette and waited, and wondered what there was in Freeman that made him go for antique stuff, jewellery and coins. Nothing that sprang from a genuine love of the past and its craftsmanship I was sure. He was just after cash. And then I thought about François Paulet. He was a likeable number. But in my profession to keep an overdraft down you had to have more than likeableness. There was a touch of music-hall about Paulet and a self-confessed habit of getting things cocked up that marked him out for the lower rungs of the hierarchy.

He came downstairs after a while, looking shocked, and shaking his head.

'*Mon Dieu!*' he said. 'It is incredible. To have affairs of the heart is natural. But to leave the evidence lying on the floor at the side of the bed for the world to see. No Frenchman would do such a thing.'

'Nor many Englishmen.'

'But some of them were clearly married women. Why' – his face cleared suddenly – 'there is enough material there to keep a blackmailer happy for life.' Then he frowned. 'It is a good thing that you and I are honourable men.'

'Personally,' I said, 'I've never ceased congratulating myself about it.' I stood up.

'You are going?' he asked.

'Back to London.'

'You could give me a lift?'

'How did you get here?'

'I am by train to Ashford. Then a bus. Then I walk.' He smiled and my heart went out to him as he went on, 'Monsieur Duchêne is not generous in the matter of expenses.'

'I'll give you a lift back to London.'

'Thank you.'

He followed me into the kitchen and then paused and nodded to a door at the far end. 'What is in there?'

'I haven't examined it because I know. It is the chemical closet.'

The toilet?'

'Yes.'

'Ah – then I will use it before our journey.'

He went over and opened the door. I must say that for a big man he was quick on his feet. As he pulled the door towards him something large and bulky fell out, and François did a backward jump of three feet.

I went to his side and looked down.

'*Merde!*' he said. 'Is it Freeman?'

'No.'

'Who is it then?'

'I don't know. Freeman is in his thirties. This man is much older.'

'He was propped on the seat, his head against the door. So when I open it – out he comes, *bim*!' Paulet sounded a bit scared.

I didn't think I had to make any comment. I knelt down by the man. I'm no expert but it was clear from the markings on the neck that he had been strangled manually. *Rigor mortis* had set in completely, so he had been dead for anything between twelve and twenty-four hours

– after this *rigor* begins to pass away. I went through his pockets, but either he carried nothing on him or someone had cleared them after his death.

Behind me, Paulet said, 'What is to do? I am in a strange country and do not wish to be involved in this kind of thing.'

'Nor me,' I said, standing up. 'We'll just go quietly away, and I'll phone the police anonymously on the way back to London.'

I looked at Paulet. He was very much shaken.

'I think,' he said, 'with an effort I shall not be sick.'

I went to the back door and opened it, letting him pass me.

'For a man who carries a gun around, I should have thought this kind of thing meant nothing to you.'

He glanced back at me indignantly. 'But that is for show. It is never loaded.'

We slithered down the muddy path in darkness and a thin drizzle to my car. All the way I was thinking of the man lying back in the kitchen. He wore a London-Scottish tie, a shabby grey suit and well-rubbed suede shoes. Even in death he maintained his beaten-spaniel look.

THREE

Neanderthal Man with Azalea

I phoned the Ashford police at a call box just outside Maidstone. Later, I dropped Paulet at the Strand Palace Hotel where he was staying.

He hadn't said a great deal on the drive to London. The sight of the dead man had shaken him. I went in and had a drink with him and he brightened up a bit. I think it was the sight of the waiters and being in an hotel. He was reminded of his old life.

I said, 'You should have stuck to the hotel business.'

'Yes, often I think that. Between ourselves, too, I made more money. You think Martin Freeman killed this man?'

'He might have done. But somehow it doesn't seem to be his style. Anyway, one thing I'm pretty certain about is that Freeman's not in England. He wrote a letter of resignation to his firm from Florence.'

'I think tomorrow I go back to Paris.'

'I should do that. If you like you can tell Monsieur Duchêne that if I ever catch up with Freeman I'll try and do something about his antique coins.'

'Thank you. And if you come there, look me up.' He handed me a business card.

The next morning from the office I phoned Gloriana and made an appointment to see her at twelve. I handed Wilkins the Bill Dawson letter and asked her to check on Sabratha, Wheelus, and Uaddan. You never knew when you might not pick up some small lead. I also gave her the Phs. Van Ommeren bill and asked her to check with them what travel arrangements they had made for Martin Freeman. When she raised an eye at this I said, 'Tell them you're speaking from the Intercontinental News Services, and it's a question of checking for his expense account. Freeman worked there.'

When she had gone I sat and stared at the wall calendar. It didn't help me beyond announcing that the day was Thursday.

Why, I asked myself, had old London-Scottish tie been strangled in Freeman's cottage? Clearly – according to Jane Judd – he had been looking for Freeman and was using a thin cover story. I thought – from his condition – that he had gone to the cottage the day before I had, and met someone who resented his presence. Really resented it, too. I resented his presence too. If the police ever discovered that Paulet and I had been there, we should both be in trouble. I was used to being in trouble with the police, but Paulet didn't strike me as the type who would handle it very well.

Thinking of Paulet, I began to go over the Duchêne antique coin angle. That sounded like Freeman, all right. Any stuff his friends left lying around he felt free to pocket. Paulet hadn't put a price on the antique coins. But at the moment Freeman had five thousand in cash from his sister, a python arm bracelet worth another five thousand, which made him ten thousand pounds in funds, plus the value of the coins which would be . . . well, I didn't know. Not knowing always irked me. I got up and went over to the low wall bookcase by the door.

Wilkins, when we had been flush once, had spent over a hundred quid on reference books, most of which we had never used. Some had never been opened. I pulled out Volume 16, MUSHR to OZON, of the *Encyclopaedia Britannica*, and looked up the article on Numismatics. Perhaps I would get some idea of the value of the coins from that.

I didn't. But I got something else. A shock. Leafing through the article I stopped at the first photographic plate. It was a full-page illustration of Ancient Greek coins, photographed by courtesy of the Trustees of the British Museum. Each set of coins, reverse and obverse, carried a number. There were twenty-two sets illustrated. Below the illustrations a legend was set out referring to the numbers. I began to read through this and before I had finished the first line a bell began to ring. The line went: i. Electrum stater of Lydia. 2. Electrum stater of Ephesus. 3. Gold stater of Croesus. 4. Daric of Persia.

I read right through and by the time I reached number twenty-two I was certain. It read: 22. Gold 100 litrae of Syracuse.

The list of stolen coins which Monsieur Duchêne had given old Paulet had been copied straight out of the *Encyclopaedia*. For my money – none of your antique Greek stuff – it had to be a phoney. I've had a few startling coincidences happen in my life, but this certainly wasn't one. Either Duchêne had given Paulet a phoney list and a phoney story to go with it, or both of them knew it was phoney. I considered the possibility of Duchêne stringing Paulet along, and then I considered the possibility of Paulet knowing the list was phoney. He seemed simple, straightforward, and a little more than inefficient. Well, that kind of act would make a good cover for whatever it was he or they wanted to cover.

I picked up the phone and called the Strand Palace Hotel. Lunch with Paulet might help to sort things out. After some hanging about, the hotel people told me that Paulet had booked out that morning.

Wilkins came back in while I was still getting nowhere.

'Sabratha,' she said, 'is the site of an ancient Roman town thirty-odd miles to the west of Tripoli.'

'It could be,' I said, 'that what is wanted on this job is an archaeologist.'

'Wheelus is the American Air Force base to the east of Tripoli. Wheelus course refers to the golf course which the Americans have built there. It's called Seabreeze.'

'Original name.'

'Uaddan,' said Wilkins, 'is the name of a hotel, which also has a casino, in Tripoli.'

'And what about the Van Ommeren people?'

'They were very helpful. Some of the account is a carryover from old travel charges, but the bulk is for air-booking from London Airport to the King Idris Airport, Tripoli. Via Rome.'

'Date?'

'He bought the ticket over a month ago and had the date left open, saying he would make his arrangements direct.'

'He must have broken his journey and gone to Florence.'

'Van Ommeren say they would be glad to have Mr Freeman's present address.'

'I'll put them on the list. When do you go to Cairo?'

'Monday.'

She moved to the door.

'Until you go – and leave a note for your sister to watch it afterwards – I'd like any press cuttings you can pick up of the discovery of the body of a man strangled to death, at Ash Cottage, Crundale, near Wye. That's in Kent.'

Wilkins looked at me. That's all. Just looked.

Gloriana mixed me a large dry martini which I sipped at gently over the next twenty minutes in order to avoid having the top of my head blown off. She drank lime juice with soda.

She had her place of honour on the large settee, one leg curled up underneath her. She wore a short blue woollen dress and a gold band around her hair. On my way in the taxi I had debated with myself what I was going to tell her. Usually I like to keep a little up my sleeve for a rainy day. However, by the time I had the martini glass in my hand, freezing my fingers off, I'd decided to give her the truth. By now I was quite sure that there was something wrong with all this Freeman business. And let's face it, because of my low iron and vitamin content I welcomed it. I was beginning to feel that maybe life still had something to offer. It's instructive, too, to lay the truth out for people. Not all of them can control the reactions they would like to control.

She listened carefully as I went through the story, every detail, and I watched her carefully. The only thing I saw of interest was the gentle swinging movement of one long nylon leg over the edge of the settee.

I finished, 'Any comments?'

She considered this for a moment, then said, 'Only that he seems to be getting himself into the dirt again. And I'll have to get him out.'

'Got a photograph of him?'

'I'll give you one before you go.'

'Would he murder a man?'

'No.'

'Bill Dawson – know him?'

'No.'

'Did you know about the country cottage?'

'No.'

'Did he ever mention any girl in Paris, probably a cabaret type? Favours Oriental gear.'

'No.'

'We're doing well. What about Leon Pelegrina who sends him a New Year's card from Florence?'

'No.'

'Tripoli – has he been there before to your knowledge?'

'Yes.'

'That's better.'

'He showed me something he did about a year ago. Some feature article which his firm placed with one of the Sunday papers. It was about the oil industry in Libya. I didn't read it.'

'Do you have any ideas about Monsieur Duchêne with his phoney list of antique coins?'

'No.'

'And you've never heard of François Paulet?"

'No.'

'And this strangled type in the cottage. From my description, does he seem to fit anyone you know?'

'No.'

'We're back on the old negative routine.'

She said, 'I know very little about my brother or his circle. That's why you're here. I want you to find him.'

'Well, one thing I'm pretty sure of – he's not in this country. How do you feel about footing first-class travel expenses all over the place? And my fee?'

'What is your fee?'

'It might be a long job, so I'll give you the monthly rate which comes a little cheaper. One thousand pounds a month.' I pitched it very high.

'That's all right.'

It's nice to be rich.

'My secretary,' I said, 'is flying on Monday to Cairo to spend a holiday with her fiancé. She could go via Tripoli, spend a few days there and check whether your brother is around. I'd only charge you half expenses for that since she's going out to Cairo anyway.' Wilkins always paid her own fare so there was no reason why I shouldn't do her some good. Whether she would take it on, of course, was another matter.

Gloriana nodded, and said, 'And what are you going to do?'

'The police', I said, 'are going to find that body in the cottage. I thought I'd hang about for a day or so to see if they issue an identification. Could help. Then I'd like to see Monsieur Duchêne in Paris, and then Signore Leon Pelegrina in Florence. After that I'll play it by ear, according to whatever my secretary turns up.'

'That seems reasonable. But I'd like you to keep in touch with me. You can always phone. I'm usually here between seven and eight at night.'

'I was hoping you wouldn't be tonight.'

'Why?'

'Because I was hoping you'd have dinner with me. I've got a much better suit than this at home. And I won't let you down with my table manners.'

She smiled, which I hadn't expected, and said, 'Just for the pleasure of my company?'

'Absolutely. I won't give a thought to the million stacked up behind it.'

'I'd be delighted. Would you like another martini?'

'Not unless you and your maid are prepared to carry me to the lift. I'm a whisky man, really.'

She nodded understandingly. I got up, patted the antique Buddha on the head, gave her my little bow and went, saying, 'I'll pick you up just after seven.'

In this business it is important to establish cordial relations with clients. It gives them the feeling that you have their interests exclusively at heart. It has other side-effects too – not always pleasant.

*

I had trouble with Wilkins. I knew I would. She was very much a creature of habit. This was her holiday. Why should she spend it working?

'All right. You can add an extra week to your leave. And don't forget you'll be getting your expenses.'

'But Olaf wouldn't like me to be alone in a town like Tripoli. He fusses, you know.'

The idea of anyone fussing over capable Wilkins was novel – but who was I to argue? I know what love can do to people.

'You'll probably be safer in Tripoli than you are in Greenwich. But if you want the anxious Swede to stop from worrying ask him to join you there. It must be less than an hour's flight from Cairo. All you have to do is send him a cable, fix rooms at a Tripoli hotel – and I suggest the Libya Palace – and change your air ticket. I tell you this Stankowski thing could be a big job. With luck I can string it out to a month. That means a thousand quid in the bank and you could have that electric typewriter you want.'

'Well . . .' It was very grudging, but I knew that I had won.

'Thanks. Anyway, you ought to do more field work. You're miles better at it than me.'

She liked that. Not that it was news to her. She had a firm conviction that she was miles better than me at everything, except a few activities which anyway she wouldn't have touched with a barge-pole.

After that I went round to Miggs' place and fixed up for a chauffeur-driven Rolls for the evening. He gave me tea out of a quart-sized enamel mug, a five-minute dissertation on the state of the second-hand car market owing to the Labour Government squeeze, flipped to a quick run-down of the present state of the Roman Catholic Church and its attitude to the Unity of Christian Churches, which – if he'd had it printed – would have gone on the Index right away and which, since he was a Catholic, didn't surprise me because they're always the best value when it comes to running down their religion or making jokes about it, and finished by asking what the hell I wanted a Rolls for.

'I'm taking a million out to dinner. Name of Stankowski, Mrs, widow, formerly Gloriana Freeman. I'm looking for her brother.'

'If that was the Stankowski who was in the scrap-metal business, watch out that she isn't like him. He was as bent as a bedspring.'

Going down the stairs, I ran into Manston at the bottom, arriving for another work-out with Miggs. He was wearing a bowler hat, dark suit, and carried a rolled umbrella, and he looked as usual like a coiled steel spring, and God help you if you were in its way when it went *zing*!

He said, 'Busy?'

'Moderately.'

'We could always give you a job. Permanently, if you like.' 'We' meant his Service, and occasionally they had roped me in to work for them and not once had I spent a happy moment on their payroll.

'I like a quiet life.'

He grinned. 'You're getting old. Sluggish too, I'll bet.'

As he spoke he raised his umbrella and swiped at the side of my neck with it. I ducked and let it go over my head. Then I went forward and got my right shoulder under his raised right arm, grabbed his wrist and let myself fall back so that I could use his moment out of balance from the umbrella blow to send him over my shoulder. It should have worked, would have done with most people, but in some odd way I found myself spun round, my face pressed against a wall and my right arm twisted up behind my back.

Still holding me, he said, 'You used to be better than that.'

'You've got it wrong. You used not to be so good.'

He released me, straightened his Old Etonian tie, and then offered me a cigarette. I lit it with a shaking hand. He saw the shake and said, 'You've been leading too sedentary a life. You really should join us and see the world. Also you get a pension at sixty.'

'Send me a telegram,' I said, 'the first time any of your blokes lives long enough to qualify for one.'

As it was a nice spring evening I walked part of the way home, from Lambeth Bridge along Millbank and past the Tate Gallery. The sky was an even duck-egg colour, and the tide was coming in fast, making up towards Vauxhall Bridge, an even brown-soup colour. A handful of gulls hung over it, scavenging. I had a growing feeling that any moment now I might feel good to be alive.

Mrs Meld was hanging over her front-garden gate, taking the air, and watching her dog take its hundred-yard evening stroll down the pavement.

'Evening, Mr Carver.'

'Evening, Mrs Meld.'

She jerked her head upwards to my place. 'You're going it a bit, aren't you?'

'You've got to be clearer than that, Mrs Meld.'

'There's another one up there.'

'A woman?'

'What else?'

'Why do you let them in?'

'What you told me, weren't it? Women can go in – not nobody else. Want to alter it, Mr Carver?'

I thought for a moment and then shook my head.

It was Jane Judd. She was wearing a light raincoat and yellow beret and was standing at the window, watching Mrs Meld who still stood at her gate.

'When that woman speaks about you,' she said, indicating Mrs Meld as I went and stood at her shoulder, 'there's reverence in her voice. Also I got the feeling that she would have liked to search me to see if I had any hidden weapons.'

'Have you?'

'Only this.'

She handed me a copy of the *Evening Standard*.

I said, 'Let's have a drink before we settle down to the crossword. And anyway I haven't got much time. I've an appointment at seven. So chat away. I presume this isn't a social call?'

'No. It isn't. I just decided that I'd been less than honest with you.'

'Don't worry about that. It puts you in the main category of my visitors and clients. Gin or whisky, or a glass of white wine?'

'Whisky. Straight.'

I poured it, straight and generous. She was putting on a good act but there was the suggestion of a shake somewhere in her voice.

'How did you get my address?'

'I phoned Mrs Stankowski.'

'And she gave it to you, just like that?'

'She did when she heard what I had to say.'

'Then let me hear it.'

She sat down on the arm of a chair and toasted me briefly with the whisky.

'I should have told you that Martin Freeman is my husband.'

I said nothing, letting it sink in. This Martin Freeman was quite a number. The more I learned about him, the more intrigued I became.

She said, 'You don't seem surprised.'

'Oh, I am. But I've learned not to show it, otherwise I'd be going round all day with my eyes popping. Why don't you wear a ring?'

'It was a secret wedding, nearly two months ago, at a registrar's office. In Acton.'

'Nice spot. What about the fiancé? PRO at Shell-Mex?'

'He doesn't exist.'

'Why did you get married?'

'On an impulse.'

'No question of love?'

'Oh, that. Yes, I suppose so. But chiefly, well . . . I like him. He's charming. Good company. Makes a woman feel good and pleased with herself. And I was tired of hotel work and just the odd dates that don't develop beyond a tatty weekend in the country. I'm thirty-five, you know. You begin to think about security, home, kids. God, it sounds conventional, but that's what all women are at heart.'

'Freeman doesn't sound the security-giving type. Pinching from his sister, and a few others; a spell in stir for some City company swindle. I wouldn't have thought you'd have been taken in.'

'I'm impulsive. That's why I'm here. I trust you.'

'Carry on then.'

'He said he was on the point of a really big deal. Something that would make his fortune. The idea was to keep the marriage secret. He didn't want publicity and he might have got some. He's a bit of a name in Fleet Street. He told me he was going off for two or three months, but he would send for me. We'd live abroad for the rest of our lives.'

'Where?'

'He didn't say. I was just to trust him and wait for his call.'

'Well, why not carry on and do that?'

She got up and helped herself to another whisky.

'Because, frankly, I'm frightened. For two reasons.'

'Number one?'

She nodded at the *Evening Standard* on the table at my side.

'I've put a mark around a news item in the paper.'

She had. It was on the back page. Just a few lines, announcing the discovery of the body of an unknown man, strangled, at Ash Cottage, Crundale, near Wye in Kent.

I said, 'He was in the chemical closet when I got down there. The type with the London-Scottish tie.'

'God.' She breathed the word quietly but there was all the feeling in the world in it.

'You don't like being mixed up in murder? Particularly if you fancy Freeman might be involved?'

'You're bloody right.' There was a flash of the forceful, competent manner I'd known at the hotel.

'Point number two?'

She hesitated, took a sip of her whisky, and then said, 'This afternoon I had a phone call at the hotel. Some man, foreign, I think, who wouldn't give his name, but said he was a close friend of Martin's. He said that if I heard in any way that Martin was dead, I wasn't to believe it. He was speaking for Martin, and said that Martin would, as he promised, eventually send for me.' She looked hard at me. 'I really am frightened, you know. I don't want to get mixed up in anything . . . well, as I said, one of the chief reasons for marrying him was this security business. But I don't want that at any price.'

'So you came to me?'

'Who else? I mean, you struck me as being a decent sort. You're already looking for Martin ... I just had to have someone to tell this to.'

'You told all this to Mrs Stankowski?'

'No. Only that I was married to Martin. What am I going to do?'

'Go home, take three sleeping pills and get a good night's sleep.'

'But what about the police?'

'If they get round to you – about the cottage, I mean – then tell them everything you've told me if you want to be out in the clear. Mind you, if you're stuck on waiting for Martin Freeman to send for you, then you'll have to make your own decision how much you tell.'

'And do I tell about you?'

'Why not? I didn't murder old London-Scottish, and I'm just trying to trace Martin Freeman. However, if they happen to catch on fast to you, you might stall mentioning me until after midday tomorrow. Not that I think they will be so fast.'

'Why midday tomorrow?'

'Because I'm going to Paris on professional business and don't want to be delayed.'

I stood up and took her arm and led her to the door.

'Don't fuss. You've done nothing wrong. Just speak the truth and shame the devil. And anyway, you'll have a new wad of material for the book *Why I Sometimes Don't Like Men*.'

She paused at the open door, smiled and just touched my arm.

'You're a good guy. Thank you.'

'If you get time, put that in writing and sign it. I'm often in need of a reference.'

She grinned, adjusted her beret with that nice little movement women have with hats, and I knew she was recovering fast. Then she held something out to me.

'Would you let Mrs Stankowski have this sometime? You needn't say where you got it.'

I had the gold ring with the jade stone in my hand.

'I'll give it to her tonight,' I said.

*

I didn't. I drove, or rather was driven, in the Rolls around to Upper Grosvenor Street just after seven. I wore a midnight-blue dinner jacket, onyx cuff-links my sister had given me, and one loop of my back braces was held on to my trousers with a safety pin because the button had gone.

I went up in the lift feeling like young Lochinvar coming out of the West – SWI, actually. This Freeman thing was developing nicely along the therapeutic lines I needed. Could be, too, that there might come a moment when in addition to my Stankowski fee, there might be a chance to pick up some side money. Oh, yes, I was recovering fast.

The Scots number on opening the door to young Lochinvar soon put paid to any nonsense about so faithful in love and so dauntless in war, and she didn't care a damn that through all the wild Border his steed was the best. She'd have known the Rolls was hired anyway.

She put a photograph in my hand.

'I'm to give you this and her apologies for being called away for the evening.' That's a translation. I worked it out while looking at the photograph – of Freeman – which I'd forgotten to take with me that morning.

'Where's she gone?'

'The devil knows. I'm not told anything in this house.' Practice made the translation of that faster.

I went back down in the lift, wondering if it were some other man, some laggard in love and a dastard in war. Frankly, I didn't care over much. Gloriana was high-flying game, too high for me in my present off-peak condition.

I got in the Rolls and had the chauffeur drive me around for an hour. Then I went home, opened a tin of ox tongue, made myself some sandwiches and coffee and sat and contemplated a bunch of mimosa that Mrs Meld had arranged in a vase on the sideboard. I considered Freeman.

For my money he was too impulsive, too careless, too given to friends making anonymous phone calls about his welfare ever to last long in the big league. He might, with luck, get away with some small racket. But I didn't read his character as closed, discreet, and contained enough to engineer anything that would give the forces of law and order more than a temporary headache.

I was in the office the next morning at half past nine – early for me. In the outer office Wilkins said, 'I've got a hair appointment at half past ten. Is that all right?'

I nodded, hoping it would be, though what anyone could do with Wilkins' hair I couldn't imagine.

She went on, 'When I got in this morning I put a call through to the Libya Palace Hotel in Tripoli.'

'Why?'

'Because I don't see why Olaf and I should go there if a simple query could be settled by a telephone call.'

'Freeman?'

'Yes. They said there was no one staying there of that name.'

'He could be at some other hotel. What about the Uaddan?'

'I've got a call booked through to them. If it comes while I'm out you can take it.'

'He might not be using his own name.'

I tossed the Freeman photograph on to her desk. She examined it and handed it back. She had a trained memory. If she ever saw Freeman now she would recognize him.

I said, 'See if you can get me a booking on an afternoon plane to Paris.'

She nodded and then handed me a newspaper cutting. It was the paragraph about the dead man at Freeman's cottage.

'Why,' she asked, 'does everything you touch start getting involved and unpleasant?'

'Which part don't you like? The involvement or the unpleasantness?'

She didn't answer, because at that moment the telephone began to ring. I went into my office. She came in ten minutes later and said, 'That was the Uaddan Hotel. I got the same answer. No one called Freeman known to them. And Mrs Stankowski is outside, wanting to see you.'

'Show her in. Don't forget that Paris flight.'

Gloriana was wearing a beautifully cut black silk suit, a mink wrap round her shoulders, a tiny little black hat with a black veil that came just below her eyes, and a different scent. She sat down on the other side of my desk and I reached over and lit a cigarette for her. The pearls round her neck were as large as fat garden peas, all perfectly matched, and evidence of the handsome profit margins in the scrap-metal business. One day, I promised myself, when I got tired of the high excitement of the struggle for existence, I would find a young, rich widow – beautiful, of course – and marry her.

I said, 'You broke two things last night. My heart and a dinner engagement.'

'Crap.' All of old Scunthorpe was in the word. But she said it with a smile.

'What happened?'

'At half past six a car called for me. It was from the office of the Lord High Treasurer.'

'Sounds like something out of Gilbert and Sullivan.'

'In the car was a man I know.'

'Young?'

'Forty-odd. His name is Apsley and he's a senior legal assistant in the Treasury Solicitor's office.'

'What did he want? To marry you or raise a loan to help pay back the war debt?' As she spoke I went over to the bookcase and fished out Whitaker's Almanac for 1965. Apsley was listed all right, commencing salary £2,391 rising to £3,135.

'I've known him a long time and I think he would like to marry me – but he's not my type. He took me back to his office where there were two other Treasury officials. They wanted to know all about Martin. Did I know where he was and so on. Apparently they've an idea that he may be mixed up in some currency deal which isn't exactly honest.'

'Did they give you details?'

'No. They've no positive evidence yet. They just wanted to know where he was. Since Dick Apsley knows me they thought an informal approach to me was the best thing. I told them I'd employed you to find him.'

'You told them everything?'

'Practically.'

'What does that mean?'

'I didn't mention about his marriage to that woman . . . what was her name?'

'Jane Judd. Why not?'

'Well, I didn't see that involving her was going to help them.'

'But you told them about the dead man at the cottage?'

'Yes. I thought they took that very calmly.'

'And what did they say about me?'

'That I could tell you of their interest – though they have their own investigators – and if I wished I could go on employing you, but they'd be glad if I passed on to them anything you found out. What the hell is that brother of mine up to?'

'I'd like to know. How long were you there?'

'Two hours.'

'And afterwards?'

'Dick took me out to dinner. But we didn't discuss Martin any more. Except that I made it clear that I wanted to go on employing you. Do you mind if I pass them any information you find?'

'No.'

'You look cross.'

'I don't like official departments on my tail. But I'll learn to live with this one. Also, since they know about the dead man, I'm going to have the police around my neck at any minute.'

'I'm sorry.'

'Don't be. I hope I'm going to be in Paris before they get to me. But I'll be back.'

'And you'll keep me informed?'

'Sure.' But not, I thought, necessarily about everything. I didn't like this Treasury approach, largely I suppose because it wasn't typical form. And I'm a great one for form.

*

I was in Paris by five o'clock. I looked up Monsieur Robert Duchêne in the directory at the airport, but he was not listed with a telephone number. François Paulet was listed at the business address he had given me. I don't know why, but in the taxi going to 2 bis Rue du Bac to see Monsieur Robert Duchêne I suddenly had a comfortable feeling because in talking to Gloriana, although I had mentioned Duchêne and Leon Pelegrina of Florence, I hadn't given their addresses to her. Frankly, there seemed something a little fishy to me in the Gloriana-Treasury tie-up. More frankly, I recognized stage two of my usual client relationship – a nagging feeling that I wasn't being told the truth and nothing but the truth, that somewhere somebody was preparing to take advantage of me.

Two bis Rue du Bac was an open doorway next to a stationer's shop. Beyond the doorway was a narrow hall with a wooden board on the wall announcing who lived in each of the six flats that made up the building. Duchêne was listed in Number 4. I went up the bare board stairs through an atmosphere thick with the smell of ancient meals and tobacco smoke.

Duchêne had handwritten his name on a piece of paper and slipped it into the card holder on the door. I rang the bell and waited. Nothing happened. I rang again, and while my finger was still on the bell push I noticed that the door was off its catch. I stopped ringing and gave it a gentle push with my toe. It swung back and I went in. There was a little hallway, two doors either side and a door at the far end. A man's bicycle stood against one wall, a raincoat hung on a peg on the other and there was a small side-table piled with old copies of *Elle* and *Paris-Match*. The coloured cover page of the top one was given up to a head and shoulders photograph of Brigitte Bardot, marred somewhat by the fact that someone had added in biro a pair of spectacles, a drooping meerschaum pipe and a fancy-looking medal above her left breast. I didn't stop to work out whether it was the Croix de Guerre or the Victoria Cross. I was just thinking that this place didn't seem the kind of pad that went with a wealthy, if unscrupulous, collector of antique coins.

The big door at the end of the hall was also slightly ajar. I pushed it open with my toe and stood waiting. Nothing happened. Inside the room I could see part of a settee and beyond it a bureau. There was a knife-slit along the cover of the settee, the material was pulled loose, and three cushions lay on the floor, with covers ripped off and some loose stuffing material which had come from inside them on the carpet. The bureau drawers were on the floor in front of the piece, and papers and odds and ends were scattered about as though a small whirlwind had hit the place.

I left a nice big interval, listening hard as a safety precaution, heard nothing, and then went in.

Someone politely shut the door behind me and something cold was pressed against the back of my neck. I didn't try to move or turn round. Facing me from the window was a number who reminded me of a full-size model I'd once seen of a Neanderthal man, only this one wore a leather jacket and blue jeans, openwork sandals, a dirty white shirt, and had in his hand a flower pot which held a red azalea.

In the politest of voices he said, '*Bon soir, Monsieur Duchêne. Nous sommes très content de vous voir.*'

He got hold of the base stem of the azalea and pulled it out of the pot, bringing the roots and soil with it. He then examined the inside of the flower pot, shrugged his shoulders with disappointment, and let the whole shebang drop to the floor. The pot shattered and the azalea scattered its petals.

In English I said, 'You've got it wrong. My name is Apsley – Richard Apsley – and I'm from Her Majesty's Treasury Solicitor's office in London.' The esses whistled a bit but I managed to sound casual. I added, 'Also, this thing at the back of my neck is making me feel very cold.'

Neanderthal smiled and from such a grotesque face it came with surprising sympathy. In good English he said, 'Then in that case, or any case, we won't concern ourselves with you any longer.' He reached out an arm about four feet long, plucked a picture from the wall and began to tear off the backing paper.

I said, 'That's no way to treat a Picasso, even if it is only a reproduction.'

I never got his reaction to this. The cold steel was suddenly gone from the back of my neck. I was hit hard and expertly above and just to the back of my right ear, and went down and out to join the azalea on the floor.

FOUR

Girl with a Python on Her Arm

Naturally, when I came to they were gone. But they'd left their mark, not only on me, but the whole flat. I knew something about turning a place over, but they knew more. It had been gutted. In the bathroom, where I staggered to get my head under the cold tap, the soap had been cut into small segments in case anything had been hidden in it. In the hall the magazines were all over the place and the tyres of the bicycle had been ripped open.

They only conceded one touch of neatness. Going back into the sitting room, I found that they had taken all the contents of my pockets – nothing was missing – and laid them out neatly on a low table. From my passport they knew that I was not Richard Apsley.

Shaky still, I went over to the telephone. Clearly this was a furnished flat which Duchêne had rented. That's why no name or phone number was listed for him. I rang Paulet's office and was lucky enough to find him in.

I said, 'I'm at 2 bis Rue du Bac. In a few moments I'm going to be strong enough to totter down the street as far as the Seine. You'll find me propped against the parapet of the Pont Royal.'

He asked no questions. Just said that he would be there. I tried out my legs by moving round the flat. I could find nothing that interested me, except a bottle of Armagnac in a kitchen cupboard. I pumped a couple of quick glasses into myself, and then went out into the world.

François Paulet, driving a small Fiat van – he apologized for it, saying that in his work it was less conspicuous than a private car (though it rattled enough to draw anyone's attention to it) – picked me up and took me down along the river to a small restaurant just off the Avenue Rapp. We ate overcooked veal and a limp salad, but the *vin blanc* was good. I told him what had happened, explaining that I had flown over thinking that a chat with Monsieur Duchêne might help me in my search for Freeman.

'You take it from there,' I said. 'What the hell were those men doing, who were they, and where the hell is Monsieur Duchêne?'

He called for the cheese board and then said, 'Monsieur Duchêne, I know, has gone to Rome. He travels much. The apartment is rented furnished and he is not often there. May I say that some of his activities – as I explained about the coins – are a little – well, irregular. But as far as I am concerned he has given me a straightforward job, to find Freeman.'

'It's not turning out like that.'

'I told him about you. Before he went yesterday. He said he would pay for any information you could give about Freeman and also that I should help you as much as possible – even to travelling, if necessary, though he warned me to keep the expenses down. What do you think? I mean about helping you?'

'I'm not doing much thinking at the moment.'

It was a lie, of course. I was. I was wondering whether I should drop into Paulet's lap the knowledge that the list of antique coins was a phoney. He might know it and he might not. I decided not to tell him. It would have been giving away an advantage which eventually I might use to my own good.

Paulet sat there, pulling at his big nose, his narrow eyes anxious to please. 'I would not get in your way. And it would be a privilege for me to observe your methods. Yes?'

'I'll think about it when my head returns to normal. What do you think these men wanted?'

He did the old Gallic handspread, palms up, and rolled his eyes. 'Who knows?'

'Have you any way of getting in touch with Duchêne?'

'No. He phones my office, or writes when he is out of Paris.'

'You've done other jobs for him?'

'A few.'

'Like what?'

'Monsieur Carvay – would it be ethical—?'

'All right.'

'If you wish, I could give you a bed for tonight. My wife and—'

'You're married?'

He smiled. 'Well, not strictly. It is an arrangement . . . well, what I mean is that I am married, to another woman, but I live with this one. She is more my type and understands me. It is expensive, though, to keep two establishments going. Soon – if things do not improve – I may have to go back to the hotel business. You wish to spend the night with us?'

'No. I'm going to get a night plane back.'

'But you will keep in touch with me? About helping you?'

'Probably.' That was the best I could do for him.

He cut himself a large slice of Camembert and shook his head sadly. 'I do hope you will. In an emergency, you know, I can be very useful.' He grinned suddenly and tapped his head. 'Not much up here, maybe – but I have a strong body.'

'We'll see.'

I got back to my flat at four in the morning and slept through until nine. Mrs Meld woke me, standing in the bedroom door holding the kitchen alarm clock which was ringing its head off.

'Shut that thing off.'

She did, but the ringing still went on. It was the telephone beside my bed. As I reached out for it she said, 'It's rung about twice in the last half hour. There was a police car round here last night, about nine. How many eggs do you want?'

'Two boiled. Three minutes.'

She went and a voice over the phone said, 'Don't take too long over breakfast. You're wanted round here.'

I knew the voice. It was coming all the way from some grim little room in New Scotland Yard.

I said, 'I didn't kill him.'

'We know that. But the Ashford police would like a statement from you. I'm interested too. It's been a long time since I listened to one of your fairy stories.'

I was round there by ten. With my friend was an Inspector from Ashford. I gave them a straightforward account of my visit to the cottage and my reason for going. I didn't say anything about the stuff I had taken from it. It took some time because the Inspector wrote it all down and then I had to read it and sign it. This done, he pocketed the statement and left. I sat and looked at my friend. He smiled at me and said, 'Like to add anything off the record?'

It's good to have friends in high places who trust you. He was a Chief Superintendent, 'C' Department, and wouldn't be bothering himself with a tatty little murder in Kent unless there was a great deal behind it.

I said, 'You whistled your country buddy off pretty smartly.'

'I wanted to make him happy. He's got your statement for his file. He can ask the Paris boys to get one from this Paulet man. Just keep the file growing fatter day by day and it feels like progress.'

'Who was the murdered man?'

'Don't know.'

'Honest?'

'Honest.'

'When was he done in?'

'Late evening. Day before you got there. What did you or Paulet take from the cottage?'

'Nothing.'

'Honest?'

I just winked, and went on quickly, 'You know the Treasury have an interest in Martin Freeman?'

'Yes.'

'Can I go now?'

'Where did you get that bump above the right ear?'

'Paris, last night. On the *métro*. An angry commuter hit me with an umbrella because I wouldn't give up my seat to a pregnant woman.'

'That figures. You're only on your best behaviour with women before they're pregnant. Thinking of doing more travelling?'

'I had it in mind – unless you're going to confiscate my passport.

Then I should make a stink. Taking away the tools of my trade. Probably sue for loss of earnings.'

He shook his head indulgently. 'You can go anywhere you want. Mrs Stankowski wants Freeman, the Treasury wants Freeman, the Ashford police want him and I'd quite like to know where he is. So carry on. Every little helps. You might turn up something, and, if you're in the right mood, you might be honest enough to let me know about it.'

He was being as bland and easy-going as butter that spreads straight from the fridge. That meant that there was a hell of a lot that he was not going to tell me.

I stood up. 'It seems to me that a lot of people want Freeman.'

'You'd be surprised. And because that's so, and because this morning I quite like you, let me give you a little advice. Just watch yourself on the *métro* in future.'

At the door I said, 'What did you get when you ran a check on Monsieur Robert Duchêne – remember, he's another who wants Freeman.'

He said, 'The Paris people have nothing on him. No record. Neither have Interpol.' He grinned. 'I checked François Paulet, too. He's about to be sued by his wife for arrears of maintenance under a legal separation order. Otherwise, nothing. Help?'

'Was it intended to?'

'No.'

I went. Back at the office Wilkins told me that Dimble had called to say there was nothing on the python bracelet and she had paid him five pounds. She then said she was flying to Tripoli the next day and that Olaf was going to meet her there.

I said, 'Look pleased about it. It'll make a change from Cairo – and your expenses are being paid. All I want to know is whether Freeman is there, or has been there recently. And anything you can get on this Bill Dawson. Why does that name seem familiar?'

'I wouldn't know.'

If we had done at that moment it might have saved us both a lot of trouble.

From my room I phoned Hawkins of the London Fraternal Insurance

Society and fed him an edited account of the Freeman affair. He said not to worry because Mrs Stankowski had withdrawn her claim against them and he would send me a cheque for my services.

I then phoned Gloriana and told her to tell her Treasury friend that I had visited Monsieur Duchêne's flat and had been banged over the head for my trouble, and that I was going to Florence on Monday. I asked her if she would have dinner with me that evening and she said she was sorry but she was going away for the weekend and, no matter where I went, would I please keep in touch with her. I promised that I would.

Then I sat and chain-smoked for a while, wondering why I was getting the feeling that somehow I was being manipulated. It was a strong feeling and – although it was a challenge and fast bringing back that old zest for living which I needed – I didn't altogether like it. It would have been a compensation if somewhere I could have glimpsed a chance to make some side money for myself. For a time I considered sending Paulet a telegram to say that I would be in Florence, Hotel Excelsior, on Monday evening, but although it was flattering to see myself in the role of a top professional making a tyro's eyes pop with my expertise, I decided against it. He'd be better off in Paris dealing with his wife's lawsuit. And, anyway, there are different kinds of expertise and some that pay off in a sounder currency than flattery.

Mrs Burtenshaw, Wilkins' sister, was in the office on Monday morning. So was her basset hound, curled up on my desk chair and defying me with hung-over eyes to do anything about it. I didn't take up the challenge as I was only passing through on my way to the airport.

I said to Mrs Burtenshaw, 'Fisk will be coming in every other day in case anything crops up.' Fisk was an ex-policeman who gave me a hand now and then.

'Hilda,' said Mrs Burtenshaw, 'was very annoyed that you wanted her to go to Tripoli. After all, Mr Carver, a holiday is a holiday and people should be free to choose where they go.'

I said, 'You think she'll ever get round to marrying Olaf ?'

'I should hope so. He's a good, sound, solid, respectable man with money in the bank.'

Practically everything I wasn't – and that's what she meant.

I said, 'If your hound in there gets bored sitting at my desk – and God knows I do at times – just give him a few of the confidential files to chew up. And thank you for coming in to help. I appreciate it very much.'

She fixed me with her steely blue eyes, sniffed and said, 'I notice that whenever I do you usually contrive to be away. I think that's a very suitable arrangement for both of us.'

The air trip produced a fine selection of irritations; fog that delayed take-off two hours, then something wrong with the plane so that we had to be switched to another, and then – because of bad weather – a switch to the Caselle airport at Turin instead of Linate at Milan, so I missed my train connexion. It was ten o'clock at night when I finally checked in at the Excelsior in Florence. I had a late meal and went to bed. It was a bad idea, because sleeping too soon after eating always gives me wild dreams and a restless night. The next morning I was bad-tempered and my eyes felt as though their sockets were too small. Leon Pelegrina was listed in the telephone directory at 23 Piazza Santo Spirito. I called him from the lobby and when a man's voice at the other end said '*Pronto*' a few times I just put the receiver down. I didn't want to talk to him over the phone. I just wanted to know he was there.

Piazza Santo Spirito was only a few minutes' walk from the hotel, over the Arno by way of the Ponte Alla Carraia, down the Via dei Serragli and then left-handed into the Piazza. At the far end of the square was the Church of Santo Spirito. It was a narrow piazza, with the space in the middle tree-lined and holding a few seats for those who just wanted to sit and stare and rest their feet. Number 23 was on the left not far from the church. A twisting stone stairway served the three or four flats into which the house had been converted. Halfway up at a turn there was a Madonna and Child set back in a wall niche decked out with some artificial flowers and lit by a weak electric light bulb. At the next turn up there was a heavy wooden door with a small brass plate carrying the name – Pelegrina. Below it was a brass knocker shaped in the form of Michelangelo's David. I took him by the legs and rapped his backside smartly against the door three or four times. I waited. Nothing happened. I repeated the treatment. This time I was rewarded with a shuffling sound on the far side of the door.

It opened slowly on hinges that needed oiling. Standing on the threshold of a small, very dark hallway was a large shape, oval, about five feet tall at its vertical axis and three feet at the horizontal. There was a round excrescence at the top of the oval from which came the glint of glass.

I said, 'Signore Pelegrina?'

'Si.'

I handed the shape one of my cards. He came forward a little into the light of the stairway to read it. The dim light threw up more details. He wore a monocle stuck in the right eye of a fat, reddish-brown face whose colour could have come from weather exposure, blood pressure, drinks or all three. He didn't have any neck, his shoulders went straight up to his ears. When he readjusted his monocle to examine the card, his mouth gaped open like a goldfish starved of oxygen. He could have been anything between forty and fifty and he had wiry, almost curly dark hair which had scattered a fine dandruff dust on the shoulders of his jacket.

'*Inglese?*' His voice was a little hoarse as though he had lived in a damp atmosphere too long.

I said, 'Yes. I'd be glad if you could spare me a few minutes.'

He let the monocle drop from his eye, and frowned. There was a strong odour of Turkish tobacco about him and stains down the front of his velvet waistcoat. One of its fancy pearl buttons was missing.

In English he said, 'It is very early in the morning.'

'Well, you know the old saying. The early bird.'

He frowned again and momentarily there was a nervous tic in his right cheek. I had the feeling that I had worried him.

'I am not dressed for visitors.'

He looked clothed enough for me. Maybe he was referring to a pair of sloppy carpet slippers he was wearing.

'I won't keep you long,' I said. 'You speak very good English.'

'I should do. My mother was English, and insisted. She was a very insistent woman. That's why my father left her. Come in.'

He stood aside for me to enter, closed the door on us, and then passed me down the gloom of the little hall. He opened the door at the far end and ushered me into the main room of the flat. From behind me he said, 'I will be back in a minute.'

I was left alone in the room. There was no gloom here. Three sets of windows looked out over the piazza. It was L-shaped, with a small fireplace set in the smaller part of the L. By the window was a large divan. In one corner stood a grand piano with a purple cloth runner on the top and a silver-framed photograph dead centre on the cloth. There were a couple of well-worn armchairs, a long narrow table and, in another corner, a small roll-top desk, open, with a typewriter on it. I walked past the fireplace and examined the bookshelves beyond it. Two of the shelves were given up to paperbacks, English, Italian, and French. The bottom shelf held a collection of English books, mostly, I noticed, about sailing or the sea. Flat on their sides at the end of the shelf were an old *Lloyd's Register of Shipping, Volume I*, 1962-3, and on top of that a *Mediterranean Pilot of the Hydrographic Department of the Admiralty.* Over the fireplace was a big photograph of a coastwise tramp steamer, and above the desk another photograph of a steam yacht. I was moving over to look at it when Leon Pelegrina came back.

He had put on patent leather shoes and a different jacket. He waved me to a chair, picked up a cigarette box and said, 'You will probably prefer to smoke your own – unless you like Turkish?'

He sat down and we both lit our own cigarettes.

Without going into a lot of side details, I told him that I had been employed by Mrs Stankowski to find her brother, Martin Freeman.

At the first mention of Freeman's name he began to pick a few bits of imaginary fluff from the sleeve of his jacket, saw me watching him and stopped. I explained why Mrs Stankowski was worried about her brother, not having heard from him on her birthday, that he had left his job, and also that he had walked off with a valuable bracelet and some money. I didn't specify the amount. I said nothing of the anonymous phone calls assuring her of his safety, and nothing about Jane Judd and the Robert Duchêne angle.

I finished, 'Mrs Stankowski is not concerned about the thefts from her. Apparently Freeman has done this before. She is genuinely worried about him. I discovered that he had a cottage in the country and I found there a New Year's card from you. Since his letter of resignation from the News Service was written from this city it seemed reasonable to come and ask if you knew anything about him. How well did you know him?'

He put his fingertips together and made a steeple, eyed it, and then let it slip into a cat's cradle. Everything he said to me, I guessed, was going to be carefully considered.

'I've known him for some years, on and off. First in Rome, I think. He has many friends there. If he wrote this letter from Florence, I certainly didn't know he was here or see him. I've been away for a long time and only got back last week.'

'Can I ask how you came to meet him?'

'Through my daughter.' He got up and went to the piano and picked up the silver-framed photograph. 'She is in the theatrical profession and Freeman did some publicity work for her. Ever since then we have kept in touch loosely.'

He handed me the photograph. She was wearing jodhpurs and a shirt and carried a saddle over one arm. It was the same girl whose photograph in Oriental get-up I had seen in Freeman's cottage.

'I see. Where is she now?'

'I haven't the least idea. We had a quarrel about six months ago. Not our first. But always when it happens' – he shrugged his fat shoulders – 'we lose touch.'

'Could Freeman be with her? Was there any romantic attachment?' It's a good phrase when you want to be polite, and I wanted to be polite with this man. I had a feeling that it would be easy to scare him and make him clam up.

'A little once, I think. But not now that I know about.' He nodded at the photograph in my hands. 'When I say that she is my daughter, let me make it clear that I have never been married. Even in that photograph you can see that she has a certain amount of, well, coloured blood.'

I nodded. It seemed an odd thing to tell me, a stranger – unless it was a way of sliding the conversation away from the main point. Dads don't usually go out of the way to explain to my kind about their bastard, partly coloured daughters. He went even further.

'Just before the war I had a business in Italian Somaliland. I met her mother there. Beautiful, beautiful. When she died I naturally looked after the child.'

Big of him.

'How', I asked, 'could I find out where your daughter is? Has she got an agent?'

'Yes. In Rome. Marrini Fratelli. They're listed in the book. Her stage name is La Piroletta. But I could probably do more for you. I could ring up a few friends in Rome who might know something of Freeman's movements recently.'

'I would be glad if you would. I'm at the Excelsior Hotel, certainly for tonight, and maybe tomorrow night. Could you ring me there?'

'Yes, certainly.'

He stood up, adjusted his monocle, and gave me a little nod of dismissal.

At the door to the stairs, he said, 'Freeman's sister – she is paying you well for your work? I understand she is a very rich lady.'

'She's giving me the rate for the job.'

He smiled, and it was the first time he'd given me that benefit. Just for a moment, I sensed, he was completely relaxed.

'It must be a wonderful thing to have much money, too much money. One could do so much with it.'

'I gather that's Freeman's angle too. And, let's face it, mine. Always the big dreamers and schemers are the chaps who lack capital.'

The smile went. He pursed his fat lips and said, '*Certo.* "*Senza speme vivemo in desio.*" That's Dante. My father made me read him. Without hope we live in desire. And that, Mr Carver, is a bad state for any ambitious man.'

He closed the door on me and I had the feeling that, despite himself, he had revealed something of the alter ego struggling for freedom inside him.

He hadn't called me by ten o'clock that night. I telephoned him at ten minutes past ten and there was no answer from the flat. I went up to my room to go to bed.

A man got in the lift just as I was about to press the button for the third floor. He was a big man with shoulders like the back of a truck. He had a large, bland face, and he wore a well-cut grey silk suit with a tiny white line in it, an immaculate white silk shirt and a yellow tussore tie. In one hand he carried a fat briefcase. There was something about him that made me think he was an actor. I'm a great one for instant diagnosis. In Rome I would have bet that he was straight from Cine Citta with his contract renewed for another three years at double the salary plus a slice of the gross.

I raised an eyebrow at the board of floor buttons.

He said, '*Terza, grazie.*'

It was a nice voice, vibrant, manly, guaranteed to send chills of pleasure down the spine of any woman who needed her head examined.

We went up in silence. The lift stopped, the doors went back and I stood aside for him to move out. He shook his head and waved me forward. We had a silent courtesy duel for five seconds and he won. I went out and he stepped after me. I went away down the corridor towards my room. Behind me I heard the lift doors close.

At the same moment something hard was stuck into my back and the vibrant, manly voice sent a chill down my spine as it said, 'Just open the door of your room and go in without causing trouble. We do not want blood on this highly expensive corridor carpet, do we?'

I said, 'Nor on the one in my room, I hope.'

He chuckled. It's a verb which is used loosely. Not many people can really chuckle after the age of four. He could – a fat, babyish sound of pure, uninhibited pleasure.

I fished out my key to open the door and decided against a quick swing round to catch him off guard.

We went through the tiny hall into my bedroom. He shut the door behind us and said, 'Go and sit in the chair by the window.'

His English was good, but the Italian accent was strong in it.

I went and sat in the chair. He put his briefcase on the bed and, holding his gun in his right hand, he opened up the case left-handed. He took out two bottles of whisky. Vat 69. For a moment hope flowered in me. He took the glass from the water carafe by my bed, poured a liberal helping of whisky and then came and handed it to me from a safe distance.

'Drink.'

I did. Not all, but a fair portion. I felt I needed it.

'Hold this.' He handed me the bottle.

'Why?'

'Because it will keep both your hands in sight.' Then as I took the bottle, thinking it might be used as a counter weapon, he added, 'Also it is a good thing to have your prints on it.'

He went and fetched the other bottle and, for the first time, I noticed that he was wearing gloves. Holding gun and bottle in one hand, he opened it and then splashed some of the contents on the bedside table and the floor around it. A nice aroma filled the room.

I flung my bottle at him. He ducked and it hit the wall on the far side of the room, smashed, and whisky trickled down the striped wallpaper.

He said, holding the gun on me, 'I was hoping you would do that. It will make it more authentic.' He tossed the other half-empty bottle at me and instinctively I caught it to save my suit being drenched.

'*Grazie,*' he said. I knew why. My prints were now on this bottle.

I said, 'Care to tell me how this scene ends?'

'Accidental death of a drunk,' he said. 'The window behind you opens on to one of the inner hotel wells. A very long drop. Nasty.

However, I'm in no hurry. Some men, knowing they were going out of the window for good, might, given the time, ask for a woman, or a good meal; some, I suppose, a priest. All I can offer you is ten minutes and the whisky from the bottle in your hand.'

He sat down on a chair by the door and kept the gun on me. From above it I had the benefit of his high-glazed smile.

I finished the glass of whisky and half filled it from the bottle. He nodded approvingly.

I said, 'I had you figured for an actor.'

He said, 'I am. People pay me and I act for them.'

'Steady work?' How did I get out of this? I was wondering. Or if I couldn't, should I finish the bottle? Why not? Where I was going, anyway, a reek of whisky on the breath wouldn't be held against me.

'Too much,' he said. 'As a matter of fact, I have to be selective nowadays.'

'Lucky you. Most of us scratch around for jobs.'

'I make plenty and pay no taxes. Also I meet interesting people. Like you, for instance. I shall be disappointed if the moment I move to hit you with this' – he indicated the gun – 'you start to sob or plead. Some do.'

'I'll try not to disappoint you.'

'Good.' He shifted in his seat to make himself more comfortable, made a flappy motion with his free hand for me to go on drinking, and said, 'It is interesting that, about last requests. I consider it often. For instance – if you had wanted a woman and I could have provided any one you wanted, which would you have chosen?'

'You're a curious bastard, aren't you?'

'Well, fundamentally my work is without much variety. I try to give it some status, intellectual or philosophical. I find it helps both me and my client. Which woman would you choose? Some glamorous film star? Or society woman? Or maybe some nothing-to-look-at number of a secretary or typist who was more a bomb in bed than any of the big names ever could hope to be. Big names, you know, are like that. They have the habit of thinking all the time only of themselves, and that is no good in bed. The ego must be swamped, the body, the senses must dominate all thought, all personality.'

'You should write a book about it. That kind of thing sells well these days.'

'Maybe I will. I have had many experiences. Once, you know, I did a job for the Mafia. It was a man, a neurotic type, but good, sincere, a sort of religious man, in a way like Billy Graham – but much smaller. It was in the south of this country, Calabria, where he was giving the *contadini* ideas. He was a peasant himself. You know what he would have liked?'

'Go ahead. Astonish me.'

'A hot bath.' He chuckled. 'Unbelievable, no? A hot bath he wants, with expensive soap, bath essence, and thick towels – because never in his life has he had such a bath. So now, which woman would you choose?'

I said, 'If you're serious about last requests, you ought to be naming yours.'

'Why?'

I didn't bother to answer. In the last ten seconds the bedroom door had been gently opening behind him and I had seen part of a face which I recognized. The door now went back with a bang and François Paulet was in the room. I sat comfortably where I was and watched. Not long ago Paulet had said to me that, although he was without much up top he had a strong body and could be useful in an emergency. His demonstration of it was a joy to watch. He wasn't handicapped in any way by the fact that my philosophical friend was as big as he was.

He smacked the man on the back of the neck and the gun jumped out of his hand and skittered across to my feet. I took my time picking it up. It was a .380 *pistolet automatique*, MAB *brevté*, model F, I discovered later. But at that moment I only had eyes for Paulet as he grabbed the man, jerked him to his feet and slammed a big right fist in his face and followed it with the left in his stomach. After that he went through a simple routine of throwing the man against one wall and then another, bouncing him once or twice on the floor and finally slinging him like a roll of limp carpet into a chair.

He stood over him and began to interrogate him in Italian, too fast for my limited knowledge of the language to give me any help. At first the man was reluctant in his replies. Paulet encouraged him with short jabs of his right fist and eventually they had a conversation which seemed to be satisfying Paulet. Paulet rounded it off by suddenly slipping his own gun out of his pocket and cracking the man above the left ear with the butt. My friend went out like a light.

Paulet turned and grinned at me.

'I did well, no?'

'It was a pleasure to watch. Have a drink.'

I held out the bottle. He drank without benefit of glass but with the thirst of a man conscious that he has done a good job and merits refreshment.

He nodded at the man. 'This *canaille* – your word for that escapes me at the moment—'

'Scum might do.'

'Yes, scum. Well, he is a professional killer who comes up from Rome today. Employed by a man here in Florence whose name he does not give. This I did not press because he has ethics like us and—'

'I know who the man is. And I think we ought to go right now and have a chat with him.'

'It will be a pleasure,' said Paulet. Then, rubbing the tip of his big nose with one finger, he looked down at the man. 'But first we must dispose of this. You think there is any more useful information to be had from him?'

'I doubt it. He was just trying to do a job.'

'You would like to hand him over to the police?'

'Don't be crazy. I wouldn't get out of this town for days with all their inquiries and processes.'

'In that case, we just get rid of him.'

He bent down, lifted the man and threw him over his shoulder. It sounds easy, but you try it. The man must have weighed over two hundred pounds. Paulet almost did it one-handed.

I followed him out of the room into the corridor. At the lift he rang.

It came up and the doors opened. Paulet slung the man inside, reached round the corner of the lift and pressed one of the buttons, and jerked his arm back as the doors began to close.

'We,' he said, 'will walk down, while he goes up to the top floor. When he is able to, he can make his own explanations.'

We went down the stairs and there was a spring in Paulet's step. He was pleased with himself, pleased that he had given a demonstration of his potential usefulness to me.

I said, 'Thank you for getting me out of that.'

'A pleasure, Monsieur Carvay.'

I said, 'My room door was locked automatically when I went in with our friend. How did you get in?'

'I have, over the years, acquired a very large collection of hotel pass keys. Maybe it was a touch of vanity, but I wanted to come in and surprise you, to impress you. Perhaps because I sensed that there was a little reluctance in you to accept my minor services.'

'How did you know I was in Florence at this hotel?'

'I telephone your London office and tell the lady there that I have important news about Freeman for you and must get in contact. She gave me your address.'

I didn't tell him that I would check that. I did the next day, and Mrs Burtenshaw confirmed it. In my book Paulet was beginning to win his spurs but I still had a lingering doubt, probably unworthy, about which horse he was intending to ride.

We took a gentle stroll through the night, over the Arno to the Piazza Santo Spirito.

Repeated banging of David's bottom on Pelegrina's door brought no response.

I looked at Paulet. 'It's a very thick door.'

'We try the keys first.'

From his jacket pocket he brought out a bunch that was so big it would have made any ordinary man walk lopsided. He bent down, examined the keyhole, and tried one or two keys experimentally.

He half turned and smiled up at me. 'Locks, too, I have studied.

This is a Continental variation of the English lever lock which your great Jeremiah Chubb invented in 1818. The important thing is not to lift the detector lever too high by using the wrong key.' He examined his bunch, selected a key and began fiddling with the lock. A few moments and two keys later, the door was open. He waved me in, beaming, his narrow-set eyes sparkling with frank vanity.

Leon Pelegrina was not there. He had packed and gone, and obviously taken his time about it. In the bedroom, which was off to the left of the hall, all his clothes had gone except an old dressing gown and a pair of pyjamas. The only things of interest – but not as far as Freeman was concerned – were the contents of the bottom drawer of the dressing table. It held a woman's silk nightdress, some female underclothes, and a couple of whippy school canes.

Paulet put on a stiff, disapproving face, and said, 'One of those.'

There was nothing to be learned from the bathroom or the kitchen. In the big main room Pelegrina had done a thorough tidying-up job. There wasn't a personal paper or letter in the desk, though there was a pile of thoroughly burnt and stirred-up paper ash in the fireplace. The silver-framed photograph of La Piroletta had gone, and the box of Turkish cigarettes was empty. Missing, too, were the framed photographs of the tramp steamer from over the fireplace and the steam yacht from the wall behind the desk. Both pictures had been hanging some time because the wallpaper was less faded from light where they had hung.

I sat down in a chair by the fire and lit a cigarette.

'Who lived here?' Paulet dropped to the divan and the springs creaked.

I told him, gave him a brief outline of my conversation with Pelegrina, and explained about the New Year's card I had found in the cottage.

I said, 'I'm sorry I kept that from you. But at the time I didn't know what a sterling chap you were going to turn out to be.'

It mollified him a bit, but not entirely.

'Let us', he said, 'have no secrets from one another in future. I wish to help and I wish to be frank with you. No?'

I nodded agreement. Well, that was all right. A nod is not binding. He could have been, for all I knew, putting some unspoken clause to the end of his declaration. If he were a good professional man he had to be, because frankness in our line never paid a dividend that raised the pulse rate through joy.

I said, 'He takes his daughter's photograph. Why?'

'Maybe it was a publicity photograph originally and would have her agent's name and address on the back.'

'You think that Marrini Fratelli are an invention?'

'I would bet on it.'

'You needn't. I checked the Rome directory at my hotel this afternoon. They don't exist. Now – why did he take the photographs? One coastwise steamer, pretty ancient craft by the look of it. Can't remember the name. And the steam yacht. I never got to have a close look at that.'

'There must have been a reason. Some day, we know. Clearly he was worried by your presence here and your questions about Freeman. Otherwise, why try to kill you? This Freeman begins to interest me.'

'That began with me a long time ago. I think you'd better get in touch with your Monsieur Duchêne and see what you can dig out of him. You can tell him about all this. In fact, it might be a good idea if I could talk to him.'

'I will try to arrange that.'

'You speak Italian well?'

'Fluently. In my youth I was a kitchen boy in the Hotel Principi di Piemonte at Turin and later a waiter at many other Italian hotels.'

It all came out pat. I knew he was a good guy, anxious to help me – but since suspicion had often meant the breath of life to me I couldn't forget the phoney list of coins.

'Have a poke around here tomorrow morning and see what you can learn about Pelegrina from the other people in the building.'

'A pleasure.'

As he spoke, an idea struck me. They did from rare time to time, out of the blue, like the first swallow of summer. I got up and went over to the bookshelves and nearly broke my wrist picking up the fat red leather-bound *Lloyd's Register of Shipping, Volume I.*

I was hoping that there would be an index of ship owners. There wasn't. The whole thing was arranged alphabetically by the names of ships. I didn't feel like ploughing through the names of nearly four thousand ships and checking the owners to see if I could find a Pelegrina among them. I didn't have to. Sticking out from the top pages of the register was a small piece of marking paper. I opened the register at the marked place.

I ran my finger down the first of the two pages that lay open and found what I wanted at the bottom almost. The ship's name was *Suna*, but in 1959 she had been called the *Pelox*, and before that in 1948 the *Nordwell.* Under her earlier names she had flown the Liberian flag, port of registry Monrovia. Her present owners – this was a 1962–3 register – were listed as 'Leon Pelegrina and Others'. Her gross tonnage was 1,366 tons, summer deadweight 662 tons. She'd been built by the Burrard DD Co Ltd of Vancouver, engines by John Inglis Co Ltd of Toronto, and her classification at Lloyds was marked 'LC class with-drawn'. A key to symbols at the front of the register said that this indicated that the class had been withdrawn by the Committee for non-compliance with the Society's regulations. From what I had seen of Leon Pelegrina, and knew of Freeman, if they were connected, that seemed about the right form. Noncompliance with regulations would have made a fine family motto for both of them. At the moment the *Suna* carried Greek registration.

I explained the details to Paulet.

He said, 'Pelegrina could still be in shipping. This I find out tomorrow, perhaps.'

I was about to tell him not to bother. I could do it by a phone call the next day to a friend of mine at Lloyd's and, what is more, have him check in the Lloyd's register of yachts whether Pelegrina owned a steam yacht. Normally I wouldn't have been at all interested in Pelegrina's shipping connexions. It was only the fact that he had troubled to take the framed photographs that made it seem possibly significant so far as Freeman was concerned. As I say, I was about to tell Paulet this when I heard footsteps coming down the small hallway.

Paulet and I stood up and turned at the same moment.

A woman appeared in the doorway of the room. She wore a loose, very short-sleeved white coat over a green silk dress that showed her knees and a nice run of legs. She held a small white pigskin case in one hand and a big white handbag in the other. Full under the light she was a treat to look at and would have passed A1 at Lloyd's or any other place. Her skin had a dusky, velvety suggestion about it, and her eyes were wide and dark. Her hair fell just short of her shoulders and had a gloss on it like fine old mahogany.

Putting in all the charm I could, I said, 'Good evening, Miss Pelegrina.'

She said, 'How the bloody hell did you get in here?' It was a beautiful voice, low, vibrant, full of dark tones that really sent a chill down my spine without making me stop to think whether I needed my head examined. She hadn't said 'bloody' either. It was something Anglo-Saxon and straight from the barrack room. I was charmed, bewitched by her.

'The door was open and – forgive us – we walked in. We had an appointment with your father.'

'Is that so? Well, the bloody door is still bloody open – so just walk straight out. I don't want any friends or business acquaintances of my father's in my flat.'

She stood back to give us room to pass. I didn't move, though Paulet shuffled a few paces.

'I understood this was his flat. It's listed in the telephone directory as—'

'If it suited him he'd list it under the name of President bloody Johnson. But it's my flat, and I want a good night's sleep, so get the hell out of here.' She dropped her case and made a gesture with her right arm towards the hall. I was going to argue, but her right arm made me change my mind. Around her wrist and encroaching on the end of her dress sleeve was a python gold bracelet which I would have known anywhere.

I glanced at Paulet. I knew at once that he had seen it.

'Come on, Paulet,' I said. 'We'll come back tomorrow when Miss Pelegrina has had a good night's sleep and is in a better mood.'

'Just get out and stay out. And when you next see my father tell him also not to come back. Tell him I'm having the lock changed.'

Her right arm waved again, imperiously, and we shuffled by. I'm good at scents, but I couldn't get hers. It was delicious, heady with all the magic and fascination of the East. I winked at her and she gave me a basilisk stare that would have put any of Wilkins' efforts in the kindergarten class.

Standing in the square outside was a white Ford Thunderbird that hadn't been there when we came in. It had a Rome number plate and thrown across the back seat was a mink coat. Before moving on I checked that the doors were locked against theft. They were.

FIVE

The Hour of Cowdust

From my room the next morning I telephoned Mrs Burtenshaw at the office. She was to contact my friend at Lloyd's and get a list of Leon Pelegrina's shipping interests if he still had any. I said I wanted a reply by the afternoon.

After that I called Gloriana and told her that I had met Leon Pelegrina but he had been unable to help me about Freeman. This was true enough and I did not bother her with the incidental details. In fact, enjoying myself as I was beginning to, feeling the *elan vital* coming back and not wanting to lose it, I had decided that I was not handing over any incidental details to anyone. I would stick to *bald* and, as far as possible, true facts. At the moment I didn't think that Gloriana was letting me in on the whole truth or, more charitably, didn't know it all herself. The Treasury angle seemed unnatural. So did the attitude of my friend the Chief Superintendent in 'C' Department of New Scotland Yard. Usually if I came up on the inside of any horse they were running I could expect to be bumped into the rails. Here they'd hauled off and let me through. Monsieur Robert Duchêne for my money was a phoney. Just at the moment I wasn't prepared to lump Paulet in the same category, but if I got a chance I was going to carry out an analysis for purity.

I phoned him too. He was staying in a cheap hotel near the Stazione Centrale. I told him to get round to Piazza Santo Spirito and keep an eye on things. Also, later, he was to try and contact Monsieur Duchêne. He said yes, yes, yes, full of eagerness. Too much eagerness, perhaps.

I gave him twenty minutes, and then I walked around to his hotel. On the way I thought about La Piroletta, and the python bracelet. Freeman was married to Jane Judd, and Jane Judd had been instructed that no matter what she heard she was to wait for the call from him to take off for pastures new. Pelegrina, I felt, could have been the man who had spoken to her and Gloriana on the phone, reassuring them about Freeman. As for Freeman . . . well, maybe he was the kind that kept one woman on a string while he played around with others, a game that usually ends up with a man getting the string snarled up around his feet and tripping over. In my book I was prepared to lay odds that the python bracelet was no love gift, but had been sold for hard cash.

At Paulet's hotel the reception desk was empty. The number of his room was 17. I took a look at the key rack. Number 17 wasn't there. Paulet had taken it out with him. That didn't worry me. I reached over and took Number 15.

On the second floor I fiddled around at the door of Number 17 with the Number 15 key, cursed aloud because I couldn't open it and then went to the chambermaid's room at the end of the corridor and asked her to open my room for me. I'd been given the wrong key at the desk. She obliged and took key Number 15 off me. The world is full of unsuspecting women always ready to help a man out of trouble.

I did a quick and neat turnover of Paulet's room. Quick, because there wasn't much to see, and neat because I didn't want him to know anyone had been in the place rummaging. I learned that he was in a poor way so far as pants and shirts were concerned, and was halfway through a *livre de poche* called *Vipere au Poing* by Herve Bazin; that his second pair of shoes wanted resoling, and that men have a way of stuffing things in their dressing-gown pockets and forgetting them. For him I suppose there was some excuse because he had actually found the letter in his pocket. It had been put there by the woman he lived with in Paris – his estranged wife would never have written in the same terms. I sat down and applied my rather fractured French to it. The first sentence explained that she was packing it, unknown to him, in his dressing-gown pocket – so that he would have a nice surprise when he found it. After that it was mildly erotic in a pleasant way. The woman was obviously stuck on him. She signed herself Therese and had added a footnote which came out in my translation as:

You rightly have a high regard for Monsieur Carver's reputation, so please be careful. Men who are both pleasant and clever can be dangerous. I know this because that is the way you are. So watch yourself. To lose you, my darling, would make life empty for me. A thousand embraces. T.

Pleasant, clever, dangerous. I didn't know whether to be flattered. It was interesting to know, however, that she put Paulet in the same category. Very interesting. I made a mental note of the address on the headed notepaper. You never knew when a detail like that might be useful. If I had been Paulet, knowing me as he was supposed to do, I would – if I'd been up to anything – have destroyed the letter. That he hadn't was a point in his favour. Or did it mean that he just wasn't quite clever enough to appreciate how clever I was? I decided to defer a decision but to keep my eyes open.

I went round to the Piazza Santo Spirito. Paulet was sitting on a bench under a tree opposite Number 23. He looked gloomy.

'*Buon giorno*, François,' I said cheerfully.

'She has gone, Monsieur Carvay.' He nodded across the street. The white Thunderbird was no longer there.

'You saw her go?'

'No. She went at eight o'clock this morning. This I learn from the woman in the opposite flat. I pretend to be from one of the city stores. Come to measure the big room for new curtains. With women it is always better to be something to do with furnishings. That is their world.'

'What did you get out of her?'

'Coffee. She is a compulsive talker and has bad breath. The woman in the opposite flat, I mean. She wants my opinion on the purchase of a new carpet, and she is watching us from the window up there now, but that is all right because I said I have to wait here for my assistant who comes from another job.'

'What did you get about the Pelegrinas?'

'The flat belongs to La Piroletta. She does some cabaret act, has money, and is not often here. Just a flying visit like this one. The woman does not like her but that is because she is beautiful and this woman is not. Leon Pelegrina was there more often, though not lately. His last visit was only for four or five days. She did not like him either. She would not want to be quoted but she thinks he is a crook and lucky not to be in prison. There was, some years ago, a scandal about him over some holiday villa development on the coast near Viareggio, but nothing was ever done about it for lack of proof. Also, she did not care for his taking women into the flat.'

'Where else would he take them?'

Paulet raised a sad eye to me. 'These women were *puttane.*'

'Well, he'd still need a flat – unless he didn't mind frightening the horses in the street. Come on, let's go.'

'You do not want to go in and have another look around?'

'It wouldn't help. Besides, I want to get down to Rome and take a plane to Tripoli.'

'Tripoli? But that will be expensive.'

'My client pays – for me. What about yours?'

'I must contact him.' He made a face. 'He hates spending money.'

'If you want results you've got to. Where is he?'

'I think in Naples.'

'What do you mean, you think? You know, don't you?'

'I am reasonably sure, yes.'

'Then ask him to meet us in Rome. I'd like to talk to him.'

'But why Tripoli?'

'Because I am reasonably sure that that is where Freeman is.'

'How you know this?'

I'd noticed that in moments of depression or excitement Paulet's syntax was inclined to slip.

'Later, perhaps, I'll tell you.'

Actually, in my pocket was a cable from Wilkins which had arrived for me early that morning at the hotel. It read:

M.F. DEFINITELY HERE SIX DAYS AGO STOP ADVISE ARRIVAL STOP
INQUIRY BLANKET LOCAL BOGEYS STOP REGARDS H.W.

It was the first time in her life that Wilkins had sent me her regards. Best wishes, of course, I got every year on a Christmas card, but that didn't count. And when it came to it she could use underworld slang with the best of them. The local police in Tripoli clearly weren't encouraging inquiries about Freeman. Wilkins didn't care for the police any more than I did, but she could be much more vocal about it, and I knew she would be – with me – the moment I arrived.

We took a train down to Rome that afternoon and we booked into the Hotel Eden together. Paulet was a bit fussed about staying in a four-star job, but I told him to relax and try and get in touch with Monsieur Duchêne. He went off to do this, while I had a large Negroni in the bar and sat considering the information which Mrs Burtenshaw had phoned me at the Excelsior just after lunch. My Lloyd's friend had said that the only maritime interest Pelegrina had at that moment seemed to be a steam yacht of some vintage called *La Sunata* – though the name had been changed a few times over the years – which was Greek registered at Piraeus, and which he let out on charter.

Monsieur Robert Duchêne arrived at the hotel at eleven the next morning. Paulet had said that he would not want to carry on a discussion in the bar or any of the hotel lounges so we held a conference in my room.

He was a tall lean man, wearing big-rimmed glasses, and he was in a bad temper. I put him at about fifty; his skin was like stained vellum and he smoked long Swiss cigars, each one having its own mouthpiece attached to it. He seldom took the cigar out of his mouth, talking expertly around each side of it, which gave a curious sideways waggle to his lips. It put them out of phase with his words as though his speech was being badly dubbed. However, he made himself clear in about ten minutes flat.

Talking exclusively to me, while Paulet sat humbly in the background, he said, 'I will be perfectly frank with you, Monsieur Carver. I understand from Paulet that following your interview with Leon Pelegrina an attempt was made on your life. Also my flat in Paris was ransacked. All this is in some way connected with Freeman, yes?'

'Yes.' His English was good, but I was trying to place the accent behind it. It didn't sound like French to me.

'Then let me make this clear – but at the same time stress its confidential nature. I am in the art and antique world. And by that I do not mean I put in any appearances at Christie's or Sotheby's. I buy and sell in a twilight world.'

'Nice way to put it.'

He frowned. 'There is always a nice way to put even the most unpleasant things. Freeman stole certain coins from me and I thought their recovery would be a simple matter. With simple matters like theft and recovery without aid of the police I am at home. Let the matter become complicated and I want no more to do with it. Frankly, the coins were illegally acquired by me in the first place. Equally frankly, I do not wish to pursue their recovery if it is to lead into deep and unfamiliar waters. In other words I do not like my flat being searched and I do not like being involved in an affair which has room for attempts on people's lives. I am dropping the whole matter. Monsieur Paulet will be paid off, and whether you find Mr Freeman is now a matter of indifference to me. Am I understood?'

I looked at Paulet. This had obviously come as a surprise to him. He looked like a small boy who has had a Christmas present taken from him because he had got it by a mistake in the first place. He didn't at that moment look like the man Therese loved and described as pleasant, clever, and capable of being dangerous. He was just crestfallen.

I said, 'Since you've never been a client of mine, Monsieur Duchêne, it is a matter of indifference to me what you decide about Freeman. I still have my own client to satisfy. Would I be right in thinking you're not in the mood to answer any questions about Freeman?'

'On the contrary, Mr Carver, I will tell you what little I do know. I met him almost a year ago in the Georges Cinq bar in Paris, and he subsequently sold me a Rajput painting of the late eighteenth century. It was of the Kangra school and was called "The Hour of Cowdust". It showed Krsna returning with the herds to Brndaban at sundown.'

He paused for me to register how impressed I was and I did register – but something quite different. I was prepared to lay fifty to one in fivers that this long streak of snap and bite had me figured for an ignoramus when it came to art and antiques. And maybe I was. But what he hadn't figured – though Therese could have given him a pointer or two – was that what I didn't know about I checked against the best references. And I was damn well going to check this Rajput load of cowdust which he was throwing in my eyes. I could do it at the British Council library in Rome. He'd slipped up over ancient coins once, he could be doing the same over old Indian paintings.

He went on, 'I met him once in Rome after that, and then not long ago he came to my flat in Paris and tried to sell me an antique Indian gold python bracelet. We could not agree on a price and he left. After he had gone I discovered that he had taken a collection of ancient coins I was holding for sale to a client.'

'And you sent Paulet off to try and find him at his cottage in Kent, a cottage which, apparently, very few people knew about. How did you know about it?'

Duchêne rolled the cigar to one corner of his mouth and the movement produced a fair imitation of a smile. 'He got drunk the evening I bought the Rajput painting and he told me about it. When drunk, Monsieur Carver, he was most tedious with his confidences. I say tedious because they were mostly about women. You will agree that women are only interesting at first hand. Is there more you would like to ask?'

'No.'

'Very well.' He looked at Paulet. 'I am staying at the Bernini-Bristol. Come there at three this afternoon with your account and I will give you a cheque on my Paris bank.'

He picked up his hat, dished out two brief nods, and left.

'I looked at Paulet. 'You expected this?'

'No.'

'Well, it's happened. I'm sorry. I've enjoyed your company.'

'You would not care to hire me as an assistant?'

'No thanks. My client wouldn't wear it and I can't afford it. Anyway, it's now the hour of cowdust in the eyes. Let's go down to the bar and have a couple of double Rajputs.'

He gave me a quizzical look, but said nothing.

I stopped at the desk and asked them to try and get me a late afternoon booking on a plane to Tripoli. Paulet and I then had our drinks and he was a very subdued man.

'Always,' he said, 'when I begin to enjoy myself, or meet someone interesting, *bam!* – the guillotine comes down.'

'Stick a ten per cent surcharge on your bill for loss of expectations.'

I skipped lunch and went along to the British Council library. It was no surprise to me to find in the article on Indian and Sinhalese Art and Archaeology in Volume 12 – HYDROZ to JEREM – of the *Encyclopaedia Britannica* a full-page reproduction of 'The Hour of Cowdust'. Well, well, even in the most careful of us there's always a point of laxness. But what, I asked myself, was it all in aid of? It wasn't the first time in my life the question had arisen and I knew that if I didn't come up with an answer then time eventually would reveal it – probably with unpleasant consequences.

The hotel desk had got me a reservation on the half-past four plane to Tripoli. I said goodbye to Paulet and made the Leonardo da Vinci Airport by taxi with ten minutes to spare.

There were not many people on the plane so there were plenty of spare seats. I sat down on the port side close to one of the wings and we took off out over the Mediterranean heading for Sicily, Malta, and then Tripoli. I settled back with a Pan book and promised myself that in an hour's time I would have a large whisky and soda. Just before the hour was up I began to get that feeling that someone was watching and taking an interest in me. It's a sense that becomes highly developed in my trade, like the sense of hearing in a good mechanic who notices at once from the note of an engine when it goes slightly off tune. I glanced across the gangway. A fat number in a mohair suit and a red fez, brown as a coffee bean, was sleeping happily. I turned to take in the seat behind him.

La Piroletta had the outside berth. The inner one held her handbag and a bunch of newspapers and magazines. She was dressed exactly as she had been in the Florence flat – except that she was not wearing the python bracelet. And she was looking at me thoughtfully. Whatever expression she had on her face suited me. It was the kind of face that could make more than the most of any expression and still be beautiful. I gave her a smile and a nod. She just remained thoughtful then she gave the faintest of nods and there was a tiny movement of her mouth which wouldn't have needed much more to make it a smile. Anyway, it was enough for me.

I got up and went back to her.

I said, 'I was just thinking of having a drink. Would you care to join me?' At the same time I handed her one of my cards.

She looked at it and then with a nice, flowing, graceful movement got up and moved to the inner berth. If you think that's easy to do, gracefully and flowingly in an aircraft seat, you can never have tried it.

I sat down and asked her what she would like to drink.

'Gin and tonic.'

I caught the stewardess' eye and gave her order and while I did I was sorting out two problems. One, the line I was going to take; and, two, this business of coincidence in life. I don't have any great faith in coincidences – though I'll admit they happen more often than most people think. But with me, so far as business was concerned, coincidences generally turned out not to be. I decided not to lay any bets either way on this one. As for the line I was to take, I thought it might make a nice change to be reasonably honest and straightforward. After all, one mustn't get stuck in one routine all the time.

I said, 'You're going to Tripoli or farther?'

'Tripoli.'

'So am I.'

'Where do you stay?'

'I don't know until I get there. A friend is booking a hotel for me. And you?'

'The Uaddan.'

'I've begun to wonder what that name means.' I hadn't, because I didn't care, but I wanted to keep the preliminaries on a drink-chat level so that she would not feel rushed.

'It is', she said, 'the Arab name for some kind of mountain goat or deer. Something like an ibex, I think.'

The drinks came. I lit a cigarette for her. She sipped her gin and tonic and there was an unembarrassed pause in the talk while we both decided the next move in the game. Daintily she picked the slice of lemon out of her drink and sucked it. That, too, she did gracefully, and with a nice little wrinkle of her nose at the citric sharpness.

I said, 'I gather you haven't a very high opinion of your father?'

She considered this, then nodded.

'Why not?'

Without hesitation, and there seemed to be no question of her sincerity, she said, 'Because he's the world's champion scrounger and he has king-sized dreams in a pea-sized brain. But that doesn't mean I haven't a protective feeling towards him – so long as he doesn't ask me for money. At least, not too much.'

'You've got plenty?'

She looked at me, smiled, and said, 'I suppose we shall come presently to the point of all this, but for the moment, since I don't actively dislike you and I like company when I'm flying to take my mind off the twenty thousand-odd feet below me, I don't mind talking. Yes, I'm very well off. And I did it all myself. How's your bank balance?'

'Reasonable at the moment – which is a rare state of affairs.'

'And you are going to Tripoli on business?'

'Yes.'

'Not, I hope, connected with my father?'

'Why do you ask that?'

'Because if you are you will either be cheated or lose your money.'

'I'm not in any deal with your father. I'm looking for a man.'

She smiled. 'I've been doing that for some time, but the quality isn't what it used to be. I suppose it's because they're mass produced or something.'

'If I can find time off from work I might take you up on that. I'm one of the last custom-built models, real leather upholstery and at a hundred miles an hour all you can hear is the ticking of the clock. How much did you pay Martin Freeman for that gold python bracelet you were wearing yesterday?'

She took it without a flicker, shook the ice around in her glass, glanced out at the strato cirrus over which the setting sun was slapping gold and scarlet in action-painting frenzy, and then said, 'In lire the equivalent of two thousand pounds.'

'It's been valued at five thousand.'

'I got a bargain then.'

'It was also stolen.'

No flicker again. 'That's his problem. Not mine.' There was a touch of the father's daughter there.

'My client wants it back.'

'Your client can have it for two thousand five hundred pounds.'

'I'll consult her.'

'Her?'

'Yes. His sister. He makes a habit of financing himself out of her collection.'

'She's wealthy?'

'Very.'

'The price has gone up to three thousand. Now ask the next question.'

'Which is?'

'Where did I get to know Martin Freeman and why did I buy it?'

'Well – where did you and why did you?'

'He once helped me with some publicity work in Rome. He's a likeable layabout and the same kind of dreamer as my father. Maybe his brain is a bit bigger. I wanted to help him – in return for what he'd done for me years ago.'

'You go for him?'

'No. Even among the mass-produced goods he's strictly a reject – with me, anyway.'

'Somali mother, Italian father, you speak English almost too well.'

'I'm a fast studier, an international cabaret star, and English, French, and German are obligatory. I weigh a hundred and thirty, have a Greek passport, and a star-shaped mole on the inside of my left thigh. If you are custom-built I might show it to you sometime. As for the Greek passport, I thought I would like to be a member of one of the most illustrious civilizations of the past. By the way, I get most of my clothes at Courrèges, don't care for oysters much, but am inclined to make a pig of myself over *pasta*. I'd like another drink and suggest that from now on we just keep to this kind of small talk. Unless, of course, you want to tell me the story of your life?'

It was a sudden dismissal, and I wondered what had prompted it. However, I didn't quarrel with it. Small talk suited me. The big fat facts of life often show for a brief, shy moment in small talk.

'Suits me,' I said. 'As for the story of my life, I really think it began when you walked into the Piazza Santo Spirito flat. Stout Cortez and a peak in Darien and all that.'

'You will have to do better than that. Why not order the drinks?'

I did and we talked. I had a feeling that I was doing better, but it was hard to tell. I didn't doubt that she felt that she had my measure. And I didn't doubt that I hadn't anything like got hers – except that she knew how to handle herself and wasn't going to let anyone else do it unless he passed muster. And nothing came out of the small talk, except the pleasure of making the time to Tripoli pass quickly and enjoyably.

As we parted in the beginning of the stampede into the customs sheds, under a dusky blue velvet sky lit with little yellow star sequins and a crescent moon to symbolize the Arab world, I said, 'Some evening soon, perhaps, we might make pigs of ourselves over *pasta* and a bottle of Orvieto?'

'Could be, but it would have to be Chianti Ruffino.'

With a smile she flowed ahead of me and I couldn't help noticing that the customs boys fell over themselves to deal with her and get her through as fast as possible.

I came out into a warm night that smelt of dry dust, burnt-up palm fronds, goats, and exhaust fumes from the waiting taxis.

One of the taxis was under the charge of the faithful Wilkins. She was wearing a woolly cardigan, a tweed skirt, sensible shoes and a wide-brimmed straw hat so that she wouldn't get burnt by the tropical moon. Just seeing her there gave me a warm feeling of belonging and nostalgia. She certainly wasn't any Gloriana or La Piroletta, but she was my girl Friday, one in a million, and that's what a man has got to have if he's going to make a success of business and have his filing system kept in order.

It was half an hour's drive in to Tripoli from the King Idris Airport. The Arab taxi-driver took it at top speed and with the radio wailing out snake-charm music at top volume. Now and again Wilkins and myself were thrown about as he deliberately just missed the odd pedestrian, goat, or camel. Conversation was difficult but we managed.

I said, 'Why didn't Olaf come with you?'

'He has a stomach upset.'

I didn't make any comment. The taxi ride was bad enough; I didn't want Wilkins turning a broadside on me.

'Where am I staying?'

'At a hotel on the sea front called Del Mehari. I got you a room with bath.'

'Why not a room at your hotel, or the Uaddan?' La Piroletta was still very, very fresh in my mind.

'Because all of them are fully booked. This is a booming oil town and hotel rooms are at a premium. And, anyway, I thought you might like to stay where Martin Freeman and William Dawson had stayed.'

'How did you find that out?'

'Olaf was responsible. I told him about the case. We checked all the hotels to see if either man had stayed recently – with no result. Then Olaf said that if Bill Dawson had said in his letter to Freeman that he could have his revenge at the Wheelus course, then – if the hotels were covering up about them for any reason, which now I am sure they are – the police or whoever it was who had instructed them might not have thought to put a cover on the Seabreeze golf course, particularly as it is American owned. So Olaf said—'

'Let's go out and see if they did play there and enter their names in the book?'

'Yes.'

'And they had?'

'Yes.'

'Clever Olaf. He's in the wrong business.'

'They played there about twelve days ago and they both gave the Del Mehari as their hotel. But at the Del Mehari when Olaf and I made inquiries—'

'They just looked blank and said no?'

'Very blank. And since they don't use a hotel registration book but do each guest on a card which goes into a filing system we couldn't ask to see the register. How long do you think it will be before Olaf and I can go to Cairo?'

'Don't tell me you're losing interest? You've done so well.'

'I'm entitled to my holiday. Also—' an even primmer note came into her voice – 'I don't like being followed by the police everywhere I go. The car behind us now is one which followed me out to the airport.'

I screwed my head round. Through the back window I could see headlights following us.

'Sure?'

'Positively.' Then disapprovingly, 'I thought this might be a straight-forward case, but I'm sure now that it isn't. You know how much I dislike complications.'

'You, and Monsieur Robert Duchêne. What's Olaf's reaction? Doesn't he find it exciting?'

'I told you he had a stomach upset. I'm sure it's a nervous one. I'm worried for him.'

She had reason to be. In a man Olaf's size a stomach upset was no minor matter.

I said, 'Did you get anything on Bill Dawson?'

'Nothing, except—'

I lost what she said as the radio began to whack out an Arab nuptial dance or something and we swerved to miss a donkey loaded four storeys high with sacks.

'Except what?'

'Except that I keep thinking that I ought to know something about him. Something at the back of my mind. It is most irritating.'

'I get the feeling too. Maybe it will come. Did you check the hire-car services? This golf course is some way out of the town, isn't it? They could have hired a car to go.'

Wilkins nodded. 'Olaf suggested that. We went round them all. And they were all very cooperative, looking through their books and apologizing when they had no record recently of a Freeman or a Dawson. All except one – it's a place near the centre of the town called the Magarba Garage. They just said at once without reference to their books that they had not hired out any cars to any such persons.'

'The police or whoever had been at them?'

'Yes. Did you bring any firearms in?'

That was typical Wilkins. She could call a spade a spade with the best of them, but a gun was always a firearm.

I said, 'Yes. It's strapped to the inside of my left leg now and damned uncomfortable.'

'Then if you don't want to become *persona non grata* I should get rid of it. Firearms can only be imported if declared on arrival and a licence obtained.'

'I'll be careful. And you've done a good job – or, at least, Olaf has. He's a bright boy. Why don't we offer him a job with us and then you wouldn't have to make the Cairo trip every year? Carver, Wilkins, and Bornjstrom. Sounds good.'

'The car behind is coming up to overtake us.'

I squinted back. It was. And it did. And then about a hundred yards ahead it pulled up and a man jumped out into our headlights.

Wilkins said, 'The firearm.'

I jerked up my trouser leg and did some quick unstrapping. Wilkins took it from me and calmly put it into her handbag like a schoolmistress coolly confiscating a catapult.

Our driver hesitated for a moment or two, considered whether he would notch up another pedestrian on his steering column, and then changed his mind as the white holster webbing, navy blue uniform, and peaked cap said 'Police' very plainly.

He pulled into the side of the road behind the police car which I saw now was a Land-Rover. The police corporal or sergeant or whatever he was came round to the side of the car and spoke through the driver's open window. Our taximan switched off 'Return to the Oasis' or whatever was playing and shrugged his shoulders.

The policeman came back to the rear window and signalled for me to wind it down. I did. A warm gust of night air came in and I gave him a big smile.

'Trouble, Officer?'

He was a Libyan, small, stocky, hard material all the way through and very correct. Even his English was correct.

'You are Mr Carver?'

'Yes.'

'And you stay where?'

'At the Del Mehari Hotel, when I get there.'

'This lady?'

'She is my secretary.'

'It is requested that you come with us, Mr Carver. Be good enough to ask your secretary to take your luggage on to your hotel.'

'I hope I'm going to be allowed to join up with it later?'

'Certainly.'

I wondered why they hadn't picked me up at the airport. The only answer I could come up with was that they wanted the minimum of public display. Interesting, since I was only looking for a man who'd stolen money and a bracelet from his own sister.

'Shall I be back there tonight?'

'Certainly, Mr Carver.'

I turned to Wilkins. 'Drop my stuff and come round and have breakfast with me in the morning. Bring Olaf if he's in a breakfast mood.'

I got out and the policeman waved the taxi on. It roared away, leaving
a dust cloud behind it and I could hear the radio going full blast.

They put me in the back of the Land-Rover and we headed for
town. One of the things about strange towns is never to reach them at
night. You have no sense of topography or direction and if you have to
take quick action you are at a loss to know which way to head. Not that
I thought this might be necessary tonight. But you never knew. Some
of the politest police opening gambits lead up to nasty end games
sometimes.

There was a nasty end game this time. But not the kind I could have
anticipated. We drove into the town and I didn't try to make any sense
out of it until for a few moments we swung along a wide esplanade with
the sea on our right and the lights of shipping somewhere way ahead
from a harbour. Then we turned into a side-street and pulled up in front
of a blank-faced building with double wooden doors. From a socket
over the door projected a Libyan national flag.

I got out with my police escort and he took me by the arm and
through the door. He said nothing and I went with him his palm on
my elbow, feeling like some old man being helped across the street by
a good Samaritan. We went down a tiled corridor that smelled of old
cooking and stale tobacco, up a stone flight of steps and then through
a half-glass door into a large, low-ceilinged room. One wall held what
looked like a collection of large metal filing cabinets. There was a bare,
chromium-topped table in the centre and sitting on one edge of it was
another Libyan in a white overall. My guide said something to him in
Arabic and the man got up and jerked a half-smoked cigarette into a
drainway under the table. For the first time I got the smell in the room
and a flicker of familiarity trembled inside me.

The man in overalls went over to one of the filing cabinets and pulled it open. It didn't surprise me now to see it come out about six feet on its rollers. He made a motion with his hand for me to come over. I did.

It wasn't a pretty sight. I stood there and took out a cigarette. The policeman who had come up alongside me held out a lighter. The man in overalls watched me guardedly. Neither of them said anything.

Lying in the container was a naked man. I inhaled smoke to get the chemical smell out of my throat and to fight down an edge of nausea. I'd seen plenty of dead men, and even a few who had been in the water a long time, but to stand there and look down at this one took more out of me than any of the others had. I let my eyes go from what had been the head down the length of the body to his feet. I did it deliberately, slowly, and with half my thoughts a long way away. Then I stepped back, turned and heard the cabinet roll back behind me.

To the policeman I said, 'What now?'

He said, 'Please to come with me.'

I did, avoiding his helping hand, moving alongside him and wondering how Jane Judd and Gloriana Stankowski were going to take the news, because tabbed neatly round the right wrist of the body had been a label, marked *Martin Freeman, British.*

SIX

The Apprentice Trail

The room, though I didn't know it then, was in the Police Headquarters on the Sciara Sidi Aissa which was a street one block south of the waterfront. Almost next door, though I didn't know that until the next morning when I got a town map and began to take my bearings, was the Hotel Casino Uaddan, and a little farther up the street to the east was the Libya Palace Hotel.

It was a small, high room with a framed photograph of King Idris of Libya over a fireplace which was piled high with old pine-cones. On the opposite wall was a framed photograph of HRH El-Hassan El-Rida El-Senussi, the Crown Prince of Libya, and just below it, flickering in the slight sea draught from the half-open window, a calendar of the Oasis Oil Company which told me that it was now April 21 and cuckoo time back home. I had to admit to a slight touch of nostalgia for the pigeons in Trafalgar Square, the tube rush in the evenings, and Mrs Meld leaning over the garden gate. I always got nostalgia when I sensed that I was getting into something deep and far from home.

The man behind the desk wore a plain navy blue suit, a white cotton shirt, and a black tie with a white stripe right down its middle. He was in his thirties, had a brown face as smooth as a pecan nut, pleasant dark eyes, a small thin-lipped mouth, and short, wiry black hair. He looked as though no one had ever rushed him in his life, or was ever going to, because he had long ago decided that, paradise as the bosom of Allah might be, he was in no hurry to reach it – so the form for longevity was a calm, even-paced life and always keep your voice down. On the edge of his desk was a little wooden board which read 'Captain Iba Asab', in English, and below some Arabic writing which probably announced the same thing.

He watched my police corporal escort out of the room, and then gave me a slow nod which was a greeting and an invitation to sit on the chair lying just off his desk.

'Mr Carver?'

'Yes.'

'Captain Asab, Libyan State Police.' He put out an arm slowly and tapped the announcement board across his desk.

'And not without a sense of the dramatic. Why this build-up?'

'You have been inconvenienced?'

'Only to the extent that by now I'd thought I'd be having a leisurely drink at my hotel and changing my socks.'

He smiled. 'Moslems are especially enjoined to be kind and charitable to the *masakeen* – unfortunate. I regret, however, I have no drink to offer you. However, I will try not to keep you too long.'

'Don't rush anything.'

He gave me a look and said, 'At the moment you are a little uncertain. Perhaps of my attitude? Perhaps of your status? Do not worry. My only wish is to give you all the information I can to help you to bring your business here to a conclusion.'

'How's your colloquial English?'

'Fair to middling. I did three years at the London School of Economics – and ended up a policeman, which just shows that you can never tell which way the ball's going to bounce. I don't myself – but light up if you want to.'

I lit a cigarette and he slowly opened a drawer as I did so.

'Where was Martin Freeman fished out of the drink?' I asked him.

He pushed an open shallow cardboard box across the desk to me. 'A little way up the coast, west of the town, two days ago. He was fully dressed, a sports jacket and trousers and so on. That's all he had on him.' He nodded at the box.

I took the box and went through the stuff. All of it had suffered from water exposure. There was a British passport in Freeman's name, a leather wallet with about ten pounds in Libyan sterling, a couple of membership cards of clubs in Rome, a bunch of keys, a Ronson leather-bound lighter, a silver cigarette case with the initials M.F. on the outside and two water-pulped cork-tipped cigarettes inside.

'Where would the rest of his stuff be? He was a visitor here. He must have had a case or something at his hotel.'

'That we have been unable to trace.'

It could have been a lie, but whether it was or not didn't seem important to me.

'How did you know I was looking for him?'

'We were informed by the British Embassy here when we reported the recovery of the body to them. I gather, too, from them that your Treasury officials in London were interested in him.'

'Why?'

'The details are confidential, but, I imagine, irrelevant now. You can go and see them, if you wish, but they asked me to tell you that Mrs Stankowski is being informed of her brother's death and she will give whatever instructions are necessary for dealing with the body. In other words the affair is out of your hands.'

'Unless – when she knows the facts – she tells me she would like to know why, before being tipped into the sea, he was shot through the head.'

'Whether it was murder or suicide, Mr Carver – that is our concern. We need no help.'

'Got any ideas on the subject?'

'At the moment, few.'

'The body floated ashore?'

'Yes.' He reached slowly for the cardboard box and began to put it back in the drawer.

'So he could have been in the water anything from six days onwards?'

'About that.'

'What did the autopsy show? About the time in the water, I mean.'

'There is some doubt. The head wound complicates it.'

'Well I can tell you he hadn't been drifting around more than twelve days.'

He looked at me calmly, but it was the kind of calm that covered surprise. Tell this man that some forgotten old uncle out in the Fezzan had left him Solomon's treasure and there still wouldn't be a flicker; in fact, you could tell him anything and he would still be the same. But one thing was for sure – he was never going to tell me or anyone else anything that he had decided was best kept to himself.

'How can you know?'

'Because he played a round of golf at the Seabreeze course twelve days ago with a friend called Bill Dawson. You got a line on any Bill Dawson?'

'No. But thank you for the information.'

'Just that? Thanks. No questions as to how I know?'

He smiled. 'Tomorrow, maybe. At the moment I don't want to delay your whisky and soda.'

'I can wait. In the visitors' book at Seabreeze they both entered their hotel as the Del Mehari – that's where I am staying – and the hotel people told my secretary that neither of them had stayed there.'

He shook his head. 'Maybe they did. Some of my countrymen, Mr Carver, are lazy and inefficient. It is a young country. I'll look into it.'

'Check the Magarba Garage too. I think you'll find that Freeman or Dawson hired a car there some time in the last twelve days.' I stood up. 'And let's be as frank as we can with one another. Okay, there are lots of things you don't want to tell me. Fine, if that's how you feel it must be. But it hardly is the way to encourage cooperation from me – that's if there's anything I could do to help.'

'If I fancy you can help me I'll get in touch with you. But please understand that I do not wish you to encroach on what is now purely a police matter.'

Encroach. It was a good word. The trouble was that I had encroached already. And it was a good feeling. My late-night and early-morning lassitude was gone. La Piroletta had been the final dose of tonic to brighten the whites of my eyes. But more than health now I could hear distantly the rattle of a cash register and that, if you've got your health and the kind of fluctuating bank balance I enjoy, is music played by the oldest siren in the world. He didn't know it, of course, but standing there looking down at him, I'd just been presented with a lead which, the moment I could check it, might prove that Bill Dawson was really the number one, gold-plated fly in this ointment. Little things tip a man's destiny. And this one was a half-folded newspaper that lay neatly to one side of his desk. Later, I learned that it was the *Sunday Ghibli*, a weekly English-language newspaper published in Tripoli. All I was concerned with was the headline. There were going to be times soon when I could have wished I had never seen it.

'So long as I keep out of your hair, that's all right?'

'Absolutely.'

'And I can stay here as long as I like?'

'I don't imagine, Mr Carver – from the information I have about you – that you will want to stay at your own expense once Mrs Stankowski terminates your assignment.'

I didn't answer.

He said, 'The police car will drive you to your hotel. As a matter of fact it is very close to the British Embassy should you want to go and see them.'

He stood up and I was surprised to see how short he was.

I said, 'Why was I picked up on the road in from the airport? All of this could have waited until tomorrow.'

He shook his head. 'It seemed to me a good thing to have it over and done with. And again I thought it might embarrass you to have a police car call for you at your hotel.'

It was weak and he knew that I knew it. A police car was going to take me back to the hotel anyway. And when the police of any country start to worry about embarrassing people like me, then it was a safe bet that the real worry in their minds was much deeper and directed elsewhere.

The Del Mehari Hotel was on the sea front to the east of the town. It was a low Moorish-style building mostly on one floor, with all the rooms set around a central hall and a couple of inner courtyards.

I took a short stroll before breakfast towards the town. Palm trees lined the long esplanade. The wide curve of the harbour was a crinkly, breeze-freshened blue. Smug-fronted Mercedes and chromium-grinning American cars made pleasant tyre noises over the tarmac. A couple of blanket-wrapped Arabs slept in a sea-front embrasure, and groups of black-dressed Arab women shuffled along in the breeze, returning from their early morning charing jobs in the government offices. The Mediterranean sky was studded with little tufts of cotton-wool cloud. Way ahead of me was the Harbour Castle and the huddle of the old Arab town. But at this end all the signals were set to GO, hell-bent into the last half of the twentieth century on the crest of the Libyan oil boom. Office and apartment blocks were reaching up to dwarf the mosques and muezzin towers, and the faithful were called to pray to Allah these days over a Tannoy system. It was about as exotic as Brighton and you could find the same things in the shops and bars but at rather higher prices. A flight of jets from the Wheelus Air Base whined through the air leaving curving vapour trails behind them. It was the same old world, distance annihilated, all services piped in, ready at the flick of a finger, and not a single real problem that had plagued the world since *homo sapiens* first planted his ugly feet on it an inch nearer being solved. Only hope can sustain a dismal record like that. Or stupidity.

I went back and had eggs and bacon and fresh rolls and coffee, and got the waiter to bring me a cable form. To Mrs Stankowski I sent the message:

Presume you have official information death brother. Cable instructions.

Knowing the efficiency of the British Post Office service, I was ready to bet that they would deliver it as a greetings telegram with a border of fluffy rabbits, song birds, and nosegays.

During my second cup of coffee Wilkins and Olaf appeared. I'd met Olaf before, but he always came as a shock to me. He seemed to have put on another two inches everywhere. His pale-blue eyes sparkled with health so that I knew the tummy trouble was gone, his pale, fair hair was ruffled from the wind, and one of his great hands grabbed mine and pumped away as though he were clearing the bilges to keep the ship from sinking. He sat down and the chair just held under his weight, and he had to sit sideways because his knees would not go under the table comfortably.

'Mr Carver – you mess up our holiday. Not the first time, eh?' He grinned and the huge brown face went into a landslide of happy wrinkles.

'How's the stomach?'

'Fine. It was temporary. Some mussels we have at an Italian restaurant. Shellfish in the Mediterranean is always suspect. I should know but I never learn. You think Hilda looks well?'

Hilda, though God knows I could never think of her as anything but Wilkins, looked well, but embarrassed at the attention directed to her. She smiled at Olaf, then frowned at me, put up a hand and touched her rust-coloured hair, and said, 'What happened with the police?'

'Freeman is dead,' I said. 'They showed me his body. Fished out of the drink. So far as I am concerned it is the end of the matter. At least, almost.'

'We can go back to Cairo?' Olaf lit an Egyptian cigarette and began to fumigate the dining room.

'When a couple of small points are cleared up. Would you have any contacts with the harbour or shipping people here?'

Olaf nodded. 'Yes. Any port on the Med or the Red Sea, I know someone.'

'Good – there's a certain Leon Pelegrina who owns a steam yacht called *La Sunata*. I'd quite like to know what the movements of that boat have been lately. Say, in the last three weeks. Can do?'

'Of course.' He rose to his feet, and grabbed the table from going over. 'I go down there now. Hilda, I come back for you soon.'

He reached across for her hand, kissed it, and was gone.

'Charming,' I said. 'He's mad about you. When you set up house see you get good, solid teak furniture and screw it to the floor.'

'He's a good kind man.'

'That's what I'm saying. And you're lucky – he comes in the king size.'

'Why are you interested in this steam yacht if the matter is finished?'

'I like to tie up the loose ends. But don't worry about going back to Cairo. You'll get there. But first I'd like you this morning to go into town and send a cable to a Miss Jane Judd at the Mountjoy Hotel in Dorset Square. Sign it in my name and ask for a reply Poste Restante here.'

'I could do it from the hotel.'

'I know you could, but anything you send from there is probably handed first to the police.'

'Look—'

'I said I was just tying up loose ends. I am. Just say Cable if M.F. has abdominal scar left-hand side.'

'I presume this body had?'

'Yes. It's about the only thing left for identification except the teeth.'

'I don't think I want to do this.'

'Why not?'

'Freeman is dead. Olaf and I want to go to Cairo. And you won't ever leave well alone. The police out here are very touchy about interference.'

'They are everywhere. Touchiness is essential. Even if you're the right height you can't get into the police without it. And there's something else.'

'I'm not surprised. You've got that look. What is it this time? Some woman – or just money?'

'Both. And in addition, a man.'

'What man?'

'Bill Dawson. Captain Asab, whom I saw at Police headquarters, was remarkably uninterested in Dawson. No policeman can be remarkably uninterested in a man who was probably playing golf with Freeman a day or so before he was shot through the head.'

'Shot?'

'Didn't I mention that?'

She looked at me with steady blue eyes and shook her head slowly, pursing her lips. Next to Olaf, but a long way behind, I was her concern. I hoped that she wasn't going to overdo it.

'You have no intention of giving up this case, have you?'

'I don't like loose ends. I'll give it up when it's all tidy. Look at this.'

I handed over to her a copy of the *Sunday Ghibli* which I had found in the hotel lounge.

'What about it?'

'Read the headline.'

She read it. Looked at me, then read it again. I lit a cigarette.

She said, 'It's a common enough name.'

'Sure. Like Smith, Brown, and Jones.'

She sniffed. 'I think you should go back to London.'

I shook my head. 'Think about Bill Dawson. William Dawson. A common enough name. Something about that keeps niggling in my mind. You could check it.'

'A call to the British Embassy would confirm it.'

'I don't want it confirmed officially yet. I just want to know privately. I thought you'd like to do it.'

'What I'd like to do is to go to Cairo, and know you were back in London. At least there your mercenary instincts are reasonably limited.' She tapped the paper. 'If what I'm thinking you're thinking is so, your plain duty would be to tell all you know to the authorities.'

'You remember the three times in the last eight years that I've done that? It did nothing for my reputation, my pocket, or my comfort. Will you check it for me? I don't want to poke around. But there's a British Reading Room here. You'll probably find it full of dead-beat Libyans having a quiet snooze, but there's sure to be some gabby type in charge of the out-of-date newspapers and magazines. Turn on the charm.'

'There could be thousands of Dawsons.'

'That's it. And some of 'em get to the top. By the way, do you still remember our private code?'

Now listen, Mr Carver!'

'All right, all right . . .' I raised a placatory hand, my left through years of practice because you always want the right free in case it doesn't work.

Wilkins stood up and gathered herself together. She could do it better than anyone I knew. The temperature dropped and from inside the glacier she said, 'I'll do this and then Olaf and I are going back. When I joined you, you know it was agreed that I should not have to do field work.'

'You make it sound as though I'm running a cotton plantation.'

'You need', she said, 'your head examined. And I wish I knew this time what you were after. I don't believe it's money, because you've got plenty at the moment.'

'A woman, perhaps.'

'No, because you would have been talking about her already and have that silly, self-satisfied look on your face.'

'What then?'

'I think you're just doing it for the hell of it. For excitement. In the same way that teenagers take blue pills and eventually find themselves hooked on heroin. If you can't get a kick out of chasing money or a woman, then you find something else to chase.'

I said, 'That's a very attractive straw hat you've got. The ribbon matches your eyes. And you are looking well.'

She didn't say 'pig', but she swept out.

From the Del Mehari to the British Embassy was about two or three hundred yards along the sea front towards the town. After the first fifty yards I realized that Captain Asab had put a tail on me. He was a young man in a leather jacket and tight black trousers, open-necked white shirt, and a very worn round astrakhan hat. He was talking to the hotel gardener who was watering the gravel of the hotel forecourt when I came out. He drifted after me down the road and I checked him by going twice round the block in which the Embassy stood. He went round conscientiously after me and then looked a bit foolish as I stood at the foot of the Embassy steps waiting for him to come by. When he came up to me, I said, 'Is the man in the black Simca your friend?'

He looked blankly at me.

I nodded across the road. A black Simca saloon was just parking across the way.

'Your friend?' I queried him.

'*No comprendo, signore,*' he said.

'Save it,' I said. 'I shall be in here for a while, then you can give me a lift down to the Uaddan. Captain Asab won't mind.'

He gave a shy little grin, then dry-washed his chin with one hand, and said, 'The signore is talking in riddles.' He ducked his head at me and moved on. I watched him go, thinking that Captain Asab must be very hard up for trained men. Either that, or he was putting a novice on to me for the experience, knowing that I wouldn't mind.

In the Embassy hallway there was a porter in a serge suit and red fez who wanted me to fill out a memo in triplicate stating the nature of my business. Instead I wrote – Martin Freeman and William Dawson – on the back of one of my cards and handed it to him, saying, 'Ask the Ambassador if he can spare five minutes.'

He looked shocked and disappeared. I sat down and watched a girl in a white blouse and check skirt arranging a bowl of flowers on a stand farther down the hall. She arranged them nicely, showing a lot of leg, one of which had a ladder in its nylon. A telephone rang twice somewhere. An Air Force officer came down the stairway and the girl moved around in her arranging so that he could see the laddered nylon. She was wasting her time. He went by her and by me and out with a glazed look in his eye as though he had just been dismissed from the service.

Five minutes later I was in a little room on the first floor talking to a secretary who had been designated to deal with me in lieu of the Ambassador Extraordinary and Plenipotentiary. There was a silver-framed photograph of a woman and two nice boys on his desk, all of them smiling. His wife and children, I presumed. It was a pity he wasn't smiling too. It spoilt the family atmosphere. He looked worried and cautious and he had the right face for it. It was clear too that he had no time for me. I was in the wrong profession and certainly wasn't wearing the right tie. His was Old Marlburian; mine was a green number with red dots on it and the silk a little frayed on the knot. Wilkins that morning had found time to give it a disapproving stare. Anxiety and caution – to them in other people I am as sensitive as a sea anemone sensing the turn of the tide.

I said, 'I just wanted to check with you whether you had had any instructions from my client about the disposal of her brother's body? Captain Asab of the police here has told me that you have already informed her of the tragedy.'

'No instructions have so far been received.'

'Will you let me know when you do receive them? I'm at the Del Mehari Hotel up the road.'

'Certainly.' He raised his bottom two inches from his chair. He couldn't wait to get rid of me.

'Dreadful thing,' I said. 'Shot through the head and then dumped in the drink. Not that he didn't have something like that coming to him by all accounts. Still – *de mortuis nil nisi bonum.*'

The tag and its sentiment didn't impress him beyond making him lower his bottom to the seat.

'I think, Mr Carver, you can safely leave everything in our hands – in cooperation with the Libyan police, that is.'

'Absolutely,' I said. 'Would you have any idea which way the sea current sets along this coast at this time of the year? East to west or the other way round?'

'I haven't the faintest idea.'

He was beginning to lift again but I stalled him.

'And what about this Bill Dawson he was last seen with?'

'How did you know—'

He broke off, not because the telephone had begun to ring on his desk, but because for a moment he had assumed that I knew something I wasn't presumed to know, and then had decided that I was probably making some kind of inspired guess. I was, of course. In fact, for inspired guessing I'm in the Olympic class. How otherwise would I make money and eat?

He picked up the phone and answered it. I sat there and listened.

His eyes kept flickering towards me as he said, 'Yes' and 'No', and then once, 'Would you mind repeating that?' It was a classical example of a guarded conversation and his eyes on me gave away the fact that whatever was being said to him he connected in some way with me.

He wrote something on a memo pad with a pencil, put the phone down, tore off the memo page, and stood up.

'Would you please excuse me a moment?'

I nodded graciously. Why not – he was on the Queen's business. I was just on my own, but I had more than an inkling even then that the two were going to be mixed. He went out of the room, through a door behind his desk. As it closed I reached over and tore off the next page of the memo block. He had a good heavy hand with a pencil when he wrote. I didn't bother then to try and decipher the markings that had come through to the lower leaf. When he came back the memo page was neatly folded in my pocket.

I said, 'You were going to tell me something about this Bill Dawson who was with Freeman sometime shortly before his death.'

Stiffly, he said, 'I wasn't aware that I was. We know nothing of any Dawson who might have been connected with Mr Freeman.' He rose smartly, no stalling him this time, but he put a patently false note of cooperation into his voice to get me eased out of the room. 'Be assured, Mr Carver – that so long as you represent Mrs Stankowski's interests out here we shall keep you informed – so far as police protocol will allow – of all developments. The death, possible murder, indeed, of a British subject is, of course, a matter of great concern to us and the local authorities.'

He had a good platform voice when he wanted, full of the deepest insincerity, but it got me out of the room and the door closed behind me.

I stopped in the hall and took out the memo leaf. It didn't need any scientific treatment to decipher it. It read:

Manston arrives Idris 19.45 hrs. Arrange car.

At that moment there could have been a harem of naked houris arranging flowers in the hall and I wouldn't have noticed them. No wonder my secretary upstairs had itchy pants and a distant manner, no wonder Captain Asab had had me picked up on the road in from King Idris Airport, and no wonder there was a cold feeling in the pit of my stomach and the adrenalin pump going full bore somewhere in my throat – because Bill Dawson just had to be what I had begun to suspect he must be. Once they had names like Pelham, Grenville, Perceval, and Rockingham, but this is the age of the common man and in have come the Browns, the Smiths, and the Dawsons to fill the high places.

I shoved the paper back into my pocket and went half-tranced out of the place. As the sea air and sunshine hit me I was telling myself that a couple of half-baked dreamy incompetents like Pelegrina and Freeman could never have dared to try and pull off something like this. Dream about it, yes. Why not, there's no law against dreams. But to try it on – and, by God, it had to be that they had . . . ! Well, they weren't even in the fourth division league for that kind of thing. In my time I'd met a few who could have tried it, even got away with it – but not those two, not unless they had all this time been hiding their real talent and brilliance.

I lit a cigarette at the bottom of the Embassy steps. For ten seconds I wondered what to do, during the next thirty I slowly came to the decision to pack up and go home, and then in the next ten I changed my mind. I couldn't go home. And leave all this? Not bloody likely. This was what the doctor had ordered for my flagging body and mind. And, anyway, leaving out health reasons, there might be other things in it . . . like money, like women, like kudos, like being one jump ahead of everyone else, like an MBE at the end of it . . . and like, quite possibly, a sticky end. Rex Carver, RIP. But what the hell, I told myself – duck a challenge and the dust settles thick on your shoulders like dandruff.

At my side, a real voice with a touch of Italian accent said, 'You really like, Mr Carver, that we give you a lift to the Uaddan?'

It was my young apprentice tail, grinning.

'Why not,' I said. 'My legs feel a bit weak at the moment.'

Obligingly they brought the Simca to the kerb for me.

They rang from the reception desk and she told them to send me up. It was a little suite on the second floor overlooking the sea. She came through from the bedroom wearing a cream silk dress that showed a lot of bare brown arm. She just stood and looked me over and I did the same for her.

She said, 'Is this business or pleasure?'

'Business first.'

She said, 'The drinks are over there. Mine is lime juice and soda water and four lumps of ice.'

I went over to a side-table and began mixing. She dropped into a little chair by the window, crossed her legs neatly and looked a picture with the sun taking the whole of one side of her body.

I said, 'What do I call you? Not La Piroletta or Miss Pelegrina.'

'So long as it is business just avoid it.'

I handed her her drink and sat down opposite her holding a gin and tonic.

I said, 'I want your help.'

'If I can. Is it this bracelet business?'

She held up her left arm; the gold python bands slid over the warm brown skin.

'Only indirectly. I want to know your real feeling for your father.'

'Why?'

'Because I think he's heading for big trouble. May already be in it.'

'That describes his life.'

'You like to see him in trouble?'

'No. As a matter of fact I am reasonably fond of him. But that doesn't stop me also being fed up with him. In the past I often helped him with money. But now – no more.'

'Has he tried to touch you recently?'

'Touch? Oh, you mean borrow money?'

'Yes.'

She shook her head. 'He knows better.'

'What is his financial position?'

'Rocky. He's been up and he's been down in his life. At the moment he's down. Mostly he's been in shipping or property development. There was a time when he was doing quite well. But it passed. What is he trying to do now that he shouldn't?'

'I'm not sure. He still owns a steam yacht, doesn't he?'

'*La Sunata*. Yes. But he's probably carrying some loan on it.'

'What about property?'

'He's not involved in any development scheme that I know about.'

I stood up and wandered round the room. A little wander often helps the thoughts. My back to her, I said, 'If he wanted to drop out of the public eye for a while where do you think he would go?'

'You mean if he wanted to hide?'

'Something like that. For instance, would he take off in *La Sunata* for a cruise?'

Her laugh brought me round to face her.

'That's the last thing he would do. He hates the sea. He's always sick.'

'Then where would he go? Does he own a house, villa, or cottage anywhere? Particularly on this side of the Mediterranean.'

She frowned. 'Why should I help you to find my father if he's in trouble?'

'God knows. I suppose, in a way, because I'd like to help him if it isn't too late.'

'Is this something to do with Freeman too?'

'I think so. I think the two of them dreamed up something which is right outside their class. Miles outside. If I can get to your father I might be able to straighten things out for him.'

'Why on earth should you? You don't care a damn for him.'

'True. But I've often straightened things out for people I don't like.'

'On the chance that it will show a profit?' She was looking at me shrewdly. Whichever way she looked, it was good.

'Yes. Why not? Good deeds are always chalked up on the credit side either in a bank book down here or in the golden one above.'

'Perhaps you'd better tell me exactly what it is that is worrying you about my father.'

'I can't because I don't know anything definite. But you tell me where

I can get in touch with him – and I promise to do all I can to help him.'

She stood and shook her head.

'Why not?'

'Because I have to think about it.'

'That means you do know where he might be?'

'Could be.'

'Then I'd advise you not to be too long making up your mind to tell me.'

'That's what I was thinking. But one has to be sure – no?'

'Oh, yes, one has to be sure – particularly in dealing with people like me.'

She stood close to me and smiled. I really was concerned about her father, even though I guessed he was a dreamy, half-baked crook. In my book he was just pathetic. I couldn't help warm generous feelings for that type because they were all victims, reaching for the moon, eyes heavenward, and bound to walk straight over the edge of a cliff sooner or later. I put my hand on her brown arm. It felt good. Man is an ambivalent creature. I worried about her father with a small part of my mind, and at the same time wanted her with a larger part, and with the part left over hoped that if any credit was to come my way it would be in cash and not a citation in any golden book.

She raised her face a little and put her lips on mine. Gently, no fuss, nothing passionate beyond my arms going comfortably round her. Then she stepped back and said, 'My friends, real friends, call me Letta. And let's face it, there are bloody few of them because I have high standards.'

'What rating do you think I'll get?'

'Come and see me after the last show tonight and I'll have it sorted out. You – and my father. All right?'

I nodded, and she went to the door and opened it for me. I gave her a big smile and went. But only twelve paces down the carpeted corridor. Then I turned round and went back to her door. I squatted down and put my eye to the keyhole. Accurate character reading is a must in my business. Letta was no girl for letting grass grow under her feet. If she wasn't sure of somebody – me, for instance – she took her time, determined to make no mistake. But if she was sure of a thing she got on with it. She was getting on with it now. She was standing by the window table, leafing through a small notebook. She put it down and picked up the telephone. She was about to speak into it when she paused and looked straight towards the room door. She began to lower the receiver to its rest.

I moved fast, down the corridor and around the corner, to get out of the way of the little bit of her character that I had overlooked, that she had read mine more accurately than I had read hers. I kept going fast – knowing she would open the door and reassure herself that I wasn't eavesdropping – until I reached the hotel hallway. To one side of the reception desk there was a girl at a switchboard. Just beyond was a glass case full of Arab leather goods, silver brooches and bangles and fifth-rate water colours. I stood and examined the exhibits and almost immediately the exchange buzzer went. The girl plugged in a lead. I listened to her speaking. It was brief and in Italian and I didn't get much of it, certainly not the number of the call that Signorina Pelegrina was booking. But I got the exchange. It was Bizerta. Well, that was enough. All I had to do now was to get a look at her address book. There couldn't be many Bizerta numbers in it. In fact, when I did come to examine it there was only one.

Outside, I declined a lift from the apprentice tail and walked back to my hotel for lunch. The first course was some fish with cotton-wool flesh full of needle-sharp bones and then a dish of mutton and rice to apply as an inner poultice to a lacerated stomach. Afterwards I lay on my bed for a couple of hours to recover and at the same time went over the tangle of Pelegrina-Freeman loose ends to see if I could sort the mess out. I didn't have a great deal of success. That Bill Dawson had to be what I suspected him to be was reasonably certain. That Pelegrina was trying to pull off a deal far too big for him was also reasonably certain. In doing this with Freeman it could be that Freeman had either become a casualty or the body I had been shown was not Freeman's but a gruesome red herring to make everyone think that Freeman was out of the picture for good. Jane Judd would establish this for me. After all, a wife ought to know whether her husband had an abdominal scar or not, and Jane had been warned not to believe anything she heard about Freeman. Yes, Freeman could be trying to set up his future life neat and tidy and without complications. As usual he wasn't being very efficient about it. Neither Manston nor Captain Asab would accept a water-sodden passport as proof of identity.

But the aspect that puzzled me most was the Paulet and Robert Duchêne angle. Just where did they feature in this, and what did they think they were going to get out of me? Or had thought they were going to get? I didn't know and I worried about it right through until it was time to have a drink before dinner.

I'd got through my first whisky and soda when the reception clerk brought me my reply from Gloriana. The cable read:

Embassy arranging all details my brother. Your services no longer required. Appreciate efforts by you to date. G.S.

Well, it was nice to be appreciated.

Halfway through my second drink Wilkins arrived. I bought her a Dubonnet and she handed me Jane Judd's reply which was:

M.F. abdominal scar right-hand side. Why? Judd.

Well, it might be some time before I could answer her 'Why?' All I knew at the moment was that it was a typical piece of Freeman care-lessness to think he could get away with a slap-dash substitute for himself.

'What about Dawson?' I asked Wilkins.

'You were right. Olaf and I are leaving for Cairo tomorrow in the late afternoon. I suggest you get a plane back to London.'

'What did Olaf find out about the yacht, *La Sunata*?'

'It was in harbour here two weeks ago and then went up the coast as far as Bizerta. A week ago it went across to Naples and is now on charter doing a trip along the French coast.'

'It went just as far as Bizerta, did it? Interesting.'

'Are you going to London?'

'I'll think about it.'

'I wish you would.'

'Don't worry. I can look after myself.'

'I doubt it.'

'Examine the records – they prove it.'

'You've been lucky, that's all. What do you think has happened to Bill Dawson?'

I gave her a smile over my whisky and shook my head. 'You're not asking me that? Not my Wilkins? You know what's happened to him, don't you?'

'He's been kidnapped.'

'Yes. By an incompetent couple who'll never get away with it the moment people like Manston—'

'Manston? Don't tell me—'

'I do tell you. What did you expect? This is his line of country. State security. No headlines. Just quiet blue murder the moment he and his crowd get their hands on Freeman or Pelegrina.'

'Or you – if you interfere. You fool.'

'I'm not interfering. I just want the missing piece of the jigsaw and then I can sell it to Manston. He'll be grateful and pay.'

She just looked at me and shook her head.

I was late getting down to the Uaddan that evening for the simple reason that I didn't want to take Letta out to dinner with a great rip in the front of my shirt. I had to come back to my hotel to change it.

The thing happened neatly, smoothly and was almost successful. One thing for sure was that I was taken completely off my guard.

It was a fine night, ablaze with stars. The lights of the shipping in the harbour and the great curve of esplanade lights lining the long waterfront reflected in the black sea, all made up a picture which pleased me and put me in a good mood. I like the sea and I like bright lights. The air was warm and I walked along happily, thinking about Letta and now and again getting a whiff of my own after-shave lotion and feeling that life was full of promise. The wide roadway was bathed now and then with the headlights of passing cars. A couple of Arab women passed me on the pavement. One was carrying a hand transistor set and the voices of the Beatles bounced into the night with a happy, hearty vitality. The world was good and I was in it. Four seconds later I was nearly out of it.

He came up the pavement towards me and I paid no attention. To me he was just a man in a suit, padding along enjoying the night air like myself. When he was level with me he turned suddenly in to me and his right arm went up. I just caught the flicker of reflected light on steel and then his hand was coming down at me fast. Miggs would have given me nought out of ten for my reaction. But then a happy man is the easiest and most unsuspecting target in the world for a fast knife man. He obviously expected some fast reaction from me – somebody somewhere had given me a good build-up, briefing him about what to expect. Maybe that saved me, for he swung, expecting me to step back fast and making allowance for it. His hand came down, allowance made for my three- or four-inch swing back, and when I didn't move he made a rapid adjustment of angle and the knife caught the edge of my collar and ripped downwards, slashing through the loose hang of my shirt front. By some miracle the blade didn't even touch my skin. But he didn't waste time moaning over his first botched effort. The hand swung again and this time I did move. I threw myself sideways, slipped, and went to the ground in the shadow of one of the esplanade trees. He came for me and side-stepped the swing of my right foot as I tried to take him off his feet. For a moment I saw his brown face, serious, intent on his work, not at all perturbed by the fact that there were a dozen people within two hundred yards' call, a workman's face, dedicated, content no doubt with the knowledge that for this sudden call to night work, he was getting double rates, and a bonus for success.

He would have got it too, except for my apprentice tail whom I had not even bothered to look for when I left the hotel. A.T. appeared out of the ground like a genie, not waiting for any lamp-rubbing call from me. Suddenly he was there, between me, the man, and the knife. I heard a grunt, the clatter of the knife dropping to the pavement and then, as I got to my feet, I saw the man running, away from the lights up a side-street. A.T. stood and watched me to my feet.

I took a deep breath and said, 'Thanks.'

A.T. just smiled.

I said, 'Was it anyone you knew?'

He shook his head.

I looked down at my shirt. Not even Mrs Meld was going to be able to do anything for it. It was good, heavy silk, handmade, one of my recent luxuries. I went back to the hotel and changed the shirt. When I came out the black Simca was parked in the hotel forecourt. A.T. stood by it, talking to the driver. Seeing me, he just held the back door open. I got in and said, 'The Uaddan.'

A.T. got in by the driver, turned to me and said, 'You were dreaming?'

I nodded.

He shook his head disapprovingly at me. It was the same kind of shake I had had a little while before from Wilkins.

SEVEN

Of Pythons and Vintage Sardines

First there was Manston. I met him in the gaming room of the hotel. The cabaret in the dining room had just finished when I arrived and Letta sent me a message that she would be with me in half an hour. I wandered into the casino, watched some oil men playing blackjack, hung around the roulette tables for a bit, and then went over and began to feed coins into a fruit machine. The gaming room could have been anywhere in the world. All I knew at that moment was that I felt a little out of it. I was suffering. Mostly from anger with myself at being caught off guard. I was puzzled, too, trying to decide who would want to put me away and why. The only person who had tried it before was Pelegrina. If this were another of his efforts, and the quick improvisation suggested it, then I couldn't help telling myself that he must have discovered that I was in Tripoli through Letta. It was going to be interesting to hear what she had to say. But first of all I had to hear what Manston had to say.

He came up to me as I stood at the fruit machine. He was wearing a dinner jacket and looked cool, confident, and in no mood for nonsense. He gave me a warm smile and a friendly nod, neither of which meant anything. With him, also in evening clothes, was an enormous man whose face was familiar. I remembered then that he had been one of the two men in Duchêne's Paris flat when I had walked in on their search. Then I had taken him for a bruiser. Now, although he was twice as big, I saw that he was out of the Manston school.

Manston looked at him and said, 'Perkins. This is Carver.'

'We've met,' I said. 'He's a dab hand with pot plants.'

'Sorry we had to be a bit rough with you, old boy.' He had a gravelly, educated voice, full of charm, reassuring. He'd probably got a blue for rugger at Cambridge. I could just see those big shoulders battering away in the scrum.

'I want you', said Manston, 'to get out of this town.'

'I'm thinking of doing that.'

'I want you, too, to forget you ever heard of Messrs Freeman and Dawson. You know why, of course.'

I nodded. 'You've done a good job stopping any publicity.'

'There's never going to be any. Also, if you'll excuse the crudity, there are not going to be any pickings in this for you.'

'I haven't been thinking along those lines. I've got plenty of money at the moment.'

'Then live to enjoy it,' said Perkins. He slipped a coin into the machine, jerked the handle and got a bigger dividend at once than I'd had so far.

'It's like that, is it?' I looked at Manston.

'It's just like that. Take a vow of silence right now – and that includes talking in your sleep. Go away and forget.'

'Do that,' said Perkins. 'We haven't got time to be bothered with any monkey tricks. Just begin one and I'll break your neck and drop you in the sea. We'll issue a D-notice so that you don't even get four lines in the evening papers.'

'Why', I asked Manston, 'have I never had the pleasure of meeting this number before? I should have thought he was too big and obvious for your service.'

'Far East, old boy,' said Perkins. 'Only just come back to home service.'

'Just forget Freeman and Dawson,' said Manston. 'That way we can go on being friends when we have to.'

'Charming. Okay – I won't say a word. But somebody will. You'll never keep this out of the press.'

'Our instructions are that we must. So we will. Understood?'

'Yes. And what happens to them when you catch up with them?'

Perkins winked. 'We break their necks and drop them in the sea, and then cover that with a D-notice.'

'I might be able to help.'

'We don't want it. Just go home and chase insurance cheats; live a full life and a long one,' said Manston.

'If you insist. How's the big man taking it? And I don't mean Sutcliffe.'

'Sincerely and frankly,' said Perkins, 'the big man is hopping bloody mad – and, of course, worried, as any decent parent would be.'

'As a matter of interest,' I said idly, 'where was the snatch made? Up the coast a bit at a place called Sabratha?'

Neither of them moved a muscle.

I grinned. 'You shouldn't have too much trouble. Not with a guy like Freeman. He couldn't even fake his own death convincingly. I'll bet he's biting his nails now to work out some fool-proof method for the ransom money to be handed over. A clever man would have had that one settled before he took the first step. Yes, I can see that you don't need my help in dealing with an incompetent like that.'

'If we ever do need you,' said Perkins affably, 'don't think we won't be able to find you.'

'You will be leaving tomorrow,' said Manston. It wasn't a question. It was an order.

I nodded, always polite, and moved away because I had just seen Letta come to the door of the gaming room.

So, secondly, there was Letta. La Piroletta. Leon Pelegrina's daughter. I wondered whether Manston knew that connexion. He would know about Paulet and Duchêne. He might know about the steam yacht *La Sunata*. But what he didn't know, clearly – otherwise he would never have been wasting any time here – was where Pelegrina and Freeman were at this moment. I might be a jump ahead of him there. But what could I do about it? I'd offered to help and had been told to go and chase insurance cheats. That hurt my pride. Not that I worried over that. The pain was minimal.

So, as I said, secondly there was Letta in a yellow silk gown, a scrap of mink over her shoulders, dark dusky skin making my fingers tremble to touch it and her dark, deep, brilliant eyes afire with the thought of a big plate of *pasta* and a flask of Chianti for two.

We got it at an Italian restaurant in the town, a jolly place with check tablecloths and little vases full of plastic flowers. Six men in from the desert, forgetting the sand and the oil rigs as they cut into big steaks and washed the meat down with neat whisky, stopped only for a moment to follow Letta with their eyes as we passed their table.

She ate *pasta* in a way that was right out of my class and she took more than her share of the Chianti, and she was bright with chatter and laughter and held my hand under the table when she wasn't holding a fork or glass. Anyone looking on would have thought there wasn't a cloud in her sky. Personally I wondered what the hell she was so determined to conceal. Much later I did find out – but not from her. I realized then that she was just hopping mad . . . with her father. Maybe that was why, on the swing back, she was so kind to me. All I needed was a little kindness to encourage me.

We walked back along the sea front, long after midnight. Although I was happy, and had one arm in hers, it was the left one. I wasn't going to be taken off my guard again. I didn't have to ask whether I had passed muster, all her actions indicated that I had been accepted as a custom-built job. She clearly was a quick shopper, knew what she wanted and when she found it paid cash down. It took the romance out of life a bit for me. Let's face it, I'm the kind whose performance is better if both parties subscribe a little to the illusion of love . . . Well, it's cosier that way at the time, even if you both know that it isn't going to last.

We had a nightcap in her room, ran pleasantly through the few, obligatory preliminaries – me, wanting to linger a bit longer over them, she not indecently hasty but anxious to have them out of the way – and then she got up, said something about giving her five minutes and went into the bedroom. I was happy to give her the time. Her handbag was on the small table and I fished out her address book. It was one of those jobs with an alphabetical cut-out down the side. I tried F for father and got nothing, then P for Pelegrina or Papa and got nothing, and then found it under L for Leon. The flat in the Piazza Santo Spirito and its number was listed, and then under that came:

Villa La Sunata, Bizerta. 27.103.

I put the book back. He had a yacht called *La Sunata,* and also a villa. Obviously the name had a sentimental or pleasing meaning for him. I wondered if it had been the name of Letta's mother. I made a note to ask her at the first chance.

The thought went right out of my head when I went into the bedroom. She was sitting on the edge of the bed quite naked, her hair tied up at the back with a broad piece of red ribbon. I didn't rush things. After all, if you're being presented with something out of the *grand cru*-class you don't gulp, you take it easy, missing none of the cumulative pleasures of sight, touch, and taste. Her skin was an even light-biscuit colour. Her breasts had a beauty which made me feel a little heady, and she had one of those narrow little waists that flowered out to broad hips and then on to long, breathtaking legs. She sat there and gave me a little smile of delight for the wonder in my eyes.

I said, 'Don't you wear a nightdress?'

'Normally, yes,' she said. 'I'm sorry. Have I robbed you of the pleasure of taking it off?'

'No, I was just making conversation.'

'Don't bother. I'm not in the talking mood.'

She put her arms out towards me and the lift of her shoulders did things to her breasts that boosted me right off the launching pad and into orbit. We went into outer space together, and I wasn't caring if we never came back.

I woke to feel her naked body pressed close up against my back. Through drowsy eyes I could see that the room was full of half-dawn light coming through the partly drawn curtains. Outside a strong wind was making a hissing noise through the palms in the garden. There was the creak and rattle of an anchor chain coming up from one of the cargo boats in the harbour. I closed my eyes and drifted back into paradise. Behind me I felt her move to readjust our combined body contours, and dreamily I thought, Why ever wake properly, why ever bother to move out into the shoddy half-baked world? The thing to do was to turn back, away from the world, and hide oneself in the tight rosebud of drowsy pleasure; to become larvae, just the two of us, hidden forever in the dark, sweet world of the ripening apple . . . I smiled in half-sleep, knowing that somewhere I was getting mixed in my thoughts and not caring. Behind me she stirred. I felt her arms move slowly, caressingly, over the bare warmth of my neck and then slide across my cheek, the long length of her arm running after it over my naked shoulder. Her hand and arm were cold. She must have been sleeping, I thought, with the top half of the covers off. Full of tenderness, not wanting her to be cold, I began a lazy turn that would bring her into my arms and let me pull the sheet up around her bare shoulder. My eyes opened slightly in the move and I found myself looking into a small, wedge-shaped head, flat and – although much thicker – about the size of an axe-head. From low on the crown a pair of yellow-brown eyes watched me coldly. A little red, delicately forked tongue flicked the tip of my nose and then the head moved with a little curving movement away and over me and I felt the dry, relaxing and then muscular constricting of the long scaly body across my bare chest.

As my hair stood on end and my body stiffened, a detached part of my mind was wondering at the association of ideas that could go on in the brain while the body slept. Paradise, the sweet ripe apple . . . me and Letta in the garden of Eden and here, to complete it, was the snake. And a damned great thing at that. Just feeling it move across my chest told me that it wasn't an inch under ten feet. It dropped off the bed with a clumsy thump – I learned later that pythons have that in common with Siamese cats, an arrogance which makes them clumsy, just going their own sweet way across tables or furniture, knocking over anything that gets in their path.

I sat up in bed with a jerk and cursed myself for not retrieving my gun from Wilkins. The python was rippling away across the room with a nice easy flowing movement. It did a figure of eight round the legs of a chair and then, unhurried, spiralled up a tall lamp standard to check that the bulb was a 120-watt.

I said with a terminal hiss that any snake could have been proud of, 'Holy Moses!'

The sound and the proceeding jerk of my body made Letta roll over. 'Whassa?' she asked sleepily.

I looked down at her. She was naked almost to the waist and her position flattened her beautiful breasts a little. The areola around each nipple was a dark, crushed-grape colour. Even with your hair standing on end you notice things like that.

I said, 'There's a bloody great snake in the room.'

She opened her eyes and smiled at me. 'There always is, darling – of one kind or another.'

'But this' – I gagged for a moment because my throat was dry – 'is a damned great python affair. You could make a pair of shoes and a couple of handbags out of it.'

She sat up, running her hands through her disordered hair. She looked across the room where the python was doing a complicated backward slide down the lamp standard.

'That's Lilith,' she said.

'What's she doing here?'

'She lives in that hamper over in the corner. She always comes out in the morning for a little exercise. She worries you?'

'Not really. It's just my hair I'm thinking about. I'll never get it to lie down again.'

She giggled, a rich, warm, early morning, dark-brown sound, and then climbed across me, almost making me forget the snake. She padded across the room, picked up Lilith by a convenient loop, draped her across her shoulders, faced me and sketched a quick bump and grind. As a cabaret act it would have given a Freudian scholar stuff for two or three chapters, and then a hefty footnote on symbolism.

She kissed the beast on the nose and said, 'You are happier if I put her away?'

'Definitely. And see the catch is secure.'

She padded to the hamper, folded Lilith away with a bending rump-and-buttock exhibition that made me reach for the water carafe to slake my snake-parched mouth.

She came back, took a flying leap into bed and lay back laughing. Then she grabbed for me and, in the few moments before speech became impossible, said, 'I will make you unafraid again. One man once, you know, had the same experience and had a bad heart attack. There was a lot of explaining to do.'

Later, lying relaxed, hearing Lilith curl and knot in the hamper, I said, 'You use her in your act?'

'Didn't you see it last night?'

'I was late getting here. But it doesn't say anything about it on the showcards in the hotel hall.'

'It is only a small part of the act. I use it as a surprise. And anyway, Lilith is sometimes in a bad temper and won't act nicely.'

'What gets her steamed up? Nostalgia for the past?'

'Guinea pigs. They are her exclusive diet. Sometimes it is difficult to get them. Then, when she is hungry, she gets temperamental.'

That wasn't hard to believe. I know a lot of people who get bad tempered if they don't get their food regularly.

'I see now,' I said, 'why Freeman had no trouble selling you that python bracelet. Is Lilith an Indian python too?'

'Yes.'

I lit a cigarette. She took it from me, had a couple of draws and then handed it back. Staring up at the ceiling, she said, 'Something else. I don't want you to worry about my father any more.'

'Why not?'

'I telephoned him yesterday.'

'Where?'

'In the Florence flat. He had returned. He swore to me he was not at the moment engaged in any business enterprise. Nor was he in any kind of trouble.'

'You believed him?'

'Absolutely.'

I said nothing. One thing was certain, however; I didn't believe her. She'd telephoned him all right. But not in Florence. He was somewhere near Bizerta. But I was prepared to believe that he had reassured her about his business enterprises at the moment. He would have to. And I guessed that she must have mentioned my name and whereabouts to him. That's why – from a piece of quick telephoning on his part – I'd had my shirt front ripped last night.

I said, 'Why did your father call his boat *La Sunata*?'

'Because of my sister. She died when she was sixteen. She was very beautiful. More than me. Also she was his favourite.'

Moving over on to one elbow, looking into her dark eyes, I said, 'I'm leaving for London today. What am I going to do about that bracelet?'

'What I said. She can have it for three thousand pounds. Make her pay – and I will give you two hundred pounds commission – perhaps.'

I grinned. 'Cutting me in, eh? You really do like me, don't you?'

She put her arms round my neck.

'I like you more than you know. You must not be upset that I show my love shamelessly. I am a very direct person. When do I see you again?'

'I don't know.'

She pouted. 'It must not be too long.'

'I'd join the act – as a snake feeder – if I didn't have to go back to London. Where are you going to be?'

'I am in Cairo next week. Then I go back to Europe. I will give you a list of my bookings for the next month and the name of my agent in Paris – so you will know how to get in touch with me.' She smiled. 'Maybe I will change one of the bookings and get a London date – you'd like that?'

'Very much.'

'Then give me a nice kiss and maybe I will arrange it.'

She got her kiss and, before I left, I got the list from her.

Unshaven, and without breakfast, I walked down to the BEA offices and booked on a flight out after lunch. Then I took a taxi up to the Libya Palace Hotel. I borrowed Olaf's electric razor and joined him and Wilkins for breakfast.

'You will be delighted to hear,' I told Wilkins, 'that I am leaving for London after lunch. I have recovered Mrs Stankowski's bracelet. Her money, I'm afraid, is gone for good. Approve?'

She dug her spoon into a large grapefruit and looked sceptical.

'We', said Olaf, beginning on the first of five boiled eggs, 'leave for Cairo tomorrow.'

'I thought you were going today?'

'We have met here a nice man, a countryman of mine – he comes from a town called Kalmar which I know well. He insists on taking us out today to see the Roman remains at Leptis Magna. Already she has seen the Pyramids. Hilda is much interested in such antiquities.'

'Are you?'

'Yes,' said Wilkins.

'Well, I never knew that.'

'There are a lot of things about me you don't know. For instance, I belong to a poetry society and a jigsaw puzzle club. I collect match-box covers and I don't care for modern art.' She jabbed the grapefruit as though she were going over a battlefield bayoneting the doubtful dead.

'You're in a bad temper too.'

'Naturally,' said Olaf. 'She does not trust you.'

'Why ever not?' I asked, wide-eyed, forcing a little resentment to make it good.

Olaf grinned and scalped an egg. 'Because you are a devious man, Mr Carver. I could not say not a good one. But devious; Hilda worries over you. Too much, I think. If she did not worry so much about you she would have married me long ago. I should be angry. Perhaps one day I will be.'

'Just give me warning, Olaf – and I'll put a lot of ground between us.' Then to Wilkins, I said, 'Don't worry. I'm going to London. By the way, I'd like to have my gun back.'

Wilkins stood up quickly. 'I knew it.' She stalked off.

I looked at Olaf, wider-eyed now, and spread my hands, puzzled.

'It is the maternal instinct,' said Olaf seriously. 'I work hard to overcome this. But it is not my forte. By nature I am the passionate, romantic type. All Swedes are, fundamentally.' He gutted a great spoonful of egg from its shell and sighed before shovelling it away.

I got my gun, and a low-pitched lecture from Wilkins in the hotel hallway as she said goodbye to me.

'Stop being maternal,' I told her. 'I'm grown up now.'

'I'll believe that when I get a cable from London saying you're there. And just for the record, don't think that Mr Manston hasn't been to see me and told me to forget all about Mr Freeman and Mr Dawson.'

'Which you will.'

'Which I shall. And so should you – unless you're a bigger damn fool than even I imagine.'

I held out my hand, Continental fashion, to shake hands with her. She ignored it.

'The gun,' I said. 'I thought the handshake would cover the handover.'

'It's already in your jacket pocket,' she said.

I looked at her, pop-eyed. I knew only one person who could have done that without my knowing, and that was Manston.

Coming out of the hotel to take my taxi to the airport, I found my A.T. and his chum waiting by their Simca. I strolled over to them.

'My compliments to Captain Asab, boys – but you can knock off now. I'm London bound.'

'It is hoped that you have enjoyed your stay in this country,' said A.T. He was a good-looking youth with a nice warm smile.

'Thanks to you, yes.' I held out a bottle of Black and White whisky which I had bought in the supermarket round the corner from the Uaddan. 'I hope police regulations won't make it difficult for you to deal with this.'

A.T.'s hand was round it so fast there was no need for words. I left them, genuinely grateful for their help and care. Boy, how wrong can you be when you fall into the trap of taking people at their face value. Olaf had called me devious. What he didn't know – and I should have done – was that there were people about who just weren't happy unless they lived in a labyrinth with a fresh peril around each corner. As some people need drink, others need deceit.

At the airport, as I came out of the ticket office with my boarding card, I found Captain Asab waiting for me. It was a blazing hot morning and he wore a heavy overcoat and a light grey astrakhan cap. His brown face was smooth with years of calm, reflective living.

He shook hands with me and said, 'I was out here on other business, so I thought I would wish you *bon voyage*.'

'Thank you. I'm off to London.'

'I am not interested in your destination, so long as you are leaving Libya. I like a reasonably quiet life, Mr Carver; just straightforward murders, smuggling, theft, and assault. But you strike me as the kind of man who attracts – could we say encourages? – unusual complications.'

'It's a dull world. I do my best. By the way, thank you for the two men you've had following me. The young one, I thought at first, was a novice in training. He's better than that. I recommend him to your notice.'

He smiled. 'You've made a mistake. I have had no one following you.'

'No?'

'No. But it could have been your Embassy, of course. After all, they have to look after their nationals.'

'Maybe.'

I gave him a big smile and moved off. But I didn't even mean 'Maybe'. The Embassy didn't give a damn about me. They went along with the Perkins theory. The sooner I had my neck broken and was dropped in the sea the better.

The aircraft was scheduled to stop at Malta and Rome on the way back. At Malta I got off and bought myself a flight on Swissair to Tunis. I got in at six o'clock that evening and had a taxi drive me up to Bizerta. I found myself a cheap hotel and lay back on a lumpy bed staring at the ceiling for about an hour before I turned out the light and tried to sleep. I didn't sleep much, but in between staving off dive-bombing mosquito attacks I did a lot of thinking. My chief worry was, who the hell had put the Apprentice Tail on me? I didn't come up with any answer and, anyway, I still thought that he had rated the bottle of whisky.

The next morning I bought myself a map and made an inquiry at the *Poste et Telegraphe* office. From the sea at Bizerta there is a narrow cut – La Goulette – that runs back inland and opens out into a wide lake. Most of Bizerta is on the westward side of this lake. You can cross this cut by a ferry and, if you're lucky, get a taxi on the other side. The Villa La Sunata was about two miles down the coast to the east.

I didn't bother with a taxi. I walked, with my jacket slung over my arm, the pocket with my gun in it thumping against my thigh bone. It was a tourist brochure day. Blue sky, sun blazing, cicadas sawing away in the umbrella pines, Arab women squatting among the myrtle and shrub watching their goats feed, a great yellow run of beach below the coast road, handfuls of terns dive-fishing in the shallow water off the sands, God in His heaven, and nothing much right with the world. You could have it all in a package tour, thirteen days, air travel included, for under forty pounds.

Personally, I'd decided what I wanted. I didn't want money, I didn't want a woman, I didn't even particularly want excitement – I was in good health now – but I thought it might be fun to have some kudos. Also it would be nice to teach Manston a lesson. I'd offered to help and been turned down. Good – I'd show him the mistake he had made, and maybe I'd collect an Order of the British Empire from a grateful government for services rendered. Possibly, too, I might be able to do something for those two incompetents, Freeman and Pelegrina. I did the last half-mile wondering why I had a soft spot for them. Perhaps it was the sheer audacity of their act which appealed. It is not every day you run into a couple of incompetent dreamers who have kidnapped the son of a British Prime Minister. Not that I go for kidnapping, of course. Who does?

Mind you, if it had been the father and not the son who had been kidnapped, I couldn't have cared less – such is the strength of political passion. They could have cut off his ears one by one and sent them to show they meant business, and slit his throat finally when they despaired of getting ransom money. Well, why not? I'm from the west of England and have been a Liberal all my life. And, anyway, if I hadn't been from the West Country I would still have been a Liberal because I just naturally gravitate to lost causes.

The villa stood up on a rising bluff of hillside surrounded by pines, scrub oak, and thickets of oleanders. The driveway was barred with a wooden gate and there was a little wooden chalet lodge with an Arab custodian sitting on the ground outside it, his back to the wall, his eyes closed and a festoon of flies at each corner of his mouth. He didn't move as I tramped by. I got a glimpse of the villa about two hundred yards back up the drive. It faced the sea. Behind it the land would slope down to the lake, and the lake was big enough to take shipping. Some night recently *La Sunata* had slipped in there and Bill Dawson had been off-loaded.

Along the road side of the property was a fence — stout posts and four wire strands. When I was out of sight of the lodge I went up the sandy bank and had a look at it. The top wire strand was about five feet from the ground. The other strands were spaced evenly down from it. The lower two strands were newer and of a different gauge from the top two. I smiled at the naivety of Freeman and Pelegrina.

I didn't touch either of the two lower wires because I guessed that somewhere up in the villa a bell would ring. In their time they must have had quite a few heart-thumping false alarms from wandering goats and sheep.

I followed the fence along until I came to a spot where it was screened from the road by a clump of hibiscus bushes, covered with brilliant flame-coloured blooms that would have made my sister in Honiton itch with envy.

I squatted down and began to scoop away at the loose sandy soil. A green lizard watched me from the top of a fence post and remained frozen until I had made a depression deep enough to allow me to crawl underneath without touching the wire. As I stood up on the other side, the lizard flirted its tail and was away down the post. I went forward through the pines. A squirrel chattered briefly at me, not inquiring but damning my business there. A yellow-and-blue bee-eater swooped from a tree and took a butterfly on the wing just for a change of diet. I took off my tie and stuffed it in my trouser pocket and put on my jacket to have my hands free. The day, I thought, that Carver won himself a decoration. I could hear the booming voice of the toast-master at the Savoy at the next annual dinner of the Association of Inquiry Agents and Private Detectives, announcing, 'Pray silence for Mr Rex Carver, OBE.' And I could see the seedy company in their rented tails, nudging one another and the whispers, 'You know why he got it. That business of the Prime Minister's son. Actually, I'm told he made a complete balls of it.' Well, there are always the envious few who try to dim your glory. I went forward in a quiet and cautious state of euphoria, which isn't easy because some kinds of euphoria have the kick of four large whiskies.

The villa was stone-built with a wooden roof. It was all over the place in little turrets and outside balconies, and the main windows on the ground floor were a curious kind of triple-pointed African Gothic with stained glass in their upper sections. From the cover of a reed-thatched gardener's shed I saw a dust-covered Humber station wagon standing below the front steps. In the cover of the encroaching trees I went in a half-circle round the place. At the back was a modern, flat-roofed addition with a wide run of french windows facing down through the trees to the lake. Green curtains had been drawn across most of the run of the windows to keep out the blazing morning sun. A door in the window entrance was half open.

I stood there watching the door and then, in a momentary lull in the cicada chorus, I caught the sound of a man's voice. It sounded like Pelegrina's. I pulled the gun from my pocket. It was the .380 model F, MAB *breveté*, which I had taken from Pelegrina's thug in Florence.

I went across the soft, pine needle strewn sand to the window, then moved along it, crouching low so that the sun would not throw my shadow against the green curtains. I reached the door on my hunkers and got a look at part of the room through the small gap the open door made above its lower hinge.

They looked as comfortable as all get-out. Freeman was lying in a cane chair which had a hole in its right arm in which rested a glass of beer. His feet were up on a small stool. I recognized him at once from his photograph. Opposite him, across a small table, was Leon Pelegrina in the same kind of cane chair, a glass of beer in his arm-hole and his feet up on the table. He was gazing at the ceiling through his monocle, his face, red and weather-tanned, screwed up as though he were searching for the answer to some quiz question. They both wore white linen suits, Freeman's neat and well pressed, Pelegrina's rumpled and a little too small for him. It was hard to believe that these two between them had done something which, if it were known, would have set the press of the world immediately rearranging its front-page spread, had radio and TV announcers breaking in on 'Housewives' Choice' and the morning schools programme for a special announcement, and made No 10 Downing Street the genuine focus of world attention for the first time since Churchill left it.

There they were, potential news dynamite, men of destiny – though perhaps not the kind they thought – relaxing before the next stage of the operation, cool beer to hand, pine-bowered sanctuary for quiet, meticulous planning – and they were talking about sardines.

At least Freeman was.

'The real difference between the French and the Portuguese sardine,' he was saying, 'is in the preparation before canning. The French always oven-grill theirs in olive oil before canning. The Portuguese just steam-cook theirs and then pack 'em in oil. There's no doubt about the superiority of the French. They use a lighter type of olive oil too. This old boy I knew in Fleet Street had a vintage sardine cellar. Laid 'em down in cases. Turned the cases over every six months to get an even spread of oil. The great vintage year was 1959. And of 'em all, the French *Rodel* sardine is the king. Cost you something like eight bob for a tin. *Marie Elisabeth*, that's Portuguese, cost less than two bob. Main thing is, there isn't a sardine fit to eat unless it's been in the can for at least twelve months.'

'You think,' asked Pelegrina, 'that there will be a reply in *The Times* today?'

'We'll know when Bou-Bou gets back from Bizerta this evening. The airmail edition will be in by then. Of course, if you don't want to spring eight bob for *Rodels,* you can go for the *Amieux, Larzul,* and *Cassegrain* types. They come out at somewhere under four bob a tin. I could eat some on toast now. Go well with beer.'

I stepped through the door, gun in hand.

'How do you like them on toast?' I asked. 'Just cold, straight from the tin – or grilled hot?'

Pelegrina jerked forward and knocked over his beer. Freeman didn't stir a muscle, except to turn his head slightly and eye me. He was a pleasant enough looking type, fair brown hair, a rather long evenly tanned face, and friendly brown eyes overhung with bushy eyebrows that went up slightly at the outer corners.

'And who the hell', he asked, 'are you?'

'Carver, Rex.'

'Oh.'

There was a silence while the penny went on dropping. I moved up to the table and sat down on an upright chair, holding the MAB *breveté* comfortably poised on one knee. There were some bottles of beer on the table and a bottle opener.

I said to Pelegrina, 'You've spilled your beer. Better have another. You can open a bottle for me too. I've had a long walk. Don't bother about a glass for me. I'll drink from the bottle.'

Pelegrina just stared at me as though I were a snake and he a mesmerized bird.

Freeman said, 'Allow me.'

He reached out for the bottle opener and began to dispense beer for Pelegrina and myself. He was cool and capable in a crisis clearly. It was a pity he hadn't the same qualities when it came to planning.

To Pelegrina I said, 'This gun belonged to your man who visited me in Florence. Don't think I won't use it. Not to kill – but just to make a nasty mess of an arm or a leg. Your knife man from Tripoli sends his regrets at having botched up his assignment.'

With my free hand I took the bottle which Freeman had opened and helped myself to a good pull. It was delicious, ice-cold.

Very slowly Pelegrina spoke. He said, *'Porca miseria!'*

I said, 'Well, that disposes of the preliminaries. Now let's get down to the real business.'

'Which is?' Freeman cocked one of his bushy eyebrows at me.

'All our cards on the table. I'll put mine down first.'

'How', said Pelegrina, beginning to function late, 'did you get in here?'

'Under your nice new wire. Happy? All right – let's get on. You two have cooked up one of the clumsiest kidnapping jobs imaginable. You've left a trail behind you three feet wide and painted red. Coming along that trail is a certain Mr Manston and a few of his friends from the dark depths of British Security, MI6, the Special Branch, and God knows what other organizations. Don't expect any mercy from that bunch. Their orders are – no headlines, get Mr William Dawson, son of the Right Honourable Henry Dawson, Prime Minister of the United Kingdom, back, and liquidate the kidnappers in such a way that they disappear without trace. That won't give them any trouble. Particularly for you, Freeman, since you're already dead and, even though the stomach scar on your body has slipped from right to left during immersion, they're not going to fuss with a little detail like that. Am I going too fast?'

Freeman smiled, but it didn't have a lot of heart in it. 'Not for me,' he said.

'Your trouble', I said, 'is that you go too fast, without enough thought. Bill Dawson was your friend, working with an oil company in Libya as a geologist. Did you think when he disappeared that you'd get away with that phoney death trick of yours? And heaven help you if any harm has been done to him.'

'He's in first-class shape,' said Freeman.

'That's more than you're going to be – unless you listen to me.'

'What do you want?' asked Pelegrina. I could see that with him I was dealing with a slow-paced thinker and not a subtle one.

'To help you. But I want a few questions answered first.'

Freeman wriggled his bottom against the cane seat and began to light a cigarette. 'Ask away – if you think it's necessary.'

'I do. Because when I get in touch with Manston – and heaven knows why he hasn't got here ahead of me, except that even the brightest of us have dull patches and this must be his first in ten years – then he's going to ask me a lot of questions when I hand Bill Dawson over and suggest a grateful government make me an OBE.'

'You go for that kind of crap?' Freeman asked.

'That noun reminds me of your sister. It's one of her favourites. So – first – you steal from her to set up this kidnapping, yes?'

'It has cost us much money,' said Pelegrina. 'Expense all along the line.'

'It could cost you your necks unless you take my advice. Where did you get that phoney body?'

'From a medical friend of mine in Athens,' said Pelegrina.

'So that Bill Dawson should think Freeman here had been kidnapped with him and then killed, so that Freeman here would then – ransom money collected – be free to go off to a happy new life with Jane Judd?' Freeman sat up at this.

I went on, 'It's obvious that you, Pelegrina, have never shown your face to Dawson so that, when free, he can't throw anything back at you. That means that the only person he's ever seen is some hireling who services him first on *La Sunata* – whose name he's never known – and then here in some handy cellar in a villa he's never seen and will never see. Let's face it, except for the wrong belly scar and a few other blemishes, it's almost reasonably neat and tidy – but how the bloody hell did you ever think you were going to collect the ransom money?'

'It's given us a lot of trouble, that,' said Freeman.

'Believe me, it's the only trouble about kidnapping. That's why there isn't much of it around. What's all this about an advertisement in *The Times*?' Some cryptic message in the Personal Column to indicate that the authorities are willing to parley with you?'

'Roughly, yes,' said Freeman.

'Roughly is the word. How did you get in touch with the authorities? Send a private letter to the PM at 10 Downing Street?'

'Just that,' said Pelegrina.

'If they agree to our terms,' said Freeman, 'they put a reply in *The Times* saying "Python Project accepted".'

I went wide-eyed. 'You called it that – and you'd pinched a python bracelet from your sister to help finance it! I'm surprised Manston isn't here already!'

'It had to have some name,' said Pelegrina.

I shook my head. They both looked at me and I could see that they were chastened. I really felt sorry for them.

'A man', I said to Freeman, 'was found dead in your Kent cottage. Strangled. You have anything to do with that?'

'No.'

I grinned. 'Not that you're against murder. You tried it on me.'

'You worried us,' said Pelegrina.

'Fair enough. If you have a worry, eliminate it. You're a right couple. But don't begin to cry about it. We might make something out of this mess yet – not much, but just something that will leave you with your skins whole so long as you start running fast and don't stop for a long time. Tell me, where does Monsieur Robert Duchêne figure in all this?'

They just looked at me blankly.

I tipped my head at Freeman. 'You're supposed to have stolen antique coins of great value from him.'

'I never heard of anyone of that name.'

'All right, we'll skip it. Here's the deal. You walk out of this villa and leave me here with Dawson. I'll give you forty-eight hours to disappear. Then I'll call up Manston and give him a cover story which he'll not believe for one moment, but which for policy reasons he'll accept. But don't think he won't be after both of you for quite a while. It's up to you to keep out of his way – for good. Seem fair?'

Freeman shook his head. 'Give it all up now! Do you know how long I've been planning and dreaming about this thing? Over two years!'

'Write it off as a bad dream. Cut your losses and run.'

Pelegrina let his monocle drop from his eye and shook his head. 'But we have invested so much money in this. You have no idea of the expense, the incidentals. Even I have to charter my own yacht under another name. Every time you turn it is money to be paid out. And that body, that was very expensive! Anyway' – there was a sudden spurt of spirit in him – 'what are we doing sitting here listening to you? Who the hell do you think you are?'

'Well, I was beginning to think I was some kind of Sir Galahad. But okay, don't listen to me. If you like I'll just get up and back out and you'll never see me again, and I won't mention a word of anything to the authorities. That'll just leave you here or wherever you choose to move to, waiting for the moment when you'll have to deal with Mr Bloody Manston. Believe me – you'd far better let me handle that for you.'

'You must have some reason other than a tinpot honour for suggesting this,' said Freeman.

'True. I'd just like to be one up on Manston and his crew for a change. And also I've a soft spot for La Piroletta, Jane Judd, and Gloriana Stankowski, whom God bless for having dragged me into this quite innocently on her part. Okay? Now, why don't you pack your bags and go fast?'

'But we might get the ransom money – we'd even give you a share,' said Pelegrina.

I shook my head. 'Tainted money, I'll be frank, I often take – but only if I know there's not going to be a kickback. Grow up – you'll never get any ransom money. You haven't even got a water-tight handover arrangement worked out. You've blundered through all the preliminaries, ignoring the big problem – and when it's the only problem left you sit down to work it out and it's so much too big for you. Your minds reject it and you end up nattering about vintage sardines.'

They looked at me. They looked at the gun in my hand. And they looked at one another. I took another pull at my beer and waited. Neither of them would have admitted it, of course, but they were both in a state of shock. They didn't have a hope. They'd both stepped into a cloud cuckoo land and they were stuck there for just so long as they could keep out of Manston's way. Once he laid hands on them life would become real and life would become earnest – and of a brief span only. To help them along, I said, 'Don't waste your time on frivolities like wondering if you can jump me, finish me off, and bury me in the backyard sand. I'm not the one you have to worry about. Keep Manston in your mind. I got the address of this place out of Letta's notebook. He'll get it too, some way or other. And forget about the money you've invested – let's face it, most of it was probably not honestly come by. All right?'

They looked at me, Pelegrina picking at his fat chin nervously, his head sunk lower between his shoulders than I had ever seen it, and Freeman tugging at one bushy eyebrow, his forehead lined with thought, not hard firm lines, but wavy uncertain ones. I was suddenly impatient with them. Damn it, I was sticking my neck out quite a bit on their behalf.

'Pack your bags and go,' I said. 'You're never going to make a cent out of Bill Dawson.'

From behind me a familiar, clipped voice said, 'That, of course, is not true.'

I began to turn quickly in my chair and then slowed up as my eyes found the doorway in the french windows and I saw that any impetuous movement might bring trouble for me.

Dark against the brilliant sunlight outside, I saw the tall form of Monsieur Robert Duchêne, flanked on the left by Paulet and on the right by my Apprentice Tail. Each one had a gun in his hand. Somewhere behind them I caught the head and shoulders of another man. For the first time ever I saw Paulet smiling broadly, a real fat blooming beam of a smile. Even Duchêne's thin lips had a little curl at the ends. Surprisingly, my A.T. looked a little sad – probably on my account, that I should have had such a touching faith in the goodness of human nature.

I dropped my gun to the floor and kicked it across to them. They let it lie at their feet.

'Don't tell me,' I said. 'Just let me guess. You're from a rival firm – and you want to make a take-over bid?'

'Exactly.' Duchêne gave me a brief nod.

Behind me I heard Pelegrina groan, and then came Freeman's voice. 'For God's sake – what a bloody morning this is turning out to be!'

Silently I seconded the sentiment.

EIGHT

Saraband Two

I was not present at the take-over discussions. I was taken away to a little room at the front of the house where, if it hadn't been for the bulk of A.T. standing guard outside, I could have had a good view of the sandy drive. In the room with me was a fourth man, whose face was vaguely familiar.

He sat by the door on the edge of a hard chair, a fidgety, nervous little man who looked as though he were waiting his turn to go into the dentist. One thin, almost feminine, hand held a big Colt Service revolver which he kept directed at me. I only hoped that the safety was on. He kept flicking his eyes at me and running the edge of his tongue between his thin lips. One of his socks had been put on inside out. I guessed that he was the talkative type. Conversation would be a way of easing his nervousness. Let him sweat, I decided. I'd got myself into this by trying to do good to those who didn't deserve it, which confirmed that there was a basic flaw in the Christian ethic. I lit a cigarette and considered the Duchêne angle. It didn't need much considering. When you look back over events from some crisis point a lot of things become clear. Being wise after the event comes easy. Duchêne had wanted to muscle in on the Dawson kidnapping. And he had let me do all the leg-work for him. That annoyed me. At least, it rated a fee. I had a feeling that I would never get one. But more important, how, I asked myself, had Duchêne or Paulet ever come to know that Dawson had been kidnapped? How had they ever come to know that Freeman was involved? I could think of two or three answers to that, but I decided to reserve judgement until I knew whether they – like Pelegrina and Freeman – were just working for their private interests or, as I suspected, representing a far from private interest.

I smoked another cigarette, and studied the one picture on the wall of the room. It showed a group of Roman matrons in and around a wide marble bath, being toileted by half a dozen handmaidens. They were having a jolly time splashing water at one another. The artist must have been Victorian because their poses were so arranged that there were no *pudenda* in the slightest bit exposed. Not that it would have cheered me up if there had been.

My guard coughed dryly and put his left hand around his right wrist to help support the big Colt.

I took pity on him.

'I've seen you before, haven't I?'

The thin face broke into a happy smile to show very bad teeth.

'On the plane from Tripoli to Malta. I got off with you.'

I remembered then. He'd looked like a worried cotton-length sales-man, fiddling around with his order book all through the flight, just across the aisle from me, and never once looking at me.

'You weren't on the Tunis plane?'

'No. Not yours. The early morning one today.'

'What happened to the Arab guard at the drive gate?'

'Paulet picked him up and wrapped some rope around him.' He giggled.

'Sounds like Paulet. What's the name of the nice boy outside the window?' I tipped my head backwards to indicate the A.T.

'We call him Mimo.'

'Nice lad. Probably the best of your bunch. What do you get your pay in – converted roubles?'

He frowned. Some things you just don't joke about.

'I'm Brown. Peter Brown.' He said it amicably to counteract the frown.

'Not with your accent you aren't. Not unless some serviceman of that name did your mother in Cyprus or Aden and then, like a fool, made an honest woman of her.'

'Please not to speak like that about my mother.' Then he smiled again, not wanting to spoil the chat. 'Ah, but I remember – you are a very flippant man.'

'But clever, no?'

'Very. But you didn't see Paulet when you arrived at Tunis last night?'

'If I had I'd have broken his neck.'

'You think you could do that?'

'I would have tried.'

He shook his head. 'Many people have – but it is still sound.' He held up the Colt a little. 'If I put this down you will be reasonable?'

'Try me.'

To my surprise he laid it thankfully on a small table at his side and began to light a cigarette. Blowing a cloud of Gitanes smoke, he went on, 'Your Prime Minister is not a wealthy man, is he?'

'No. He's against it on principle. Capital is a dirty word to him – at least in public. And, anyway, with your name, he's your Prime Minister as well. Or do I just say "ha-ha" to that? Further, as a matter of ethnological interest, if things keep going the way they are and all British troops are withdrawn to the other side of the English Channel, your kind is doomed. Unless the package-tour tourists take over.'

He smiled. 'You have it wrong. My mother was a Miss Sylvia Brown of Wimbledon. My father was a foreign student at London University. I took her name.'

I didn't believe a word he said. He just liked talking. But the conversation was cut off by the entry of Duchêne and Paulet. It had taken them two hours to wrap up their negotiations with Freeman and Pelegrina.

Mr Peter Brown of Wimbledon was dismissed. On a tray François Paulet had a couple of bottles of beer, a glass, and a plate of sandwiches. He put them down by me and – he'd been a waiter once at the Principi di Piemonte – he opened a bottle adroitly and poured a glass of beer for me. Over his big de Gaulle nose, his close-set eyes twinkled and he smiled.

'You see how I look after an old friend?'

'If the sandwiches are cheese and tomato you can take 'em back.'

'Pâté .'

Duchêne went to the Roman picture and stared disapprovingly at it, ignoring me.

'Hardly in your class, is it, Duchêne? Not phoney enough. Like those antique coins and all that herd-returning-at-cowdust crap, straight from the *Encyclopaedia Britannica*. I shouldn't have thought you would have made an elementary mistake like that.'

He turned and said severely, 'I didn't. It was some fool in the Central Bureau who has never done an hour's field work in his life. But they insist that they should provide the background and cover stories.'

'He'll be shot, of course?'

'Probably. You wish to eat first, or talk business at the same time?'

Mouth full of sandwich, I said, 'Carry on.'

He adjusted his big horn-rimmed spectacles, lit himself one of his Swiss cigar jobs, rolled it comfortably into the left corner of his mouth and said, 'May I say first of all that you have nothing to worry about. Actually we are very grateful to you.'

'So you should be. You used me to make contact with Freeman and Pelegrina – and I was fool enough not to know what was happening. But I still think you have something to worry about. By tomorrow morning anyone left in this house is going to be sitting on dynamite. Manston may have been a bit slow off the mark for once, but he'll be here.'

'I know all about Manston.'

'I'll bet you do.'

'This house will be empty by four o'clock this afternoon. Everyone except you will be moving to another and much more secure hiding place.'

'And me?' I finished the first glass of beer and Paulet poured me another.

'You like the pâté?'

'Excellent.' I looked at Duchêne. 'Well?'

'You are going back to London.'

'Good. I'll be glad to wash my hands of the whole affair.'

'Hardly. Though eventually you will.'

'I knew there would be a catch.'

'Please don't think we have used you without any intention of rewarding you. All you have to do is follow your instructions – simple ones – and in six months' time five thousand pounds will be deposited for you in any bank you like to nominate in any country.'

'I don't think I want your kind of money. And believe me, that's right out of character.'

'You are free to refuse it.'

'But not free to disobey my instructions?'

'No.'

'Perhaps you'd better tell me what they are.'

'You go back to London, to your office, to your home and you wait for a telephone call or some communication arranging a meeting with someone who will identify himself as Saraband Two.'

I groaned. 'I'll bet that name was made up by your Central Bureau too.' He nodded sympathetically.

Paulet said, 'It is always the same. The people who sit in offices, they are incurable romantics, no? We who live in the smoke of battle have a more elemental approach.'

I cocked an eye at him. 'Your approach seemed just clumsy to me. But I must say I took it for real. The world's full of clumsy people. By the way, when did you strangle our friend with the London-Scottish tie?'

'The evening before you came. He was one of Manston's men and I did not want him to have the various bits of information lying about the cottage. It was a highly regrettable thing to have to do.'

'But you gritted your teeth, said "*pour la patrie*" – or whatever the Slav equivalent is – and did it.'

Paulet looked at the stern-faced Duchêne. 'He jokes, always, Monsieur Carvay; he jokes. I like him so much for that.'

As he finished he whipped out his right hand, hit me on the side of the face and knocked me from the chair.

As I picked myself up he said very sincerely, 'There was nothing personal in that. Monsieur Duchêne just wants you to realize that this is a serious matter.'

'As indeed it is,' said Duchêne. 'And please, I wish to have no more references made to my government. Not that I am admitting that you are right as to which one it is.'

'So I go back to London, wait for a call from Saraband Two, and then do exactly as I'm told.'

'Exactly.'

'And what happens if I go back and refuse to play ball? I could go right to Manston's boss and tell him everything.'

'You are referring to Mr Sutcliffe?'

'Yes.' There was no surprise in me. The intelligence services of all countries kept directories and dossiers of the top boys on each side. I wondered sometimes why they didn't all meet once a year for a jolly reunion dinner on some neutral ground like Switzerland or San Marino. They were all inhuman bastards, anyway, and if I could have known the date and place of the next meeting I'd have put a bomb under the table and cleaned the world up a little.

'You will make no approach to anyone, nor tell anyone anything until you have spoken to Saraband Two. When you have met — you will do exactly as you are told.'

'And you think I'll do this – just because you tell me to? You're crazy. Paulet, tell him he's crazy. You know me – only wild horses can make me do anything I don't want to do, and it takes a lot of them, big, fat Percherons weighing two and a half tons each.'

Paulet shook his head. 'They are splendid horses, but rapidly dying out. It is the growing use of tractors in my country, you know.'

Irritably Duchêne said, 'Enough of this. You will do as you are told, Monsieur Carver, because if you do not then someone very dear and near to you will be killed.'

'You must mean me.'

'No.'

'Then you're living in a dream. All my life I've avoided having anyone near and dear to me. They're always coming for loans or something.'

Duchêne rolled his cigar to the other corner of his mouth. Paulet picked up a sandwich which had fallen on the floor when he had hit me. Outside the window Mimo began to whistle gently 'Winchester Cathedral' as he watched the Arab porter, who had got his feet free of his bonds, come shuffling urgently up the drive, the rest of the cords round his body making him look like a walking mummy. Mimo fired a shot into the sand a yard to his side. The Arab sat down and stayed sat as Mimo went down to him, still whistling. You couldn't help liking Mimo, you couldn't help liking Paulet – but it was easy to dislike Duchêne.

Fishing in his jacket pocket, he pulled out a letter and handed it to me.

'Read this,' he said.

I did. It was from Wilkins:

Dear Mr Carver,

Olaf and I were stopped on the road to Leptis Magna. I am not allowed to tell you more. I do not know what has happened to Olaf – but I am being treated with every consideration.

Shocked as I am by this turn of events – the result entirely of your egotistical stupidity – I beg of you at least from now on to act as the bearer of this letter would wish.

I am told that if you do not I shall suffer some mishap.

Return to London and do as these people say. This is not a time for any of your obstinate heroics. Please be wise.

Distressed though I am about my personal predicament, I am much more concerned about Olaf's.

Tell him, if he is free, not to worry too much about me, or to blame himself for being hoodwinked by his false countryman into making the trip to Leptis Magna.

Calmly though I write, I am naturally very angry at what has happened. When I am free I shall have to consider very seriously whether I shall return to my present work.

Bluntly, do as these people request, since I am assured by them that it will not involve you in anything criminal.

Unless you do this, they have made it very, very clear that the consequences will be serious for me.

Both of us have had our disagreements in the past and usually in your pig-headed fashion you have ignored my advice. Why is it that you have always to make a mess, not only of your own life, but of other people's? None of this would have happened if you had gone straight back to London from Libya.

No rash action on your part can help me now. Frankly my life is in your hands. For once please, please, do exactly as you are told.

Yours,
Hilda Wilkins

I read it twice. It was Wilkins' handwriting without doubt. It wasn't Wilkins' style, quite. Any communication she made to me, verbal or written, was usually briefer and quick to the point. But this time – since she was in a dangerous position and worried about her beloved Olaf – she had let herself go.

I said to Duchêne, 'If she comes to any harm, and I get the chance, I'll gut you!'

'No harm is going to come to her – so long as you act sensibly. She herself tells you to do that too.'

'You give me your word?'

'I do.'

Paulet said, 'The moment you have completed your mission, she will be set free.'

'This was your idea?'

Paulet nodded. 'Central Bureau were opposed to it until we pointed out its advantages.'

'We have got to have a go-between', said Duchêne, 'to carry out negotiations for us. Someone who knows the other side is trusted by them, and someone we know and can trust because he understands the consequences of keeping faith with us.'

'You've bought Freeman and Pelegrina out?'

He nodded. 'For a substantial sum. After all, they did the preliminary work, clumsily but effectively.'

'And what's happening to them?'

'That is not your affair. What good is money to them unless they have security as well? We have made an honest bargain with them. We do the same with you.'

'And Bill Dawson?'

'He is in this house. We have seen him and he is in good health.'

'I don't care so much about his health – though I'll hand the good news on to his father. What I want to know is what kind of deal you're thinking of making for his return? Not just a cash transaction, surely?'

'Clearly not, Mr Carver. Equally clearly, your curiosity will have to wait until you meet Saraband Two. Only one point remains to be stressed. So far the British authorities have kept this whole matter a secret. The press and the public have no idea he has been kidnapped. For our purposes it must remain that way. If you say or do anything which will bring this affair into the open – then you know what will happen to Miss Wilkins and to yourself.'

He didn't have to stress that to me. It was obvious. And there were two or three kinds of deals he could make over Bill Dawson. What I wanted to know – but wasn't going to ask him because I didn't want him to realize the point had occurred to me – was how, if the affair had been kept quiet so far, he had come to know about it and had decided to take advantage of it, staying in the background until the last moment and using me hard all the time. There was something very fishy there.

'Where's Olaf?'

'We held him for a while after we took Miss Wilkins, then we released him on the coast road some miles from Tripoli.'

'What, to go back to the police and make a stink about it all?'

'He won't get far with Captain Asab. The Libyan authorities have instructions to keep this quiet.'

'Olaf isn't the kind to stay quiet. And, by God, if he gets near you he's capable of doing things to you which would make any efforts of mine seem charitable.'

Duchêne shrugged his shoulders.

Paulet said, 'All you have to do is be sensible and wait for Saraband Two. If Manston gets in touch with you when you return to London, you know nothing. Nothing until you receive your instructions from Saraband Two. You can say that you were late getting back to London because you broke your journey in Rome for a day or so.'

'You think I can get away with that – or with not telling him about you?'

Duchêne shrugged. 'Who cares? You will get instructions on those points from Saraband Two. You will not, I imagine, be asked to perform too complicated a dance.'

I stared at him. For the first time since I had known him he had allowed himself a touch of humour. Not that there was any hint of it on his face. But he had to be feeling good to have gone so far out of character.

'Ha-ha,' I said flatly.

It was practically the last thing I said to them. I was kept another half-hour in the room. I didn't see Freeman or Pelegrina. Finally Mimo and Peter Brown of Wimbledon drove me back to Tunis to catch a plane to London. They had collected my cases from the Bizerta hotel and had paid my bill. Decent of them.

It was a hard drive for both of them. By nature they were affable souls who liked nothing better than a little light gossip to make the miles spin by without tedium. But Duchêne must have given them instructions not to talk. Maybe he thought they might let something slip, something which I could use. If one thing was for sure, it was that Duchêne was not trusting me an inch. The only hold he had over me was Wilkins – and it was a sound one. When Wilkins came out of this one safe and well, I knew that I was in for the worst half hour of my life. Worse still, long before she got at me I knew that I was going to have Olaf to deal with. All I could hope was that he would leave me sufficiently in one piece to be able to deal with Saraband Two and then the Sutcliffe-Manston outfit. I had a dark future ahead and my face must have shown it, because as Mimo and Peter Brown left me at the airport, Mimo patted me on the arm and said, 'Do not worry too much. Everything will be all right. One day you tell your children about this and have a big laugh.'

'Children? I'm not even married.'

'Is that necessary?'

I went into the airport buildings, tempted to phone the police, or Manston at the Tripoli Embassy, and put them on to the Villa La Sunata. Temptation lasted only a few seconds. The villa would be cleared by now and I should only be making things impossible for Wilkins. I was sitting in a big cleft stick and any move I made was just going to be from one discomfort to another.

However, on the plane I found some comfort. Not much, but enough. I knew my Wilkins and I knew her philosophy and her literary style. To begin with she was not afraid of anything that walked on two legs, and she had a sturdy conviction that melodrama was not something that could touch her life. She didn't believe that she could be kidnapped. If it happened she would still refuse to believe it. The only real affliction in her life was a tendency to catch colds easily, a sniff her only valid protest against fate.

As for her literary style, it was anything but long-winded. Short, tart, and to the point was Wilkins' style.

Eighteen thousand feet above the Gulf of Tunis I opened her letter – which Duchêne had left with me, since he knew eventually I would have to show it to Manston as part of my credentials and serious intent as a go-between – and began to work out the simple code which Wilkins and I had established long ago. I'd had the devil's own job to persuade her, years ago, that one day it might be useful. This was the first time in two years that she had ever used it. All I had to do was to list in running order the first and last letters of each paragraph. That gave me ONSHIPREDSTACKBLUEBAND. Which gave me ON SHIP RED STACK BLUE BAND.

Clever Wilkins. Somewhere, at least to begin with, she had been held – after the hijacking on the Leptis Magna road – on a ship whose funnel was red with a blue band round it. Single funnel, probably. Probably, too, a cargo boat of some kind. Well, probably again, that ship could have been in harbour in the last week in some port between, say, Alexandria and Sfax, maybe as far up as Tunis. If Olaf came raging after me, I could hand it to him and he could postpone killing me until he had tried to trace it.

I got in late, poached myself a couple of stale lion-stamped eggs and ate them on two toasted pieces of ready-sliced, untouched-by-hand, flavourless loaf. I washed it down with half a glass of milk that probably came from a cow untouched by human hand, finished up feeling slightly sick and, as a specific against indigestion and growing gloom, made myself a very strong whisky and soda.

I sat and stared at the telephone, willing it to ring and Saraband Two to announce himself. I wanted action to chase away the blues. I didn't get it.

Mrs Meld, seeing the light on when she put her cat out for the night, came in, eyes puffy from watching television, and said, 'Have a nice time then, Mr Carver?'

'Splendid.'

'That's the spirit then. I'll be in to do your breakfast in the morning per usual. See what happened to the bedroom ceiling?'

'No; I haven't been in there.'

'Part of it fell down. Just like that. While I was hoovering. Meld says he'll fix it. Save you a big builder's bill.'

'Did he say which year he would do it?'

She laughed. 'That kind of mood, is it? Well, we all feel down in the mouth after a holiday.'

She hadn't got it right by a long chalk. I wasn't down in the mouth. I was right down in my boots.

I was in the office by half past nine the next morning. In the outer office Mrs Burtenshaw put down the *Daily Telegraph* and greeted me without enthusiasm. Business was at a standstill, she said, and she had had a nice postcard from Wilkins two days ago. I didn't comment that she might never have another if I didn't play my cards right.

In my own office I had to use both hands to get the basset hound off my chair. He hit the ground with a thump and promptly went to sleep on the carpet under the desk so that I had no room to stretch my legs out.

I reached for the phone, feeling as gloomy as a Great Dane, and called Mrs Stankowski.

The glorious Gloriana answered it and seemed delighted to hear my voice. It did nothing to cheer me up. All I wanted was contact with Saraband Two and to be on my way. I told her about La Piroletta, that she had the python bracelet and was willing to sell it back. I gave her the name and address of Letta's Paris agents so that she could get in touch with her. Gloriana said she would consider what to do about the bracelet, and then asked me to come and have dinner with her that evening in her flat. I said I would, forcing some enthusiasm into my voice out of politeness.

I put the receiver down and sat there wondering if they had tapped my phone, and, if they had, how long it would be before somebody was around to see me.

It took an hour, actually. Mrs Burtenshaw rang through and said there was a Mr Vickers to see me. I told her to send him in. I knew Mr Edwin Vickers and where he came from – and I knew now that they were running a tap on my phone.

He came in fish-faced, drifting like a dried leaf in an idle breeze, eyes mournful, mouth turned down, and his suit needing a good brush and pressing, a troglodyte from the submerged two-thirds of Whitehall.

He took the chair across the desk and competed with me and the basset hound for leg room under the desk.

'The last time I saw you,' I said, 'you were going to retire and help your brother-in-law run a hotel in Scotland.'

'Brother. He decided he didn't want me. We never got on, anyway. And anyway, they held over my retirement date. Shortage of trained operators.'

He was flattering himself. He could have fallen down a drain opposite the Cenotaph and nobody would ever have missed him.

'What's the big message this morning?'

'I'm requested – by you-know-who – to check your itinerary back from Tripoli. Seems to have taken a day or so longer than it should.'

'I stopped off in Rome for a night. Eden Hotel. Had a customer I thought I might sell the Coliseum to.'

'Keep the hotel bill?'

'No.'

'Why not? You were on expenses, weren't you?'

'No, I wasn't. My services were terminated in Tripoli by my client. Anyway, what's the big interest?'

'I wouldn't know. Check your movements, they said.'

'Well, you've checked them. Anything else?'

He nodded. 'They want you to sit tight in London. If you try to leave the country you'll be stopped.'

'I could write to my MP about that.'

He stood up and helped himself to a cigarette from my desk box.

'Do that – if you know who he is. That your dog?'

The basset had come out from under and was rolling leisurely on his back in a patch of sunlight by the window.

'No. He just appears every morning in early spring – and then suddenly he's gone for another year. Away mating, I suppose.'

He bent down and rubbed the back of bis hand along the length of the basset's tummy. It was a long rub.

'I'm fond of animals,' he said.

'How do they feel about you?'

He straightened up, gave me a sad look, shook his head, and backed to the door as though he feared either the dog or myself would go for his lean throat. At the door he said, 'They said to keep your nose clean for once if you know what is good for you.'

'In those words?'

'No. I colloquialized them.'

Colloquially, I told him to get out. He did, looking a little shocked. He was too meek, that was the trouble. His kind might eventually inherit the earth but before they did people would always be trampling on them.

After he'd gone I sat there for a long time worrying about Wilkins. Yes, worrying. It was no good not admitting it. I was worrying about her. I'd got her involved in this and although I'd been told she would be safe as long as I played ball there were certain aspects of the situation that nagged at me. This had gone from a simple kidnapping-for-cash case right up to the high levels of security double-dealing and ice-cold bargaining where ordinary mortals begin to gasp for oxygen.

Half an hour before midday Olaf burst in – straight from the airport. He hadn't shaved and his eyes had a murderous glare in them. His pilot's pea-jacket swung open over his barrel chest and he thumped it with one big fist as he came up to the desk.

'I want Hilda,' he said. There was a faint odour of rum on his breath.

'So do I,' I said, 'but shouting won't get her back.'

'She not come back and I break your neck and all the necks I can find.'

'Sit down and stop behaving like a walking volcano.'

'Something is to be done right away. The police in Tripoli are useless. Polite but useless. Everyone is useless. I am looking forward to the Roman antiquities at Leptis Magna and so is Hilda. This worm who says he is from Kalmar – his neck, too, I break eventually.'

'Sit down.'

Surprisingly, he did. I got up and went to the special clients' cupboard and came back with a bottle of Bacardi and a glass.

'Carry on the treatment and listen.'

He poured himself a liberal glass and drained it before I had even got under way. I didn't worry about his drinking (though Wilkins would have given him hell had she been there) because he was clearly the type who could drink rum as though it were milk – and did, when he had to keep up his strength.

Before I could get going he helped himself to another glass and said, 'In five years we are to be married. By then I have saved ten thousand pounds. This holiday it was all arranged. We looked forward to great happiness to come and now, what?'

'Just listen,' I said patiently, 'and when you've listened don't ever repeat a word of what I've said to anyone under any conditions. Okay?'

'I should trust you, is that it?'

'It may be hard, but try. In fact, you've got to if we're going to get Wilkins back.'

'Why you call her Wilkins always? Her name is Hilda. It is not right to make a woman sound like a man.'

I sighed. Love and anxiety were mixing up his thought processes. 'You call her Hilda', I said, 'because you love her and she loves you. But to me she is Wilkins, because I have a great respect and affection for her and she is my business partner. Carver and Wilkins. And, for God's sake, let's stop quibbling over points of chivalry. Now just throttle back on the rum intake and listen.'

He did both. I gave it to him straight. The full and complete story. I didn't keep a thing back from him and that was paying him a compliment which I handed out to very few in my life. Always I had found it paid to keep a little back as a form of insurance, but with Olaf glaring at me from his red-rimmed blue eyes I dished out the full truth, and I finished, 'The first thing you have to do is try and trace that ship. Red funnel, blue band. I've a friend at Lloyd's and I'll make an appointment for you. He'll fix it so that you can see the shipping movement lists for the last two weeks. From your own sources you can find out what shipping lines operating in the Med carry those funnel markings. Can you do that?'

'Yes, possibly. Yes, certainly.'

'Even if it's an Iron Curtain vessel?'

'They are all registered.'

'Good. Let me know where you are staying and don't ever telephone me – and don't telephone anyone else unless you do it from a call box.' I flicked my hand to the desk phone. 'That's tapped.'

'It's not possible! In a democratic country?'

I didn't answer because both statements were wrong and there's something touching about the naivety of nice people who think they live in the best of all possible worlds.

I got rid of him at the cost of half a bottle of rum and told him to come and see me the next day if he had anything to tell me.

When he had gone I went out, exhausted, bound for Miggs' place and a quiet glass of Guinness. In the outer office Mrs Burtenshaw said, 'That was Olaf, wasn't it?'

'You know him?'

'Hilda has shown me photographs. What is he doing here, and where is Hilda?'

I didn't feel up to another involvement, so I said, 'He had to make a flying visit to London on business. Something extremely important. Hilda's waiting for him in Cairo.'

'That sounds very odd.'

I knew it did. It was the first time I'd ever called Wilkins Hilda in front of her sister or anyone else.

'He's going back, probably tomorrow. I think it's something to do with him trying to get a job in this country with the Port of London Authority – he couldn't ignore it. If he gets it and can live here . . . well, that would be fine, wouldn't it?'

She looked at me doubtfully, and then said, 'Hilda never told me he was a drinking man. I'm rather surprised.'

'He's not usually. It's just that he's come from the heat of Africa and needs a little rum to keep out the cold in England.'

It was the best I could do. I went out before she could develop any further lines of inquiry.

I fell into the battered cane chair in Miggs' office over the garage and gymnasium and, limp as a rag, said, 'I've changed my mind. Fix me a stiff whisky and soda, and don't ask a lot of awkward questions. Just let's have a little normal chit-chat about the market price of hot cars and the current rate for heroin.'

Miggs grinned and began to set out the drinks.

'You look flaked,' he said as he put a drink in my hand.

'I am.'

'I'll give you an hour's work-out after lunch.'

'You won't.'

He sat down opposite me, his big red face like a fat autumnal sun, and fished in one of the waistcoat pockets.

'Got a message for you. Someone phoned here, yesterday. Didn't know you were interested in cage birds.'

'I'm not. Though I did once look after Mrs Meld's canary for two weeks while they went to Southend.'

'Ankers, his name is. Keeps a pet shop up near St Giles' Circus. The address is there.' He handed me the slip of paper.

It just had the name and the address on it.

'He must have got me mixed up with someone else.'

'No. He said he had a new consignment of African finches and other stuff in and thought you'd like first look at them.'

'He's mad. I don't know any Ankers, and I don't want any birds, caged or otherwise.'

'Come off it – you don't have to let me in on your secrets. You must know him. He said he'd got a copy of that book you wanted too.'

'What bloody book?'

'Wrote it down on the back of the paper.'

I turned the paper over. Written on the back was 'Saraband Two by R. Duchêne'.

I sat up smartly and said, 'Well, I'm damned!'

Miggs grinned even wider. 'He said you would be pleased. What is it – some dirty piece of work, guaranteed to rouse the dullest appetite?'

'Something like that,' I said.

'Any time between two and three of an afternoon, he said.'

'Thanks.'

'When you've finished with it I'll borrow it.'

'You won't.'

He reached for my glass which, to my surprise, was already empty. I was getting Olaf's complaint – but I made no struggle against it. A little Dutch courage was just what I needed at this moment.

NINE

Blowing Hot and Cold

I was there at fifteen minutes past two – and left at fifteen minutes past three. In that time I had been given my instructions by Saraband Two, and also had been forced into buying an African parrot for the knock-down price of ten pounds. Its vocabulary was knock-down too; limited but forceful. I gave it to Miggs on my way home.

The pet shop had two dirty bow-fronted windows, and inside it was as dark as a cave and smelt like a kennel. The doorbell rang as I went in and closed the door behind me.

A raucous voice screamed, 'Shut it! Bloody shut it!'

I said into the gloom, 'If you use your eyes you'll see I've shut it.'

'Sad thing! Bloody sad thing!' the voice screamed.

I saw then that the owner was a parrot in a large and tarnished cage hanging just inside the door. In a tall, wire-framed enclosure that ran down the middle of the shop five or six dozen small tropical birds huddled together in groups, swopping chirping, nostalgic memories of their homelands. Bags of hound meal, fish and bird food were stacked on the floor and dusty shelves. Dog leads and collars, rubber bones and poodle jackets hung from the ceiling. On either side of the door at the back of the shop were cages with long-haired rabbits and short-haired guinea pigs. In a long glass tank a shoal of goldfish moved slowly round and round in an endless gavotte.

The parrot yelled, 'Get that hair cut! Get that bloody hair cut!'

For want of company, I said, 'I like it this way.'

For answer it blew me a raspberry. At this moment a man about three foot six high, bald as an egg, with a badly coloured shell, shuffled out of the gloom to one corner of the far end of the shop, and blinked at me through steel-framed glasses. He wore a green baize apron of the kind that went out with butlers' pantries, a wool cap, khaki-coloured, that went out with the First World War, and a collarless shirt that had once been white. He could have been any age from seventy up.

He squinted at me, and then at the parrot, and said, 'Dirty-mouthed little sod, ain't he?'

'Company to have around, though.'

'Come off an Esso oil tanker. Second cook 'ad 'im. Been all over the world, 'e 'as, and talks like it.'

The parrot, knowing he held the centre of the stage, said sadly, 'Nellie . . . Bloody Nellie . . .'

'Are you Mr Ankers?' I asked.

'Unhappily, yes.' He had a gulping kind of voice, as though he were holding back a sob all the time.

'I'm Carver. You left a message with a friend of mine.'

'Ah, yes. In that case you won't want to be bothered with small stuff like Zebra finches or black-headed mannikins, will you. Not even a Spreo starling or a Shama. Right?'

'Right.'

'No. The one for you is Alfred there. Genuine African, five years Esso-cook trained, live to be a 'undred. Company for yer old age. Gentle in 'is ways, too. Only bites when 'ungry. Fifteen pounds knock-down price.'

'I don't want a parrot. You know what I want. I'm Carver.'

'I know you don't want a parrot, but you got to 'ave one or you don't get through that back door. I 'as to 'ave my perks, don't I?'

'Do you? I'm here by invitation.'

'Makes no odds.' He switched from a sob to a sigh, shook his head, and went on, 'It's an understandin' I 'ave with 'em. Got into trouble, I did, years ago with 'em. 'Ad a 'old over me since and used me. Used me cruel. But I said that's all right – just so long as I get me cut off that kind of visitor. So don't ask any that won't act straight and upcoming about buying. Fifteen pounds. Last a lifetime. Give all your friends a good belly laugh.'

'I should buy a parrot when I don't want one? Just to get through a door to see someone I don't want to see?'

'That's the long and short of it, mate. Anyway, what's wrong? You taken against Alfred?'

I looked at Alfred. He pulled the skin down over one eye in the lewdest leer I've ever seen.

'I think he's charming. You take a cheque?'

'Cash.'

'You guarantee if he bites I don't get psittacosis?'

'If he bites it'll be bleedin' painful – that's all I guarantee.'

I handed him two fivers.

'Fifteen,' he said.

'Ten is what you get. You've led me enough of a dance.'

For a moment his eyes came up to me, the glance shrewd, calculating and a little unsettling – and at that moment it wasn't taking much to unsettle me. Then he shrugged his shoulders.

'All right. Bloody soft-hearted I am. Through the door, up the stairs, first door on the right.' He put a hand on my arm. 'Listen, you look a spunky kind. Cheeky, sort of. Don't try nuffin'. Saraband's very high up, and they got ways. Nasty ways if you come the old acid. I know.'

'Thanks.'

I made for the door.

From behind me Alfred shouted, 'So long, old cock!'

'Don't worry,' I called, 'I'll be back – I hope.'

I went up a stairway lit by one bulb. The wall on my left was covered with graffiti which normally I would have spent some time over. All I got was one gem – *The Pope is the secret head of the Mafia.*

Two flights up, a radio was going full blast. Clear above it a voice yelled, 'Charlie! Bloody Charlie – where are you?' It could have been another parrot.

I found the first door on the right, adjusted my tie nervously, took a deep breath and went in without knocking.

The room was neat and tidy; just two chairs and a kitchen table. Anyone could keep a room like that shipshape. There was a window that looked out to a blank wall three feet away. Sitting behind the table was a grey-haired woman who must have been in her sixties. She wore a neat blue suit and a tan-coloured blouse and there was a small blue hat on the table in front of her. She had one of those healthy, wise, happy faces that belong to favourite aunts, and on one hand I saw a nice dress ring, blue-enamel set with a cluster of pearls. Her earrings matched the ring. A wealthy favourite aunt who didn't neglect her looks and spent freely on clothes. She gave me a charming smile and put her cigarette down on the ashtray in front of her.

'Mr Carver?'

'Yes.'

'Do please sit down – and get over your surprise.'

I sat down on the other chair and began to get over my surprise.

'Did that horrible Ankers make you buy something?' Her voice was strictly Cheltenham and Girton and stands-the-clock-still-at-ten-to-three-and-will-there-be-honey-or-something-for-tea. Maybe, I thought, I am dreaming and back to the age of fourteen and she's going to take me out to a matinee of *The Sound of Music*, and then tea at Fortnum's afterwards.

'A parrot,' I said. 'Called Alfred. Ten pounds.'

'He's incorrigible. If you wish we'll refund the money. We're glad to always . . . that is, with our more indigent callers.'

'Don't bother. I'll send the parrot to Mr V. E. Semichastny. Its language should be useful in brushing up the idiomatic English of his KGB boys.'

'And girls.' She gave a clear tinkle of laughter – bright, and even a little coquettish, the way aunts are with favourite, and fast-growing nephews. Damn it, I was beginning to like her. To keep things in perspective, I deliberately thought of poor old strangled London-Scottish tie, and of Wilkins. My frown showed.

Full of understanding, she said, 'Now the surprise is over and you want to get down to business?'

'That's why I'm here. For instructions. Though personally I can't see why one of your Embassy people from Kensington Palace Gardens couldn't have gone straight to Sutcliffe with whatever proposition you have to make.'

'No? It's simple. If anything goes wrong we wish to be able to say truthfully that there has been no official contact at any state department level. And anyway, most successful diplomatic matters are usually initiated by an unofficial, private approach.'

'Since when was kidnapping classified as a diplomatic move?'

'Since, I suppose, Mr Carver, Helen of Troy's time – or well before, no doubt. Do I detect a note of antagonism in your voice?'

'I'm trying to get it there. I think this whole business stinks.'

'Naturally. But that's another argument. However, let me assure you that as long as you do as you are told, no harm will come to your secretary. You have a deep feeling of affection and loyalty to her. That's nice to find these days—'

'And very convenient for you.'

'Naturally. One must make the most of the means at one's disposal. Do smoke if you wish.'

I lit a cigarette. As I did so she reached down to the side of her chair and brought up a blue suede handbag and opened it. She pulled out an envelope and slid it across to me. I saw that it was unsealed.

'Are these the instructions?'

'Those are the terms of the settlement which we wish to make with your Mr Sutcliffe.'

'He's not my Mr Sutcliffe. I like people who find they can only function if they have hearts.'

She smiled, and nodded indulgently.

'You can read them at your leisure. Of course, you won't show them to anyone else except Mr Sutcliffe. I'd like you to deliver them within the next twenty-four hours.'

'And when I see him – how much am I supposed to know? I mean about Duchêne and the other people involved? He's quite capable of putting me under the lights and beating the facts out of me. I might have to tell him about this place and you.'

'Yes, I understand that. I suggest you tell him all you know. There's no need for deceit – and Mr Sutcliffe well understands the conventions which have to be observed. He is not going to do anything that will put William Dawson in jeopardy. This affair has now gone far above any cloak-and-dagger level. I rely not only on your good sense, but on that of Mr Sutcliffe as well. And believe me, Mr Carver, we have made a close study of both of you.'

'Anybody who thinks he understands Sutcliffe is in for a shock. For instance, from what I tell him he might pick you up and make you say where Dawson is being held.'

'It would be a waste of his time, because I don't know where Dawson is – yet.'

'I'll bet.'

She gave a graceful little shrug of her shoulders and stood up. 'You're from Devon, aren't you?'

'Yes.' I was on my feet for a lady, a nephew well aunt-trained. 'Honiton.'

'Ah, yes – that's where they make that lovely lace. Daddy used to take us to Devon for holidays when we were young. Torquay. They were wonderful days.'

'Aren't they now?'

She gave me almost a roguish look. 'Oh, yes, indeed.'

I moved to the door to open it for her. 'How did it go?' I asked. 'Cheltenham? Girton? Nice upper-class family?'

'Yes.'

'And how the jump from there to the KGB?'

'It was a personal matter – and a painful one at first.'

'But not now?'

'No. I thoroughly enjoy it.'

'Even though you go round carrying a spray gas gun in your handbag?'

She laughed. 'You have quick eyes, Mr Carver. Yes, even though I do that. After all, you might have turned out to be an unpleasant customer.'

'I might still.'

She looked hard at me then, and something was touched off within which wasn't often allowed to show in her face, but for a moment it was there, and it was something I'd seen before in Sutcliffe and Manston, something that gave one the feeling of standing naked, half-dead with fatigue, looking down into some greeny-blue ice gorge which just offered coldness while you fought off vertigo, and death when it overcame you . . . They all came from the same mould.

I opened the door for her and as she moved the look was gone. She gave me a charming, polite inclination of the head so that I almost put my hand out to thank her for a pleasant time.

She said, 'If you wish, you can stay up here and read the contents of the envelope. No one will disturb you.'

'Thank you.'

She went and I closed the door on her. I stuffed the envelope in my pocket, gave her three minutes and then went out myself. In the shop I collected Alfred. Outside the shop I picked up a taxi. As usual I got a talkative driver.

'Where to, sailor boy?'

He got more than he bargained for because Alfred took my side and suddenly began to scream at the top of his voice, 'Bloody! Bloody! Bloody! Bloody!'

He kept it up at intervals all the way to Miggs' place. Happily Miggs was out, so I left Alfred for him with a note. As I went out, shutting the door behind me, I heard Alfred scream, 'Shut that door. Shut that bloody door!'

I went weakly to the tube station. Alfred and Saraband Two and Ankers in one afternoon were proving that I didn't have the stamina I thought I had. And, to cap it all, there was Sutcliffe to come. The cup of life was fairly brimming over with dirty water.

It was half past four. I kicked off my shoes and flopped on the bed with Saraband Two's letter in my hand. I stared at the ceiling, knowing that I didn't want to open the letter, knowing that I wished now that I had never got myself and Wilkins involved in this, knowing that this time I had really gone too far – and couldn't now avoid going farther, right out of the daylight into the jungle gloom and menace of Sutcliffe's world. Frankly, Sutcliffe frightened me. Manston I could take. But Sutcliffe, no.

The plaster that had fallen off the ceiling had left a lath-striped patch the shape of Australia. That's where I should be, I thought. Somewhere in the outback, safe. But not even that would be far enough away.

I stacked the pillows up, propped myself against them, lit a cigarette, and opened the letter. It was typed on foolscap sheets of paper, water-marked *Abermill Bond. Made in Gt Britain*. And it read:

For the attention of Robert Cledwyn Sutcliffe, OBE, MC

(Well, that was something. I'd never known his second name. The bastard was Welsh. Not that all Welsh are bastards. And he was an OBE. I could think of lots of other orders he merited, none of them likely to appeal to his vanity because, of course, he was vain. It was the odd quality that supported his ruthlessness, efficiency, and labyrinthian thinking. Military Cross too. Well, he could bring that out for an airing on St David's day and parade it around Whitehall with a leek stuck in his hat. Shut up, I told myself. You're only going on at him because you're scared stiff of him.)

I read on:

1. The bearer of this communication is well known to you. He will explain his participation in this matter, and that he is acting under duress.

2. It is requested that you bring the following information and suggestions to the attention of the Prime Minister and First Lord of the Treasury, The Rt Hon James Freemantle Dawson, OBE, MP.

3. The Prime Minister already knows that his son, William Freemantle Dawson, has been kidnapped. This was done, purely for monetary gain, by two private individuals. These individuals have now sold out their interest in this operation to another party, who now wishes to open negotiations for the return of William Dawson, subject to suitable exchange arrangements being con-cluded. These will not, of course, involve any financial payments.

4. At the moment the Prime Minister's son is in good health, being well cared for, and allowed reasonable facilities for exercise

and recreation. It is hoped that no cause will be given for this state of affairs to be changed.

5. At the moment the following individuals, of special interest to the party who has now taken over the care and custody of William Dawson, are held in one or other of Her Majesty's prisons.

(*a*) Henry Houghton, Admiralty clerk. 15-year sentence. 1961.

(*b*) William Vassall, Admiralty clerk. 18-year sentence. 1962.

(*c*) Frank Bossard, guided missile researcher, 21-year sentence. 1965.

(*d*) Peter Kroger, bookseller, 20-year sentence, 1961.

(*e*) Helen Kroger, wife of above, 20-year sentence, 1961.

6. The safe return of William Dawson is proposed on the basis of the following conditions:

(*a*) Any exchange would include the automatic return of Gerald Brooke, British subject, now held in the labour camp at Mordva since his removal from the Lubyanka prison, Moscow.

(*b*) Any exchange must, from your side, include two of the persons listed under para 5 above, one of whom must be one of the Krogers.

7. In order to maintain security, and avoid damaging publicity for either side, it is essential that the Prime Minister's personal interest in this matter be kept strictly secret and that no leakage should ever be allowed of the fact that his son was kidnapped.

Further, to avoid public agitation over the exchange of one of the Krogers, it is suggested that a well-authenticated cover be arranged to show the Kroger chosen had died in prison. A guarantee is given that this cover will be strictly honoured by the party of this side. In this manner the only public announcement necessary, and an acceptable one to the world press, will be a straightforward exchange of Gerald Brooke and whichever individual is chosen from para 5 above in addition to the Kroger selected. This open and public exchange can be arranged along similar lines to that of the Greville Wynn–Gordon Lonsdale affair of 1964.

8. A reply to this proposition can be made through the bearer of this communication. Or, if it is considered politic that he should have no further part in this proceeding, then an advertisement should be inserted in the Personal Column of *The Times* to read: 'Saraband Two: Come Home' – followed by a telephone number. The party of this side will establish *bona fides* when answering by announcing himself as Mr Wakefield.

(That gave me a dry laugh. Wakefield was the prison in which Peter Kroger was being held.)

9. In the event of these exchange proposals being rejected out of hand, the party of this side – on receipt of such positive refusal – will allow a grace period of ten days before the regrettable elimination of William Freemantle Dawson. On the other hand, in the event of agreement being reached for an exchange, it is stipulated that all arrangements shall be completed for the necessary handovers within thirty days of final agreement of details.

And that was it. And I was sweating. Lots of side-issues had occurred to me as I read it through – and they were all unpleasant so far as Wilkins and myself were concerned. And Sutcliffe! He'd go up in smoke. The party of this side had him on toast . . . unless the Prime Minister was prepared to sacrifice his son. Well, he might be a tough cookie as a politician – how else can you be one unless you are? – but, as a father, he would feel the same as any other father. Why, just to get Wilkins back I would have handed over the whole of MI6 and the CIA if I could.

I rolled off the bed and stuffed the letter into my pocket. It was still early but a drink was essential.

Before I could get a drink the telephone rang. It was a telegram for me from Letta. She was going to be in Paris the next week and looking forward to a happy reunion. The telegram gave the address of the apartment where she would be staying, and finished 'Love from Lilith too'.

I went gloomily to the decanter. I couldn't see happy reunions being part of my lot for a while.

I was putting soda in the whisky when there was a knock at the flat door. I finished the soda job, took a deep swig, and then went to the door and jerked it open with a touch of bad temper, the kind that comes from having that little-boy-lost feeling and knowing that all the world is against you.

Standing outside was Jane Judd, looking full of the joys of spring, dark-haired, dark-eyed, wearing a black tailor-made and a daffodil-yellow blouse.

'What the hell do you want?'

'To see you – even if you are going to be damned bad-tempered about it.'

She moved past me into the room. She moved nicely and dispensed a passing whiff of perfume, but neither did anything for me.

'How did you know I was back?'

'I rang your office.'

'All right – let's have it.'

'I want to know what your cable about belly scars was all about.'

I picked up the whisky glass and gave her a pugnacious, Churchillian scowl over the top.

'Has anybody been asking you questions about Freeman?'

'No. Like who? What are you so bad-tempered about?'

'I've just been elected patsy of the year.'

'Good. You shouldn't have any difficulty holding the title for quite a while. Why the cable?'

'Because your precious Martin Freeman – whatever he was or is up to – tried to fake his death. As usual it was a pretty poor effort. So no need for tears. You're not a widow – yet. When did you hear from him?'

'How do you know I've heard from him?'

'Inspired guess. Also, you've got an inquiring mind. You're trying to figure him out. You want to know what he's up to. You want to know what you might be getting into. You're uncertain. You don't want trouble. You just want marriage and security. You've got my sympathy and come to think of it – I'll add a little good advice. Get unmarried and forget him.'

As I finished speaking I reached out and took the long, slim, black patent handbag from under her arm. She made a move but I waved her back.

I opened the bag. Inside was a coloured picture postcard. There was other stuff as well, but I didn't bother with that. It was dated the day I had left the Villa La Sunata. It had a Bizerta postmark, and showed a nice view of a mountain called the Jebel Something-or-Other. It was addressed to her at the Mountjoy Hotel and an unsigned message read: 'From July 1, book one week Doré Hotel, Barcelona. Will contact you there.'

'How do you know it's from Freeman?' I asked.

'I know his handwriting.'

'My advice to you is to ignore it. It's a pretty ordinary hotel, anyway. No bridal suite. Not even a restaurant of its own.'

'God, you are in a mood.'

'I am. You sure no one's been asking you questions about him?'

'Absolutely.'

I handed her back the bag but kept the postcard.

'What are you going to do with that?'

'Burn it,' I said, and got out my lighter.

'But it's mine!'

'You can remember it. July 1, one week, Doré Hotel, Barcelona. Take my advice, don't go.'

I lit the edge of the card and carried it to the fireplace. I dropped it in and watched it flame away. One thing I was pretty certain about was that Saraband Two and company were never going to let Freeman reach Barcelona. Or Pelegrina reach wherever he wanted to reach.

They might be jollied along for a while: but in the end they would be eliminated. No publicity, no leaks . . . these were the essentials of the exchange deal. The professionals involved had to be trusted, but out-siders were unnecessary risks. That's why I was scared stiff for Wilkins – and myself.

Jane's eyes came back from the fireplace to me. From the look on her face there was no doubt now that she knew she was in something big.

'It's as serious as all that?' she asked.

'More than that. I suggest you forget all about Freeman.'

She began to move to the door, then paused and looked back at me. 'You're involved, too?'

'A little – but on the right side. By the way, if he does get in touch with you again, let me know. But come here. Don't use the phone.'

She nodded and went out, no longer full of the joys of spring. I was sorry for her, but I couldn't waste much time on it. The best I could do for her was not to tell her the truth.

I went to the phone and dialled a Covent Garden number. It wasn't listed in the directory, but it was a number I was never likely to forget.

A voice at the other end said, 'Yes?'

'Carver here.'

'Yes?'

'I've got to see him. Urgently, importantly, and vitally.'

'Tell me where you can be reached in the next six hours.'

I gave my phone number and the number of Gloriana Stankowski's flat.

I had a bath and changed, drank two more whiskies and then walked down to the corner of the street to the Embankment and got a taxi. Any other time going to have dinner with Gloriana would have been a pleasure that would have driven all gloom from my mind. Tonight gloom was four lengths ahead of pleasure and going well on its second wind.

Gloriana opened the door to me herself, gave me a neat little kiss on the side of the cheek which surprised me, explained that the Scots maid was out – her evening at the cinema – ushered me through the narrow hall and settled me under one of the porcelain lemon trees in the sitting room, and quickly had a large drink in my hand, all with the charming expertise of a hostess anxious to please a favourite guest. I wondered what favour she was going to ask me. It wasn't a big one, and it came almost at once.

She settled on the monster divan across the way from me, wearing a crushed-raspberry silk blouse and dark, Victoria-plum-coloured trousers, stuck an elegant finger in a large glass of gin and campari and twiddled the ice cubes around so that they chinked musically against the fine crystal. Three block-busting drinks like that, I thought, and she would be flat on her back – and I too gloomy to take advantage of it. Her hair was spun red-gold and her lips were as pretty and knowing as a Cupid's. There was a little dimple on her chin. I took a good pull at the whisky. It was strong and it hit me, as drink always does when the mind is unsettled. Maybe, I thought, she'd been playing cards with some Cupid for kisses and won the coral of his lips, the rose of his cheek, and the crystal of his brow. 'O Love! has she done this to thee? What shall, alas! become of me?' Maudlin, too – that's how drink takes the enfeebled spirit.

She said, 'You look scared to death.'

I said, 'I am.'

She said, 'Tell me what is all this secret service crap?'

'Tell me,' I said, 'what anyone has said to you.'

'The man I know in the Treasury has told me that any communication I get from Martin must be passed on to him, and that I am to inform him of anyone who comes asking questions about him. Including you. What the hell has that bloody brother of mine been up to?'

'That's no way to speak of the dead.'

'Dead?' She laughed, a silvery sound that rivalled the ice music against her crystal glass. 'Martin's kind don't die. They go on into their nineties, still making a nuisance of themselves.'

'Sure?'

'Dead men don't repay a ten-thousand-pound theft in notes, delivered anonymously in a brown-paper parcel.'

'You told the Treasury boy this?'

'Yes. But he won't tell me anything, except to forget Martin for quite a while. That's why I asked you here – surely you can tell me something? If you don't you don't get any damned dinner; oysters and a beautiful salmon trout and a bottle of Montrachet between us. Come on, give. One thing I can't stand is mysteries. Certainly not the kind you stupid men cook up between you. What's that bastard Martin up to?'

'I don't know. He tried to fake his own death in Tripoli. Don't ask me why. Anyway, he's paid you back the money he took and, as I said, if you get in touch with this dusky number' – I got up, went and sat by her and took out one of La Piroletta's business cards – 'you can buy the python bracelet back. She bought it off Martin for two thousand quid. You'll have to make your own price with her.' I wrote the Paris address of Letta on the card and handed it to her. 'She's going to be in Paris next week.'

'Why should I have to pay anything?'

'Because La Piroletta is that kind.'

'Was she kind to you too?'

'I'm giving a strictly professional report.'

'Then tell me what all the mystery about my brother is.'

'If I knew—'

'You know—'

'I still wouldn't tell.'

'Go to hell.'

'I'm halfway there. Any messages?'

'Yes. When you meet my old man tell him he didn't beat Martin hard or often enough.'

'Does this mean I don't get dinner?'

'It depends on whether I can manage three dozen oysters by myself.'

'I'll have another drink while you're making up your mind.'

I leant over and kissed her gently on the coral pink lips, briefly, and wondered if they were soft with promise or disinterest. Then I went over to the bar.

My back to her, I said, 'Has your only contact with the authorities been this guy in the Treasury?'

There was a little pause, and she said, 'Yes.'

I said, 'I'll send my account in to you tomorrow – if I live that long.'

She said, 'You'll live. You've got the same survival factor that Martin has. What have you told this Jane Judd?'

I turned, fat drink in hand. 'To forget him. Approve?'

She nodded.

At that moment the telephone rang. I reached out for it, looked at her, and said, '*Permesso?*'

She nodded.

I picked up the receiver.

A voice at the other end said,

'Mr Carver?'

'Yes.'

'Mr Rex Carver?'

'You don't have to be so formal, you know it bloody is.'

'Report here immediately.'

'Can't I finish my drink?'

There was a click at the other end.

I looked at Gloriana and she looked at me.

'The dark clouds might', I said, 'have rolled away and it could have turned out to be a wonderful evening. As it is, you're stuck with three dozen oysters and a bottle of Montrachet.'

'Where are you going?'

'To the Inquisitors. To the dark shrine of Security. To the devildom of men without hearts. Into the crêpe-festooned shadows of the underworld, where all is cold and bleak and there is a human sacrifice every hour on the hour.'

'You're tight, love.' She sounded genuinely sympathetic.

'I know. But the moment their door closes on me, the cold inside will shrivel every particle of alcoholic warmth from my blood, every soft and comforting whisky fume from my brain.'

She giggled, stood up, and came and took the glass from me. 'Don't have that. You don't need it. Certainly not for yourself. You're not even worried about yourself. I know you well enough by now. Who is it?

Who is it you're really worried about?'

'Certainly not your bloody brother.'

'That's good, because he wouldn't be damned well worth it.'

I took the glass from her and drained it.

'Don't worry,' I said. 'It could be my last.'

She took the empty glass from me, put it down, and then reached her arms around me and gave me a hug.

'You're nice,' she said, and kissed me, good and hard and lovingly. Then, releasing me, she added, 'But too damned dramatic.'

'We can only be what we are, only do what we have to do, only end as it is foreordained.'

'Crap. And if you get away before midnight come back.'

She kissed me again and then I tore myself away and stumbled out into the night.

I got the taxi to drop me on the corner by Moss Bros, and then walked through into Covent Garden. Having a taxi right up to the door would have been *lèse-majesté* and bad security. Anyway, one had to approach as a penitent on foot; barefoot, if the weather was right. The door to Robert Cledwyn Sutcliffe's flat looked like the entrance to some seedy publisher's offices.

I rang the bell and after an interval Hackett, his manservant, opened it. Before he did so I knew that he would have checked me over the monitoring system from inside.

'Hullo there, Mr Carver,' he said cheerfully. In itself a bad sign.

'Hullo there, Hackett, old cock,' I said, following him in.

He turned from shutting the door, and said, 'You've bin drinking.' It was a statement, not a question.

'Yes, I bin drinking, Hackett. What you bin doing? Getting the torture chamber ready?'

Hackett shook his head. 'We're in that kind of mood, are we, Mr Carver? I don't think he'll like it. He's been off his food for three weeks.'

'Good. Let's hope he keeps it up and starves to death.'

'Oh dear, Mr Carver, I would advise you to take a brace.'

'Give me a stiff one, neat, before I go up then. Who's with him?'

'Mr Manston and Mr Perkins.'

'The unholy trinity.'

He winked and nodded me up the stairs on my own. I took a three seconds' brace outside the door, knocked, and walked in.

The only light in the room came from the brackets over his half a dozen paintings. They were always modern and were always different each time I came. Facing me on the far wall was a red-and-blue Francis Bacon job of a nude man who looked the way I felt, all twisted up. To one side of it stood Manston; tall, well-built, in evening dress, a red carnation in his buttonhole, his face tanned and giving me a mild smile. He looked disgustingly healthy. Perkins, in a stiff Donegal tweed suit, had his great bulk collapsed into a leather armchair. He had a fat cigar in his mouth, jutted his chin at me like the prow of a cruiser in welcome, and reached an arm about five feet long out to a side-table to retrieve his glass.

Sutcliffe was sitting in another armchair, a plump, dumpy man, face big and bland like a Buddha's. A blue smoking jacket was rumpled up over his shoulders and his small legs were thrust out for his tiny feet to rest on a footstool. He looked at me with calm, cool, grey eyes that had behind them over fifty years' experience of not being fooled or ever indulging in the stupidity of being warm-hearted. He went on looking. Nobody said a word. I shuffled my feet and looked at the sideboard. There was a lot of bracing material there. In the past they'd indulged me with the odd glass of Glenlivet – when they had wanted me to feel at home. There were no signs of real welcome now.

I said, 'It's pretty cold in here for the time of the year.' I pulled Saraband Two's letter from my pocket.

'We're in no mood for any of your low-level social chat,' said Sutcliffe. He said it quietly, but each word had a vibrant core of ferocity.

'Well, here's something on a very high level for you to get your teeth into.'

I handed him the letter. He looked at the letter, and then at me, pursed his plump lips in a prissy little movement and then said, 'God help you, Carver, if you're up to any of your old tricks.'

'I'm as pure as driven snow. And driven is the word. Read this after you've read that.' I handed over Wilkins' letter. I glanced at Manston. 'You're reasonably fond of me. Don't I get a drink?'

Perkins said, 'Just be content with breathing.'

Sutcliffe sunk his head into his shoulders and began to read. I watched his face. It showed no emotion whatever. It wouldn't. He had been training it that way for over fifty years.

Tired of Perkins and Manston, I stared at one of the modern paintings beyond Sutcliffe. The canvas was covered with irregular coloured squares and triangles, and in the top right-hand corner was the word *Hommes* and in the diagonally opposite corner the word *Femmes*. I didn't try to work it out. I was just content to be a bloody-minded Philistine.

Sutcliffe read through the two epistles, held the various sheets up to the light, squinted at them, fingered their texture and then read them all through again. This done, he said to no one in particular, 'Get Hackett up.'

Perkins reached out a long left arm and thumbed a bell push in the wall. Ten seconds later Hackett came in without knocking.

'Sir?'

Sutcliffe swung his head round slowly and gave Hackett a smile. 'Take Mr Carver down to the waiting room and make him comfortable.'

'Yes, sir.'

'And see that he doesn't panic.'

'Yes, sir.'

Hackett came over to me. An automatic had suddenly sprouted out of his right hand. With his left he ran expertly over my jacket and trousers.

'Nothing lethal,' I said. 'Except a nail-file in my ticket pocket.'

Hackett led me out and shut the door.

'They must be cross with you, Mr Carver. Never sent you down to the waiting room before, have they?'

'No.'

But I knew all about the waiting room from hearsay. Personally I would have been glad to leave it that way.

We went down into the basement. Hackett unlocked a green baize door at the end of a little corridor and waved me in. He did it with the automatic, so I had to obey.

The door closed behind me and I was alone. It was a big room without windows. The floor was tiled, plain white tiles. The walls were sound-proofed, leather panels covering whatever they had used for insulation. When you touched the stuff it gave gently. In a recess at the far end of the room was a bunk, screwed to floor and wall. At its foot a little washbasin was set in the wall. Behind a plastic curtain in the right-hand wall was a recessed toilet. A plain wooden table and a kitchen chair stood in the middle of the room. Set in the ceiling behind an iron grille was a light. Above the doorway almost at ceiling height was a row of small portholes, some glass-covered and some covered with perforated brass discs. From one of them now was coming the gentle hiss of air being forced into the room. Looking up at it, I caught the blast of hot draught funnelling down at me. As I stood there the noise of the hissing increased.

I went over to the bunk and sat down on the low pile of folded army blankets. I've lived in some odd rooms in my time, most of them crumby hotel rooms, and generally managed to make myself comfortable. In this room I knew I was never going to be comfortable. Nothing would ever make it sing for me – and why should it? The purpose of this room was to make people sing loud and clear if they had any sins or deceits to be purged.

Within five minutes the temperature had gone up to tropical level and I had my jacket off and my collar loosened. Within the next ten it went down to freezing point so that I had the blankets huddled round me and my breath hanging in cold clouds before my face. This hot and cold sequence went on for about an hour. It was nothing serious. It was just annoying. But I knew that it was no more than a mild foretaste of unpleasantness to come unless I decided to behave myself. They needn't have bothered. Within reasonable limits I had already decided to behave myself. Like Martin Freeman, I had a high survival factor and meant to protect myself.

From a loudspeaker in one of the portholes over the door Sutcliffe's voice suddenly came out cold and clear into the room.

'We'll be down later, Carver. Don't rely on any sentiment about the help you've given us in the past – almost outweighed, of course, by the trouble you've given us too. You don't come out of that room alive until we have the last scrap of truth out of you about this business. Think about it and prepare yourself for confession.'

I said, 'Can you hear me?'

He said, 'Yes. Why?'

'Because in that case I won't speak my deepest thoughts about you out loud. I'll just be polite and say, "Drop dead, you stinking bastard!"'

I heard someone laugh. It could have been Perkins or Manston. It certainly wasn't Sutcliffe.

TEN

Next Stop Hades

At no time were they all three in the room together. Sometimes there were two, usually only one, while the others, I guessed, watched and listened on the closed-circuit screen in Sutcliffe's room. Or, if they had any sense, took a nap . . . because what was there to get from me?

But they obviously thought that there was something.

Manston, alone, started the ball rolling. About four hours after my being shown into the room, Hackett let him in. From the moment of his arrival the air-conditioning went back to normal.

He sat on the kitchen chair while I lay on the bunk.

'All right,' he said, no emotion in his voice, no encouraging look on his face, 'just tell your story from start to finish – and omit nothing.'

I sat upright and told him. It took quite a while and when I had finished he said, 'That's all?'

'Yes.'

He shook his head. 'You mean to say it was just pure chance that you were given a commission by the London Fraternal Insurance Society to recover Mrs Stankowski's property – and this led you, again by chance, into this Freeman business?'

'Yes.'

'And it was just some little bell ringing at the back of your mind that began to warn you that Bill Dawson might be the Prime Minister's son?'

'Yes. The name worried me. Then in Tripoli I saw a newspaper headline about his father. In Captain Asab's office, actually. I got Wilkins to check. Dawson isn't interested in politics. He's an oil geologist or whatever you call it and he was employed by an oil exploration company in Libya. It had been in the press at some time.'

'Why didn't you come to me with the information you had about the Villa La Sunata? We could have had Dawson back home by now.'

'I didn't know about the villa when I met you. And you made it clear you needed no help from me. When I did know . . . well, let's say I was silent out of pique, or vanity—'

'Not cupidity?'

'I've often wondered if that word had anything to do with cupid.'

He got up slowly and came towards me.

'It has. From the Latin *cupere*, desire. It's a capsule description of your basic motives – money and sex.'

'So, I suffer from a common disease.'

'How much did Saraband Two say would be put in your bank account?'

'Five thousand pounds. But it was Duchêne who said it. I refused.'

'Sure it wasn't fifty thousand – and you haven't refused?'

Light dawned.

'You think I'm in on this job?'

He reached down and got me by the shirt front. He was nothing like as big as Perkins. He wasn't much bigger than me. But I was moved, jerked up, swung round, and then thrown to slam up against a wall, my head thudding against it. I lay where I had fallen.

'That's what we think,' he said. 'We're just waiting for you to confirm it.'

He moved to the door, paused by it, and said, 'By the way, there's nothing personal in my actions. I just want you in the right frame of mind.'

'That's what Paulet said. Thanks. It's nice to know this isn't going to spoil a beautiful friendship.'

He went out. I went back to the bunk. In the next hour they rang the changes between equatorial and arctic temperatures until my body responses would have sent a Pavlov off his head with delight. I swear to God they got me so mixed up that sometimes I sweated when it was freezing and shivered when the place was like a bakehouse.

Then Perkins came, big, bluff, and genial.

He lit a cigarette and sat on the edge of the table.

'All right,' he said, 'just tell your story from start to finish – and omit nothing.'

I told him. It took quite a while, and when I had finished he said, 'That's all?'

'Yes.'

He shook his head.

'Jane Judd visited you because she was worried about Freeman and wanted to know if you knew what was happening?'

'Yes. And I told her I didn't know what it was all about.'

'Why didn't you tell us about the postcard you took from her bag?'

While I was down here they were obviously doing some fast checking outside.

'I didn't think it was important. You don't want Freeman. You want Dawson. They won't be in the same place. Freeman and Pelegrina have sold out to the KGB boys.'

He moved fast and sledge-hammered me on the chin with his right fist. I went to the floor and stayed there.

He went to the door.

'Think the story over again and try to remember *all* the details.'

He went out. I got up. The temperature changes started again and this time went on for two hours. I thought over the details between shivering with heat and sweating with cold. Surely, I told myself, a man must be allowed to retain something, just something, which he could use in a *cupere* way.

The next time it was Sutcliffe. He had changed into a neat blue suit and wore his Etonian tie. He sat on the kitchen chair and pouted his plump little lips at me.

'All right,' I said, 'I will now tell you my story from start to finish – and omit nothing.'

'Good.'

I went to the little washbasin to get a drink.

He said, 'The water's cut off. It won't come on again for some time.'

I told my story with a dry mouth. When I had finished, he said, 'That's all?'

'Yes.'

He said, 'You were at Gloriana Stankowski's yesterday evening?'

'Is it tomorrow already?' I looked at my watch. It was.

'She told you that she had received anonymously ten thousand pounds in notes from Freeman. Why haven't you mentioned that?'

'Because you bloody well already know.' I could afford to lose my temper with him. At least he wouldn't try any strong-arm stuff on me. 'You've got a Treasury hyena on her tail and he knows.'

Sutcliffe shook his head. 'You must try and understand. When we ask *you* for *your* full story we mean the full story even if some details of it are already known to us.' He stood up. 'By the way, I made a mistake about the water not being on. You can have a drink if you wish.'

I went to the basin, grabbed a glass – plastic – and held it under the tap. As my right hand closed over the metal tap to turn it I got a shock up my arm that jolted me three feet backwards. I lay on the floor and wasn't aware of Sutcliffe going out.

When I found the strength to get up I flopped on to the bunk.

For the next three hours I did the arctic-tropical trip so many times that I lost count. But that didn't matter. From the moment of Sutcliffe's going a brass band had started to play over the loudspeaker. It was a good band – mad about Sousa – and played at top volume for the full three hours. Heat, cold, and sound. Simple little things. They kept them going. I slowly began to go mad. I put it off for a while by chewing up medicated toilet paper from the loo and wadding the wet pads into my ears. They finished the recital with 'Sussex by the Sea', and then a slow funeral march.

I lay on the bunk like a piece of chewed string.

Manston and Perkins came in together and propped me up.

'Shall we', said Perkins, 'go through your story again?'

I looked at him with a limp smile. 'Do we have to? I was just beginning to enjoy the music.'

Manston said, 'The general opinion is, Carver, that while you may be holding back a few details . . . you know, magpie stuff, little bright bits that you can't bear to part with . . . the serious aspect is that you are refusing to admit the overall truth. You can keep your little bits. But you must give us the basic truth.'

'You've had it.'

'No. I'll admit the truth of your story, right up to the time you went to Tripoli and discovered that the Dawson who had been kidnapped was the Prime Minister's son.'

'Thanks. Can I get a drink now without electrocuting myself?'

Perkins, a true white man, got up and filled the plastic tumbler for me. Then he drank it himself and leaned back against the edge of the basin.

'When you learnt that, you realized why Duchêne and Paulet were stringing you along with a phoney story, and you made a good guess as to their interest. So—'

'Let me tell it, please.' I got up and went to the basin. I looked at Manston. 'Tell this gorilla to get out of the way. I want a drink and if I don't get one I'll tear his stupid Anglo-Saxon head off his over-muscled rowing shoulders.'

Manston looked at Perkins, and Perkins stepped away. I drank like a camel. I probably sounded like one as well.

Bloated, I turned. 'So,' I said, 'the moment I'd got the dope about the Villa La Sunata from La Piroletta, I did a deal with Duchêne and we all went up there together. Right?'

'Right.' Manston nodded. The carnation in his buttonhole was wilted. Not so much as I was.

'And we worked out a plan to keep me in the clear. A phoney kidnapping of Wilkins and so on. And me to come back here and play the man under duress to you. And eventually the prisoner exchange deal would go through and I'd get a whacking great secret payment for my services and Wilkins would come home, safe and sound, and never know what a triple-crossing, corkscrew-minded man she had for a boss. Is that it?'

'Precisely,' said Perkins.

'You believe that?' I asked Manston.

He nodded. 'Knowing you, yes. It measures up to your kind of morality.'

'Oh, sure. No real harm is done to Dawson or Wilkins. Brooke comes back from Russia, and the British taxpayer is saved the expense of keeping two people in prison here, and by now anyway they have no vital information to hand over to Mr V. Semichastny – he only wants them as a matter of face. So what harm is done to anyone? And I get fifty thousand pounds in a numbered Swiss account. It's all been good clean fun. You believe that?'

'It's the truth, isn't it?' said Perkins. 'And, now that you've got it off your chest, why don't we go on to the main point? Where is Dawson? Don't tell us you don't know that.'

Standing there by the bunk, I raised my eyes to heaven and clamped my hands to my brow in a gesture of despair. The trouble was, I was so fatigued that the movement made me collapse on the bunk. Leaning back against the wall, I said, 'This government spends eight million pounds a year, openly acknowledged, under State Expenditure, Class XI, Miscellaneous, for its Secret Service – and you two morons draw part of it in salary. Stick with it. Don't go out into the big, hard world of industry and commerce. You'd never survive. You've got to have intelligence and common sense to hold down a pay-packet out there. Go away, you bother me.' I rolled over and lay down. I was tired, too tired even to be angry. Too tired even to be afraid. Heat and cold and brass-band music can do that to you.

Manston said, 'All right, Perkins. He's yours for five minutes. Don't mark his face, that's all.'

He didn't. I tried to kick him in the groin as he came for me, but he grabbed my ankle and damned near broke my leg as he jerked me off the bunk. Then he worked me over, strictly for five minutes, which is a long time when you are being bounced from wall to floor. It might even have been from wall to floor to ceiling towards the end. I wouldn't have known, because I passed out without a mark on my face.

When I came round my watch said twelve o'clock, but whether it was midday or midnight, I had no idea. Hackett appeared with a tray and no consolation. On the tray was a glass of milk and three very dry cheese biscuits.

I stood up from the bunk as he put the tray on the table. My body was so stiff and bruised that I functioned like a badly manipulated puppet. Hackett waved me back with one hand.

'Don't try nothing like jumping me, Mr Carver. There's someone outside the door.'

'Don't worry,' I said. 'I couldn't jump over a matchstick.'

'That's what you get for being difficult. You really ought to understand, Mr Carver, that you're in deep. The boss is still off his food. Not like him a bit.'

He came over and handed me the glass of milk.

'Why don't you be a good boy and tell 'em what they want to know?'

'They've had the truth. Why can't they be content with that?'

'There's truth and truth. Mind you, I got to say that whichever one you stick with it won't do you any good. The boss, he's always had it in for you because you would never come and work for him. And because the times you have come in on a part-time basis you've always played it your own way. Bad, that. He likes things done proper even by temporary staff.'

I said, 'Is it day or night outside?'

'Midday. Lovely day, warm and bright. All the girls with skirts right up above their knees, birds singing, and even the cab-drivers with grins on their faces. Pity you'll never see any of it again.'

He meant it. A cold spasm wriggled through my guts.

'Cut it out,' I said angrily.

'It's the truth. Yours won't be the first body I've carried out of 'ere. Proper routine we got. No trouble. Just a quick injection and you're out like a light. No trouble about disposal, neither. Ambulance waiting at the back, nice little drive down to just below Greenwich and you get dumped in the tide. Nice pub in Greenwich, The Ship, 'spects you know it. We always stop there on the way back for a couple of quick ones. Let's see, be three weeks since I was there last.'

'Go to hell.'

'Frightening you, am I?'

'Of course you are, you bastard.'

He chuckled and went, and I sat and munched the dry biscuits. Before I had finished they started up the tropical-arctic treatment again and after an hour a colliery brass band came on, blaring away at Colonel Bogey for a start and carrying on with a two-hour repertoire. And after that it all started again, the full story and omit no details. First with Sutcliffe, whose fat lips had started to be a little twitchy, then Perkins, who picked out a few spots on my body not already bruised and made a tidy job of filling in. I slugged him once when he got a bit careless, but my fist bounced off his jaw as though it had been made of india-rubber. Then Manston came, wearing a neatly pressed, Savile Row, grey-flannel suit and smelling of Tabac aftershave lotion.

He was sad and gentle, but adamant; the full story and omit no details.

Lying on the bunk, chewed up, battered up, heated up, cooled down, eardrums aching from brass-band music, I said, 'For God's sake, you're a reasonable guy, you know me. I'm not part of the Saraband Two set-up. If I had been I'd have admitted it ages ago. I'm no hero. I want to get out of here.'

He said, 'We've had people in here who've said just that. Little shrimpy types, hardly any blood in their veins, skinny types, fat types, tough types, and angel-faced, wide-eyed innocent types. All sorts, and you could have got lovely odds that they were innocent – but they weren't. Any more than you are.'

'Just assume I am.'

'Makes no difference. The innocent have got to suffer with the guilty in this. Get it into your head – this is a State affair of the highest secrecy. It's the Prime Minister who is involved personally. Already his bottom is itchy with anxiety because one slip-up, one line of publicity, could blow this thing open. Can't you see that? He wants his son back. That means a deal with the other side. Let that story break and God knows where the consequences would end. So . . .'

'So what?'

'So, it's obvious – whether you tell us the truth or not, you're not going out of this room alive. Do you think Sutcliffe would let you wander around with a scoop like this in your hands? In a year's time you'd be turning it into cash some way.'

'You really mean that?'

'Yes. And if I didn't, I couldn't help you.'

'Why not?'

With all the cold calmness in the world, he said, 'Because we've already made preliminary contact with your Saraband Two crowd. They insist – for the common good – that a rider be added to the exchange agreement. We have to eliminate you – and they will eventually do the same for your Wilkins.'

'The bastards! You're not taking that, surely?'

'Why not? We don't want publicity now or later. Anyway, it's now part of the deal for Dawson's return.'

'And you're accepting it?'

'Of course, and the PM wants his son back. Naturally, he won't be bothered with *all* the details.'

I was silent for a long time, largely because my throat was too dry to let me say anything and my heart was pumping away so loudly that I doubt whether he could have heard anything I said.

Finally I said in a very small voice, 'Can't you do something about Wilkins? She knows how to keep her mouth shut.'

He shrugged. 'No. It would be the same for Olaf, Gloriana Stankowski, and Jane Judd, if you'd told them the real facts. I tell you the lid's going to be put on this pot for good. You think, for instance, that Saraband Two and that lot will ever let Freeman or Pelegrina go free?'

'No.'

'Of course not. They're giving them that impression right now, even letting them pay back money, send postcards, and so on – but they won't ever get away. Now do you get some idea of the kind of fix you're in? Once this exchange goes through, both sides have every reason in the world to eliminate all the fringe types who know anything about it. Certain professionals are going to know – but then they're professionals, trained not to open their mouths. Pity you didn't join us years ago – we might have treated you differently.'

I stood up. I hated his guts. I hated Sutcliffe, Perkins, and the whole cold-blooded lot of them – and I was scared stiff for myself.

'Don't try anything,' he said.

'I'm not, not for myself. But do one thing for me – try and work it for Wilkins. She's a professional, all right. You tell her to keep her mouth shut, and shut it will be for the rest of her life. Do that for me, you high-class, ice-cold security bastard. Just one favour.'

He stood up and moved to the door. 'I'll put it to Sutcliffe – he's listening now, anyway – but it will be entirely his decision.'

He went. The brass band came on. The heat and the cold started up, and eventually they came again, by themselves, in twos, in threes, pumping away, the whole story, omit nothing, not even the smallest detail this time – if it had not been for Manston's talk about Wilkins and what would happen to her, I might have disgorged the few tiny details that I had been keeping back. Not that they would have helped much. But now they were unimportant. I was going and so was Wilkins, so what was the good of saying anything? Let them rot.

Then I was left alone. My watch said seven o'clock. The girl secretaries home from work would be taking their geyser-fed baths in Notting Hill Gate, the chaps from Lloyd's, the Stock Exchange, and the City offices would be suburb-bound through all points of the compass to their mock-Tudor villas and Kent farms, or be in their London clubs, hot hands already round their third whisky, Miggs would be in his office, feet up, listening to Alfred's scurrilities, Mrs Meld would be leaning over the gate waiting for Meld to come back with the evening Guinness, Olaf, tired from badgering Mrs Burtenshaw for news of me, would be sunk in a rum depression, the Prime Minister would be struggling with his dress studs before going to a City Livery dinner, and clouds of starlings and pigeons would have settled around Trafalgar Square to unload another night's guano harvest, and the world would go on turning, slowing down a little each minute but not really worried about deceleration. That was my worry, unique and unavoidable, I was decelerating fast. I would never sleep with another woman, never have a drop too much to drink again, never take that first morning draw on a cigarette and lie coughing happily in bed listening to Mrs Meld giving out with 'Old Man River' – I suppose I should have been preparing my soul for the final fence. I even considered it, and then said, What the hell? My soul had been a non-runner for too long to think it could start steeplechasing at this late hour. I turned over and went to sleep ... sleep ... chief nourisher in life's feast. Well, tomorrow I would be absent from the board.

They woke me at nine o'clock. Four of them, Manston, Perkins, Hackett, and a bloke I'd never seen before who had a long, drawn, hanging face and bad teeth. Sutcliffe no doubt was watching over the closed-circuit television.

Hackett and the strange man had me flat on my bunk the moment I made a move. Perkins stood by with hypodermic syringe while Manston slowly rolled up my right shirt sleeve.

'Usual disposal, Mr Manston?' said Hackett.

'No.' Manston shook his head. 'We've used Greenwich enough lately. Take him up river. Above Richmond.'

Hackett beamed. 'Right you are, Mr Manston. Make a nice change. Jim and I can have a drink at Kew Green on the way back.'

I started to fight but they held me down. I started to shout and they let me. Alfred would have been proud of me. Perkins leant over and jabbed the syringe in my arm. The fighting and the shouting died – and so did I – amazed how quick and painless it all was, and with no time to speculate on my destination.

It was the wink that did it. A little muscular flick of the eyelid that briefly spelled hope, a tiny signal picked up and registered within a tenth of a second.

Rooks were cawing. There was the noise of a tractor, distant, ploughing the Elysian fields or more likely carting away clinker from the great fires of Hades. Water was splashing somewhere, but was probably unreachable, a diabolical tantalization. Warmth and comfort. Maybe a gentle initiation that would rise to red-hot discomfort. Naked, of course. Naked ye come and naked ye go. Music, too. Organ music, deep, welling up, fading, a long slow monotony of sound. No brass bands, thank God or, more probably, the Devil. Voices, too. Probably the central bureau of registration, manned by trusties, privileged types who were allowed a long drink once every decade. Church bells, distant, subtle torture since to have heeded their call in the old days would have changed one's ultimate destination. A dog barked, a long, fierce, gritty sound prefacing the biting of some toiling buttock, some pain-wracked body.

I lay there, eyes shut and in no hurry to open them. I considered the wink, that last-moment act, obscured from all the others as Manston leant over, watching me. It had to mean something, surely? Or had it just been a nervous tic? I didn't want to open my eyes in case it had been. The beds in the place were comfortable anyway, even if they did tuck you in without pyjamas. I felt well, but bruised, rested but not eager for action. A telephone rang, distantly. That didn't surprise me. From the tractor I knew that the place was modernized.

I stretched, took a deep breath and got a whiff of tobacco in the air. Snout. That meant I would have to get on the right side of the barons.

A voice said, 'Why he so long?'

Nobody answered. The voice was familiar. I ignored it. I was comfortable.

There was the chink of a glass and then the long, slow hissing of a siphon. A delicious sound. Not to be ignored. I opened my eyes and sat up, naked.

It was a nice bedroom, diamond-paned windows, a candlewick bedcover, white carpet, a bow-fronted Sheraton chest of drawers, some tapestry-covered chairs, and a little Regency desk by the window. From a transistor set on the desk came the sound of organ music. Through the window I could see a row of elms, rooks flying around their crests, and a stretch of hop garden with the bines well up the wires.

Olaf was standing by the window. He reached out and switched off the set. He looked absolutely miserable. Manston was sitting in a chair by the desk. He had a glass in his hand. Close to him was a low table, sunlight streaked across it, sparkling on crystal of decanters and glasses. A silver-meshed siphon stood on a silver coaster.

I said, 'Is it Sunday?'

'Yes,' said Manston. 'The bells are from Sissinghurst church. Wind's in the west. Morning service.'

'It's a bit early for a drink, isn't it?'

'If you lead a conventional life, yes.'

He reached out for a decanter of whisky.

'Three-quarters of the way up the glass. The rest soda. Lazarus special.'

He fixed the drink for me and brought it over.

'How was it down there?' he asked.

'They all sent messages. Freeman's father runs a tobacco ring. He's disappointed in his son, but looks forward to seeing him soon and expressing his displeasure in person.'

I drank. It was a real corpse-reviver. I shivered with the shock, looked down at my naked, bruised torso, and said, 'Why naked?'

'Because,' said Manston, 'all your clothes were put on another cadaver, now going up and down with the tide somewhere between Richmond and Westminster Bridge.'

I said, 'You did wink, didn't you?'

'I did. It was the one moment when I could risk spoiling authenticity. I felt you merited it.'

'Big of you.'

I took another drink. It was good, but I had it tamed this time.

'You did well,' said Manston. 'I was afraid you might ask the one question which would have spoiled it all.'

'How did Duchêne and Paulet, in the first place, ever get on to the fact that Freeman was mixed up in the kidnapping? How, in fact, did they ever know there was a kidnapping?'

'Yes. They knew long before you did.'

'How did they know?'

'From someone in our department – we think. Not sure, though. Freeman sent a letter to the PM. It was opened by his personal secretary.

The letter, of course, was not signed by Freeman. It just stated the facts and gave instructions for a code advertisement to be inserted in *The Times*. The letter was handed to Sutcliffe by the PM. Five people only knew the facts right up to the time that one of our agents was murdered in Freeman's cottage. Five. The PM, his secretary, Sutcliffe, myself, and Perkins.'

'But there was a leak.'

'Clearly.'

'Perkins?'

'Who can tell?'

'It could have come through Captain Asab or one of his men in Tripoli.'

'No. Duchêne was operating before Captain Asab knew.'

'How did you know it was Freeman?'

'Through a letter that Bill Dawson sent his father – unknown to Freeman, obviously. He said that Freeman was coming out to spend some time with him. He'd got leave from his oil company and they were going to do a tour of the Roman antiquities in Libya ... Leptis Magna, Sabratha, and so on. Freeman has a record. We checked him and it seemed likely that he was the man. Perkins, in fact, did the checking.'

'You were a bit late getting on to his country cottage, weren't you?'

'That's the way Perkins – if he's the one — would have worked it, giving it to us late, and having Paulet there to put the clamp on our man.'

I looked at Olaf, big, moon-faced, standing unhappily by the window. 'Why don't you say something?'

'My heart is choked. I think only of Hilda.'

I looked at Manston. 'I've an idea that we're going to do something about that, aren't we?'

Manston stood up and smiled. 'You'll find a complete change of clothes in the bathroom. We'll talk it over before lunch.' He looked at his watch. 'You're due at Lympne at three to catch a plane to Paris. You can't stay in this country – since you're supposed to be dead.'

Showered, shaved, dressed, resuscitated, I sat on the loggia of

Manston's country house and watched the year's first swallows dipping over the swimming pool while Manston laid it on the line for me. His analysis of the situation was clear, but bleak, and very direct.

First, Perkins. He was only a few months back from a Far East tour. He might or might not be a double agent. Lacking proof yet, it was assumed that he was. Even so, it had been decided to let him run for a while. If he were a traitor, then through him they could be sure that the Saraband Two crowd would have written me off for dead. He, himself, had administered the injection of poison to me – only it had been, unknown to him, a nicely judged dose of pentothal, and Hackett and his friend had whisked me away before Perkins could become suspicious. The rest had been easy; another body in the river with my clothes on, and it might be some time before the body was found.

Secondly, Saraband Two had been contacted through a *Times* advertisement and Perkins was acting as the link man. Saraband Two had been told that the exchange deal was on, and that I had been eliminated, as requested, because it was vital that no outsider should be allowed to wander around with such high State secrets as I knew.

'In fact,' said Manston coolly, 'Sutcliffe was actually rather in favour of killing you.'

'He always was fond of me.'

'But I persuaded him that you might have a use.'

'Well, he can always kill me if it turns out you're wrong.'

Thirdly, they had picked up Olaf – unknown to Perkins – just after I had gone to them, and he had stubbornly insisted that all he knew was that Wilkins had been kidnapped and that I had asked him to trace a certain ship.

'Just as you never let on that you had told him about the kidnapping of Dawson, so he never admitted that he knew. In fact—' Manston glanced across at Olaf – 'his mind has room for only one thought at the moment. Wilkins.'

'What about her?'

Manston considered this. 'At the moment there are thirty days in which to arrange the exchanges. I don't think they will start wiping out

Freeman, Pelegrina, or Wilkins until they are absolutely certain that it is going through. They don't present any security risk at the moment because they are being held.'

'Which brings us to the real reason why you didn't kill me. No?'

He nodded, and explained, 'The Prime Minister has agreed to the exchange. He wants his son back. Nothing must go wrong and there mustn't be even a rumour about the affair. You can imagine Sutcliffe's private reaction to that one. His hands are tied officially. You know how big a part pride plays in an organization like ours. We don't like to be outmanoeuvred by another organization. It hurts. We'd like to go on with the exchange arrangements, but also in the thirty days do our damnedest to find Dawson and upset Saraband Two's apple cart. But if we do that and anything goes wrong – then the PM will have heads rolling. You get the dilemma?'

I not only got it. I could imagine how Sutcliffe was squirming. He had been outsmarted by Saraband Two. It was a rare discomfort for him – and I couldn't shed a tear about it. Wilkins was the only person on my mind.

'So what's the score with me? Your hands are tied. And I'm back from the dead.'

'With a new identity.' Manston flipped a passport across to me. I opened it. There was the usual bad passport photograph of me, and I had become Duncan Hilton.

'I don't care for the Duncan,' I said.

'You're on your own,' said Manston. He handed me a sheet of paper. 'Olaf traced the ship for you. There's a list there of her ports of call and route over the last two weeks. At the moment she's coaling in Algiers. My bet is that Dawson and company have already been shipped ashore somewhere. If we can arrange it, we're going to get a customs or quarantine check on her in Algiers – but it won't be easy because our hands are tied officially. Meanwhile, as I say, you're on your own.'

'And what the hell do you think I can do?'

'You want Wilkins back—'

'She must come back or I kill someone,' said Olaf in an angry-bear tone. We both ignored him.

'Think of something,' said Manston. 'There's money waiting for you in Paris. Credit Lyonnais, Place de l'Opéra. You've got a little under thirty days. Get to work. You're an inquiry agent, aren't you? And we're employing you on this job – it took me a long time to get Sutcliffe to accept that. Find something, anything, any lead. The moment you have anything get on to me, or the nearest British consulate, and give the code word 'Python' and he'll pass the message. That's the most we can do for you.'

'And if it comes to nothing?'

'Then it comes to nothing.'

He looked uncomfortable, and I knew why, but I saw no reason to spare him. All right, in his way he liked me, even regarded me as a friend of a kind, but his true love was the damned service he worked for. That, first, second, third, and always.

'Let's get it straight,' I said. 'I'm a big boy and used to hard facts. If I fail, the only person who's going to come back and keep a shut mouth forever is Dawson. Right?'

'I'm afraid so. It's no good trying to make any deal about Wilkins. You know that.'

'Come on, Manston. Spill it all. If I don't find Dawson for you, then pretty soon after the thirty-day limit Olaf and I will go too – won't we?'

He looked at me, tight-mouthed, but he said nothing. He didn't have to. We would go, in a car accident, somehow, somewhere. And he was tight-mouthed because it wasn't his decision – but Sutcliffe's.

'Remember one thing,' he said. 'It's vital that the Saraband Two people get no idea you're alive. You go to Paris this afternoon by yourself. Olaf can join you tomorrow. You've both got rooms at the Hotel Balzac. Know where that is?'

'Yes. And blast you and Sutcliffe.'

I stood up and did a bit of angry pacing. Manston watched me. Olaf sat with his big head hanging down, staring at the pavings. A wagtail flirted along the edge of the pool and a few busy bees mined away at a row of tulips. A warm, late spring day, birds fidgeting on their eggs, water beetles skating on the swimming pool, church service just over, and a thousand Dads putting their two thousand feet up with the *News of the World* while Mum sweated over a hot stove ... and Carver sweated over an impossible job. Oh, I knew how the minds of men like Sutcliffe worked. He didn't think I had a ghost of a chance. But he was prepared, just prepared, to give me any kind of chance if by a long shot it would save his departmental pride. But if it didn't come off – then he would want all record of that long chance expunged from the book. The last bell would ring for me. Hear it not, Duncan, I told myself, for it is a knell that summons thee to heaven or hell – and when that came there wouldn't be any reassuring wink.

Olaf stood up. He glowered at the both of us and then said, 'I think I go back to London and see the Swedish Embassy. Maybe they can do something. After all, Hilda is my fiancée.'

I went over to the cane drink table that had been wheeled out, poured him a stiff rum, and handed it to him.

'Just drink that, Olaf. And do exactly as you're told. Wilkins is coming back – and you're going to help me get her.'

'I suppose', said Manston, 'that after all that treatment at Sutcliffe's place, there isn't anything you're holding back. Anything vital?'

'If there is,' I said, 'I can't think of it. But there is one thing which hasn't been settled.'

'Oh?'

'Sutcliffe is employing me. We haven't discussed terms.'

Manston smiled. 'You must be feeling better. Anyway, you know the usual rates. Plus expenses, of course.'

'Stuff the usual rates. This is an unusual job. If I don't pull it off ... well, there won't be any question of payment.'

'And if you do?'

'Five thousand pounds and an Order of the British Empire.'

Manston's mouth gaped, which was unlike him, for he was a well-brought-up chap.

'You mean that?'

'I do – and you're going to fix it. Five thousand pounds for me – and the OBE for Wilkins. Right?'

He paused, tickled his chin with the tips of his well-manicured fingers, and then said, 'Yes. My personal promise.'

ELEVEN

Sic Transit Gloriana

A hired car from a local garage took me to Lympne, and from there I got a plane to Paris – only it didn't go to Paris, it went to Beauvais, and then there was a long coach ride in.

A fourteen-year-old boy sat alongside me in the plane, going through a pile of Batman comics. He passed a couple over to me and I leafed through them. They didn't give me any ideas that I thought would work.

I got into the hotel around seven, and flopped on the bed with my shoes on, too tired and depressed to order myself a drink. I pulled the list of ship details from my pocket and went over it again. It wasn't any more helpful than staring at the ceiling but it made a change.

Olaf had done a good job. The ship was the *Sveti*, cargo boat, timber trade from Odessa, Russian owned. She did a regular route to Istanbul, Athens, and through the Mediterranean to Algiers, where she now was Olaf had made a note that she had arrived two days over normal schedule at Algiers. In the coach air terminal in Paris I had picked up a BEA red-white-and-blue flight brochure – About your flight, *votre vol, ihr Flug* – which was full of good maps. From Athens through the Mediterranean the *Sveti* had to pass between Sicily and North Africa. That brought her route very close to Bizerta, close enough for Duchêne to have quietly slipped his party aboard. The run from Bizerta along the coast to Algiers was straightforward, but somewhere along it I guessed that the *Sveti* had made a two-day diversion. That put within her range Sicily, Corsica, Sardinia, Majorca, and the rest of the Balearic Islands, even Spain itself – though I had an idea that the USSR did not trade with Spain. Even so, that would not have stopped the *Sveti* heaving to at night off the coast while a party went ashore. I dropped the brochure and asked the ceiling how in hell one man, and a love-stricken

Swede, could cover that area of possibilities? Looking for a needle in a
haystack was easier. At least you only had the stack to deal with. The
Prime Minister's son could be in any of dozens of haystacks. I settled
back on the bed and considered praying for the miracle of second sight.
I even considered taking a pin and trying a jab over the map. In fact I
did it. The oracle announced that Dawson was a hundred miles south
of Rome in the middle of the Tyrrhenian Sea. Rome made me think
of Duchêne. Duchêne made me think of Paulet. Clever Paulet, who
kindly brought me beer, sandwiches, and a backhander – yet still I liked
him. Not that that was going to stop me breaking his neck or putting
a bullet into him if it would get Wilkins out of her jam. A dead Paulet
would upset his girlfriend Thérèse. *To lose you, my darling, would make
life empty for me. A thousand embraces.* That's what she'd written to him.

I sat up suddenly. Manston had asked me if there was any detail I
had not mentioned. Well, there was – because I had forgotten it myself
until now. Paulet's office address I'd kicked over – they knew it, anyway.
And they knew his real wife's address. But only I knew Therese's address.

I got a cab to the top of the Avenue Wagram, and then walked down
to the Place des Ternes. I went into a bar and had two *pernods*. Suddenly
I was feeling good and hopeful for no reason at all.

I went out into the velvety, spring-warm, Gauloise-flavoured Paris
evening. It was an old house on the Avenue des Ternes, turned into
apartments. There was no concierge. Just a row of name plates in the
hallway with bell pushes alongside them. Mademoiselle Thérèse Diotel
was apartment Number 3. I went up two floors. There was one door
on the landing with Thérèse's card slipped into a brass holder. There
was a fanlight over the door. No light showed through it. That didn't
mean she was not in. She didn't know me – but she was a clever girl,
would have to be to be hitched up with Paulet. Any excuse I made
would have to be a good one. The trouble was I couldn't think of a good
one. Nobody comes to sell Larousse dictionaries on a Sunday evening,
and I couldn't say I was an old friend of Paulet's from the KGB training
school in Moscow. So I did something which I hadn't done since my
small boy days. I rang the bell good and hard and ran away. Up the next

flight of steps to the turn where I could just hang my head down and watch the door. Nothing happened. I went down and repeated the performance just to be sure. She could have been taking a bath or even entertaining a lover – after all, Paulet had been away some time. Nothing happened.

I went back and did the door lock with a piece of perspex. The small hallway was in darkness. I let it stay that way and went through into the main room, after checking a kitchen to the left of the hall and a bathroom to the right. The main room was in darkness. I pulled the curtains and switched on the light. A door across the room led into a bedroom. I could see the end of the bed, and a red dress draped over a small chair. I went in, pulled the curtains, and switched on the light. The bed was made and had a frilly sort of canopy over the top end. There were frills like candy floss over the dressing table, and a yellow-and-black stuffed Esso tiger sprawled over a little sofa. Everything was neat and tidy. I did a quick tour again of the kitchen and bathroom and main room. The whole place was neat and tidy, and with the feeling of not having been used for some time. No washing-up left, no evidence of meals, nothing in the kitchen bin, half a carton of sour milk in the fridge and a packet of sausages; no cigarette stubs in the ashtrays, no newspapers; on the table in the main room a vase held an arrangement of wilted mimosa. I had the conviction that Therese was away and had been for some days. So I took a good look around. One of the things I enjoy is going over other people's rooms. In ten minutes you can often learn more about them than they could tell you themselves in an hour.

She was a great one for Colette, had all her books in paperback. Her favourite aperitif was something called Ambassadeur – three bottles in the sideboard. There was whisky as well, half a bottle. I made myself a drink and carried it with me on the tour of inspection. She used *Jolie Madame* scent, favoured short nightdresses, one of them a rather nice number in blue and white spotted silk. She kept Paulet's love letters – about twenty of them – in a bureau drawer, tied up with a red ribbon that had Galerie Lafayette printed on it in gold. I struggled through them; they were dated from long before the Dawson affair and were mostly repetitious – Paulet, even my bad French told me, had no literary style or true lover's felicity of expression. In fact he was mostly quite earthy and direct about his need and feeling for her. There was only one thing of interest in them. It was in a letter just over eighteen months old, written from Rome. Just one sentence which read, translated, 'J. has died suddenly so the whole D. business has been cancelled.'

I stood there, pondering this. D. could, of course, have stood for Dawson. Who was J.?

I put the letter back. Under them, wrapped in a yellow duster, was a 9 mm Browning pistol – obviously a spare to the one Paulet carried – and some ammunition. I took the gift without leaving a thank you card.

I washed my whisky glass in the kitchen and put it back in place and made for the flat door, head down with the dejection of failure. It was just as well, otherwise I might not have seen it. On entering, the opening door had pushed it back far to one side from where it had fallen through the letter box on the thick carpet. It was a confirmatory cablegram in a little envelope – the kind they always send you the next day to confirm a telegram which has been passed over the phone.

I opened it. It was in French. Translated, it read: *We need a good cook at V.V. immediately. Meet Mimo, Tristan's Bar, any midday next three days.* It was signed François, and had been sent from Bizerta the day they had released me. Thérèse had received it – over the phone – late the same day, and had been away early the next morning before the postman had dropped the confirmation through the letter box. But where the devil were V.V. and Tristan's Bar? I went to the flat telephone and called Directory Inquiries. There was no Tristan's Bar or Bar Tristan listed in the Paris area.

I went back to the hotel and to bed, but not to sleep. I stared at the ceiling and kept saying to myself, 'J. has died suddenly so the whole D. business has been cancelled.' If D. stood for Dawson, could it have been that Saraband Two and company had had this affair lined up – maybe a straightforward job they were going to do themselves nearly two years ago? And if so, why was J. so important that his or her death had made them cancel the deal?

The next morning – Olaf wasn't arriving until after midday – I went round to see Letta. I needed company and also I hoped that I would get some information. All right, so I was breaking a Manston rule not to let anyone know that I was alive. But I was prepared to break all the rules in the book if it would give me a chance of getting Wilkins back. And, anyway, if I told Letta to keep her mouth shut she would.

She was having breakfast near a wide window, the sunlight gold-leafing her skin, her dark hair piled up close around her head in some morning coiffure that made it look as though she were wearing a cossack hat. She wore a loose morning coat, red and white stripes, had her legs up on a stool, and her feet were bare. She looked so good to me that I wished this were just a social call and that I had all the time in the world and no worries and could start off on a little interregnum of pleasure and dalliance such as a man must have now and again to rejuvenate the mind and the spirit.

It was clear, too, that she felt the same way. She came out of her chair in one long graceful movement and her arms went round me in a warm tackle. It was nice to know that I meant so much to her. I just let the mutual disentanglement come gently and in its own sweet time. Then I sat down on a chair and lit a cigarette. She sat on the arm and with the tips of her fingers did things to the top of my head. It was pleasant but made thought difficult.

I said, 'Can we talk frankly or are there any snakes around?'

She nodded towards the top of the window. Lilith was up there, coiled around a fat transverse curtain pole.

'Poor Lilith,' said Letta. 'At the moment, you know, she is not well. She won't eat and is so irritable. She is all nervous and tensed up and I cannot use her in my act. Last night she kept me awake for hours, twisting and rattling in her basket. Why should she be off her food – the guinea pigs in Paris are very good? And now she won't come down from there.'

She leant over and kissed me on the cheek. The housecoat flapped open and I put a hand on the golden brown curve of one of her breasts to steady her from falling into my lap.

Her flesh warm under my palm, I said, 'Officially I'm supposed to be dead. You haven't seen me. You won't say anything to anyone about me. Okay?'

'For a dead man, you look very healthy.'

'Tell me,' I said, 'have you heard from your father recently?'

'No. You are still playing around with that old business?'

'Yes, I am.'

I was disappointed. Freeman had got in touch with Jane Judd, and paid Gloriana back and out of it had come Barcelona. I had hoped that Pelegrina might have made some semi-revealing communication to Letta.

She kissed me again and this time slid into my lap. 'Tonight, after I come back from the Scherezade, I make you come alive again and forget all this business. I give you a key so that you can come in and wait for me, yes?'

With an effort I came back to the business in hand. 'But you did lend money to your father for his last venture, didn't you?' I asked.

'Yes, and positively for the last time. I made that clear. He's a man who can complicate people's lives. I like mine straightforward. Just like now. You and me.'

'You called him on the phone from Tripoli at the Villa La Sunata, didn't you?'

'Yes, to ask him what the hell he was up to. You went there?'

'Yes.'

'And he is in trouble?'

'Bad trouble.'

'Something you can do nothing about?'

'Would you want me to?'

'Yes, if you could. After all, I am his daughter and, although he is such a stupid old fool, I have some feeling for him.'

'You ever heard of a place called Tristan's Bar or the Bar Tristan? Your father ever mentioned it? Or a place . . . house or something . . . whose initials might be V.V.?'

'No. Such mystery. This, for you, is life, no? Always mysteries?'

'It could be my death.'

I said it lightly, but I don't think if I said it seriously it would have got through to her. Her lips were nuzzling the side of my neck and I needed all my willpower to keep my natural anxiety in the foreground. Up above the window Lilith lazily adjusted a couple of coils and eyed me biliously.

She didn't know it but there was a prize guinea pig sitting down below her. Me. Manston had turned me loose, a human guinea pig, into an experiment which didn't seem to have a hope of succeeding. And when it failed the chopping block would be waiting. It was this kind of thought that made it difficult for me to go along with Letta's present mood. There's nothing like worry to inhibit a man.

Before I left, she gave me a key to the apartment. I took it. Why not? I might feel a different man by the evening.

'You come and sit and have a drink,' she said. 'Always I am back by half past one.' She had her hand on the door when she turned back and went to a bureau.

She came back and held out the gold python bracelet.

'You do me a favour?'

'Of course.'

'I have had a telephone call from your Mrs Stankowski. She is staying at the Georges Cinq. We talk about the price for the bracelet but do not agree. You go and see her and get for me three thousand pounds. Then I give you ten per cent. She's fond of you, no? She will not haggle with you' – she smiled – 'and I do not mind if you humour her a little to get the right price.'

I nodded and sighed. Women.

Letta laughed, reached forward, kissed me and said, 'But you do not humour her too much. She likes you, I know. When we talk over the phone she asked if I had seen you. She sounded worried about you.'

So she might be. I had walked out of her flat, away from cold salmon, oysters, Montrachet, and what could have been a pleasant aftermath, into limbo.

*

The thing about my kind of job which makes for the occasional success is the inability of the most intelligent human being, the Sutcliffe or Manston or Saraband Two types, to control or foresee every little circumstance that lurks on the fringe of a complicated affair. Somewhere somebody is going to make a mistake, and somewhere somebody is going to take advantage of it. Small things in the right place can have big potentials. Take a beer bottle, for instance; full of beer it has no room for anything else. Empty, well, it can be packed with all sorts of things. And master minds, thank the Lord, have occasional moods of uncritical acceptance like normal, uncomplicated people.

I didn't indulge in this piece of pretty ordinary philosophy as I was going to see Gloriana. It came afterwards. If I'd had any sense I'd have taken it a step or two further but I suppose at that time, after leaving her, I mean, I was in a deep state of uncritical acceptance of life.

Why I went to see her I don't really know. I had time to waste until Olaf got in, and with time to waste I felt life was a vacuum unless I filled it. Though what I was going to do when Olaf got in I couldn't think – except that I didn't mean to hold his hand through any maudlin rum-drinking bout. I suppose, fundamentally, being a great believer in survival, I went to Gloriana to tidy up the python bracelet deal and make sure of my ten per cent commission. Thinking about money, though it wasn't any great sum, kept me from thinking about other things.

At the Georges Cinq the reception clerk rang through and asked Mrs Stankowski if she could see a Mr Duncan Hilton about her brother. Mrs Stankowski said she would and up I went.

Was she surprised to see me! Her beautiful cornflower blue eyes popped and she nearly dropped the dry martini she had just mixed for herself. We just stood there looking at one another. After the dusky, Oriental charm of Letta, she was the fresh, pink and white, red-gold and blue of frank, Anglo-Saxon womanhood, and I wondered what it was about me that, even in this present crisis, could always be happy with either, were the other dear charmer away.

'You bastard – what happened to you!'

She came to me, arms outstretched, making me feel like the sailor home from the sea and the hunter home from the hill. Her arms went round my neck and she kissed me, spilling dry martini down the back of my jacket. I didn't mind. It was nice to be wanted. We let the kiss run for a bit and I smoothed the hollow of her back, appreciating the high-quality silk of the little shantung jacket she wore. After all, I had permission from Letta to humour her a little.

Stepping back, I said, 'I'm dead. This is Duncan Hilton. You never saw Rex Carver again after he left your apartment. Just be content with the new *persona* – and ask no questions.'

She nodded, content for the moment, but in time I knew that the questions would come. I went over to the cocktail shaker, added more gin and poured myself a drink.

She sat back on the settee, curled her legs under her and watched me. I had a curious feeling that she was waiting for something – perhaps for me to get a drink inside me before she felt ready to hand me whatever there was to hand.

'This whole affair', she said, 'is really something stinking big, isn't it?'

'Yes. What are you doing over here – apart from getting your bracelet back from Letta?'

'My Treasury friend advised me to get out of England for a while. Go somewhere quiet and rest, he said.'

'Paris is hardly quiet and rest.'

'I'm going to Cannes.'

That hardly qualified either, I thought, but I didn't bother to say so.

'What is it all about?' she asked. 'Something quite out of the ordinary? And that damned brother of mine mixed up in it. Though he's a complete fool, he's still my brother and I'm beginning to get very worried about him.'

I sat beside her and smoothed the back of her hand. 'Gentling' they call it with animals. I had a feeling she needed it. She was all worked up. I pulled the python bracelet from my pocket and handed it to her.

'Give me a cheque for three thousand pounds and it is yours. Letta won't take a penny less.'

'You've seen her?'

'I had to. I'm her business agent.'

She fingered the bracelet and then slipped it on her arm. 'I'll give you a cheque before you go.'

That was unusual. No haggling. She clearly had something else on her mind.

'What's bothering you?' I asked.

'I don't know what you mean.'

'Come on, yes, you do. You're as nervous as a kitten.'

'Crap!' She smiled.

'Even that doesn't sound as authentic as it used to.'

'They gave you a rough time, didn't they?'

'The bruises don't show when I'm dressed. What's the matter with you?'

'I suppose it's because they wouldn't tell me a damned thing about what's behind all this. Go away and forget, they said.'

'Then do it. Head for the sunshine at Cannes. The peace and calm of the five-star Carlton and the healing solitude of the Boulevard Croisette.'

She sipped at what was left of her martini, eyeing me over the glass.

'Tell me,' she said, 'have you heard from your secretary, Miss Wilkins?'

I just stared at her.

'Have you?' she asked.

'Why on earth should I? Heard from her from where? What's Wilkins got to do with anything?'

'That's what I've been trying to make up my mind about, ever since you walked in here. You see, I was told to pass anything I got straight to them. You see . . . I only got it this morning. It was sent on with other mail from my London apartment. By the maid. Oh, hell . . . perhaps I oughtn't to—'

I took her glass from her and put it on a small table. Then I grabbed her arm.

'Try starting at the beginning. And get this straight. You can trust me. You won't be disobeying any order. I'm working for them. They've given me just a handful of days to bring home the bacon. If I don't, then leaving aside my funeral arrangements, there's going to be a lot of other work for the undertaker.' I shook her arm. Putting it in words had brought a quick freeze in my stomach. 'I'm in a fix. If you've got anything that will help – let's hear it.'

She got up, retrieved her glass, sipped, then walked away from me and stared at a Corot reproduction on the wall. Without looking at me, she said, 'I'll give you a cheque for the bracelet.'

'I want more than that from you. If I have to squeeze it from you. Come on now.'

Turning, her face worried, she said, 'They were most emphatic about anything I got going straight to them.'

'You're scared of them. I don't blame you. They scare me. But if you know anything it ought to come to me first. Hell, I'm the one who has been turned loose to do their work for them. Now tell me what all this is about Wilkins.'

She came back, stood above me, and took the plunge. 'I've had a letter from her,' she said.

I just looked at her.

Then I heard myself say, 'You've had a what?'

'A letter. It's on the desk over there. I was just going to send it off to them.'

I got up, and as I walked to the desk, she said, 'I got it this morning forwarded with the rest of my mail.'

I went to the desk. There was an opened envelope lying on it. As I picked it up, I heard Gloriana pouring herself another drink behind me.

It was a long envelope, foolscap size, addressed to her and marked *Confidential,* and it had a fancy Spanish stamp on it. Inside were two sheets of paper. One was ordinary cheap letter paper, and the other was a large piece of brown wrapping paper, torn off rough around two edges. I tackled the brown paper first, carrying it to the light of a table lamp. On it was written in block capitals:

TO WHOEVER FINDS THIS –

YOU WILL GET FIFTY POUNDS – 8,500 PESETAS – IF YOU SEND THIS LETTER TO MRS J. STANKOWSKI, EATON HOUSE, UPPER GROSVENOR STREET, LONDON, ENGLAND.

YOU MUST TELL HER EXACTLY HOW AND WHERE YOU FOUND IT AND WHEN.

MRS STANKOWSKI: WHEN YOU RECEIVE THIS AND ITS COVERING LETTER PLEASE GET IN TOUCH WITH MR CARVER. I AM DOING THE SAME THING IN BEER BOTTLES FOR HIM.

WE ARE NOT ALLOWED OUTSIDE, BUT THIS HOUSE IS ISOLATED AND NEAR THE SEA, EITHER SPAIN OR ONE OF THE SPANISH ISLANDS. B.D. IS HERE. TREATED WELL. I SEE ONLY A MAN CALLED PAULET AND A WOMAN – THERESE.

TO WHOEVER FINDS THIS I SAY THIS IS NOT A JOKE. IT IS A VERY SERIOUS MATTER AND YOU WILL GET FIFTY POUNDS IF YOU SEND THIS TO MRS STANKOWSKI.

It was signed, in her ordinary hand – Hilda Wilkins.

The other letter, written in rather a schoolboyish hand, was also in English, and the address at the head was 7 Paseo Maritimo, San Antonio Abad, Ibiza, Islas de Baleares.

Dear Lady,

Very much I hope this no joke because I can be very useful for fifty pounds but would like it in the pesetas. I am student but work evenings in the San Antonio supermarket, chiefly washing bottles and opening crates. This letter I almost do not see, but am curious when I do. It is in a beer bottle, a large one, in two dozen returned for the consignment. Only we take back the bottles which are from us and they are for beer, mineral acqua, and wines. It is good I find it because I am study the English language because there is so much tourism here and should hope one day to be in the hotel trade, not as waiter, but at the reception, perhaps rising to manager. So I hope this is serious about the fifty pounds (8,500 pts). This I find yesterdays ago at 1800 hrs. Also, I find same kind of letter for Mr Carver and write him, also in London. This way, perhaps, it is permitted I get 17,000 pesetas?

> Your obedient servant, esteemed lady,
> José Bonifaz.

The date on the letter was four days old.

I sat back and lit a cigarette. Gloriana came and put a fresh martini alongside me but said nothing. She was still probably wondering whether she had done the right thing. I was way past worrying about that. I had a nice warm feeling about Wilkins. What a girl. I could see her. Wilkins cooped up a prisoner. That was enough to make her mad anyway. She'd be in a filthy temper, but that wouldn't stop her thinking and scheming. It would only put an edge on her brain. It would be hot and the prisoners would be supplied with beer. Big fat brown bottles that when empty would be cleared away, and finally carted back to the supermarket for a fresh supply; big, fat, empty beer bottles going back so that the *consigne* could be allowed on them. And they'd be brown bottles. Wilkins had used brown paper so that it wouldn't show up when Paulet or Thérèse collected them. Oh, yes, she was my girl, all right. Tough, capable, bad-tempered Wilkins who never let anything in life get on top of her but a cold. Block letters to make her letter easy to read for a foreigner. And no wonder José Bonifaz preferred to be paid in pesetas – they would come to more than fifty pounds . . . The other letter from Bonifaz to me was probably on my desk in London now. Since it would be marked 'Confidential' Mrs Burtenshaw would not have opened it. Everyone, Manston, Sutcliffe, and myself, working from the outside in, and suddenly Wilkins coming up trumps, working from the inside out.

Gloriana sat on the arm of my chair, and said, 'Does it help?'

'It's going to. It's got to.'

She gave me a quizzical look. 'You didn't get a letter from Wilkins also? This José says he has written to you.'

'It's probably lying on my office desk unopened.'

'Are you going to let them know?'

'Them?'

'You know. The Treasury man.'

I stood up. 'To hell with them. I'm not going to shout for them until I really have something to shout for. Do you know Ibiza?'

'Yes.'

'San Antonio?'

'Yes. It's a nice place spoiled by tourists. Jan and I spent a week there once. Don't you think you ought to tell them? I mean, if it's all so serious?'

'Forget them.'

She looked doubtful but she kept at it.

'Is this Miss Wilkins being kept there . . . you know, against her wishes?'

'Yes.'

'And who's B.D.?'

I put my hands on her shoulders and looked straight into her blue eyes. 'Look, I don't want you to ask questions. The less you know, the better for you.'

'You're not going to keep me out of it – are you forgetting my brother is probably there, in danger?'

'You don't care a damn for your brother.'

'Not for some of the things he's done. But I do care for him as a brother.'

I shook my head. 'I don't want you mixed up in this. They've told you to go away and forget it all. Do that.'

She shook her head. 'You ought to tell them if it's so serious.'

'I'm going to – in good time. But first I want a chat with José Bonifaz, and I want to find out if there's a Bar Tristan in San Antonio. Is there?'

'I wouldn't know.'

I said, 'I'll keep these letters. You forget about them. And if I can possibly do anything about your brother I will.' I put the letters in my pocket. 'You've never received them. Your conscience is clear.'

'And you're going to Ibiza?'

'As soon as I can get a flight. No hope today. But I ought to get off tomorrow.'

I went up to her and gave her a light kiss on the cheek.

'Don't worry. You're doing the right thing. As soon as I have any positive information I'll let the right people know about it.'

If I told them too soon I knew what might happen. Somebody might try to put a stopper on it. The PM might not want to take any risks with his son. But if I wanted Wilkins back I had to take risks. By shouting for Manston now there was too much chance of some high-level decision blocking any further action.

I began to move to the door.

Gloriana said, 'Don't forget the cheque.'

'What cheque?'

'For that mercenary snake-charmer of yours. Don't you want an excuse to go and see her again before you take off tomorrow?'

'Well . . . I suppose it will help fill in time. I'll give it to her this evening.'

She grinned at me, raised a hand to touch her red-gold hair, and said, 'Just try and keep things on a purely business level, otherwise you'll spoil our beautiful friendship.'

She moved to the bureau to write the cheque. As she wrote she said, 'If you get any news about my brother, let me know. I'll be at Cannes. Not at the Carlton – but the Reserve Miramar, Jan and I always stayed there.'

In my business one should always listen carefully to what people say. Very carefully. I didn't know it then, but I was going to make this mistake twice. Listen, don't interrupt, and then do a lot of careful thinking. After all, I wasn't selling soap or potatoes – I was selling expertise. Now, hours later, seeing this same woman sitting opposite me, I had the tardy conviction that maybe I would have done better with soap and potatoes. She had her hands cocked up on her crossed legs, and the right hand held a gun – a gas gun; no noise, deadly effective within two yards and we were less than that apart. 'Life is very sweet, brother; who would wish to die?' And, to continue with the borrowing, it was no consolation to think that while 'every dog has his day, and mine has been a fine one', I was content for it all to end then and there. And all for the want of a little thoughtful listening.

But first there had been Olaf at the airport. I didn't tell him about Wilkins' letter. There would have been no holding him. We got bookings on a direct jet flight to Ibiza for early the next morning. Normally one had to go to Palma, Majorca, and make a change to a local flight to the island, but now the airfield on Ibiza had been lengthened and strengthened to take jets. That suited me; every hour saved could be important. Olaf stormed a bit about the mystery, but I told him that I would put him in the picture on the plane. Until then he was to go to our hotel and keep sober for the next day's trip.

'Just tell me there is some hope for us to get Hilda – then I'm content.'

'There is some hope. All you have to do is to stay in your room and don't drink more than half a bottle of rum.'

I had dinner with him, and left him about half past nine and went along to Letta's flat, deep in thought, but all along the wrong lines. I had decided that I would put a call through to Manston from the airport the next morning just before we took off. I wasn't going to run the risk of any of his Paris men blocking me from getting on that Caravelle.

I fixed myself a whisky and sat in a chair near the window and planned what I would do. It was simple. The moment I had established where V.V. was – and I was sure that Wilkins and Bill Dawson would be there – then I would call up the cavalry. I was really quite happy and pleased with myself, and full of admiration for Wilkins' cleverness.

What the hell would I do without her if she ever got round to marrying Olaf?

And now here, sitting in a chair a few feet from me, was Gloriana Stankowski smiling, self-composed, and dedicated to the business in hand . . . her right hand.

I'd left the apartment door unlocked and she had walked in and taken a seat opposite me. She was wearing a smart, black tailor-made, with black velvet trimmings on cuffs and neck and a white silk blouse with an antique silver brooch of some Indian god with about six arms – Siva, probably, representing the destructive principle in life. She was always very studied in her dress. And she'd fooled me completely.

I said, 'I presume whatever that thing in your hand holds, you mean business with it?'

'Unfortunately, yes, but—'

'Please,' I interrupted, 'don't say you hope I won't take it personally.'

'I don't care how you take it. I'm only thinking of myself. I was given a promise that I wouldn't have to take part in active operations of this kind. The promise has been broken twice since Jan died. Now, because of Wilkins' letter and the fact that you are still alive when you should be dead, they say—'

'Saraband Two or Duchêne?'

'Does it matter?'

'Not really. I'm beginning to see light.'

J. was Jan, of course.

She shifted her hand a little, and said, 'I don't even know what chemical it contains. But it's effective. I've used it before. I had to do a course after I married Jan.'

She must have known damn well what was in the pistol. You don't take courses without being told. It was probably potassium cyanide. Maybe she just didn't want to confuse me with science. Maybe she just didn't want to think too much about what she was going to do.

I said, 'Was Jan very fond of your brother Martin?'

'Yes – oddly enough. Although Martin never knew the truth behind it, they had this thing to kidnap Dawson fixed up over two years ago.

There was no Pelegrina in the picture then. Jan saw it as a way of fixing up Martin with some money. They would do the kidnapping between them – it arose because Martin was so friendly with Dawson and had the opportunities – and then Jan's real lot, mine, too, of course by then, would take over. Martin would think the take-over genuine and would go off happy with his money. Unhappily Jan died.'

'Martin had no idea that you and Jan worked for Saraband Two?'

'No. Nor does now. You like her? She gives me the creeps. In fact, I've wanted to get out of the whole thing since Jan's death, but I wasn't allowed. Anyway, you can see that you have to go. It's most important that this deal goes through on the terms already agreed.'

I moved one hand, just a fraction, hoping I might be allowed a last cigarette. She stopped me with a gesture of her hand and a shake of the head.

I said, 'But your brother, after Jan's death, still nursed the idea of kidnapping Dawson, said nothing to you about it – because right from the start he had never known that you were in on the original idea, or even that you and Jan were agents?'

'That's right. The whole thing was called off officially. But Martin went on nursing it. When he disappeared, stealing from me, I knew what he was after. I went down to his cottage – oh, I knew about that – and saw the letter from Dawson inviting him to Tripoli. So I was instructed to make a fuss with the insurance company, knowing you would be called in. They were very clever. They thought Martin would try and set it up some time on his own, so they made me transfer my insurance to the London Fraternal – just so that it would be you on the job.'

'Flattering.'

She shrugged her shoulders. 'All they wanted was for you to do their work – that's all they ever want. Somebody to do their work . . . somebody expendable or docile. I'm fed up with it. I only went in because Jan persuaded me, and with him it was fun. Nothing's been fun since. I really loved him.'

'You're breaking my heart.'

She gave a ghost of a smile. 'I like you. But you don't begin to compare with Jan. Nevertheless, I like you . . . I suppose that's why I'm talking so much, working myself up to it. The other two times I really disliked the people involved.'

I said, 'Why ever did you show me Wilkins' letter?'

'They said I was to make sure you hadn't received one and passed it on. I knew you wouldn't tell me if you had unless I showed you mine. And now – I've got to kill you.'

I said, 'Why not put that stupid thing away and have a drink? Maybe we could work something out? Why not?'

She shook her head.

'Jan's gone, but I still like living. If I disobeyed, I wouldn't live long.'

'Maybe we could fix something up. Look, other people are involved. Wilkins – and, could be, your brother. They might not let him off the hook. You wouldn't like to see him go under.'

Her face stiffened. 'I don't care what happens to him. He was worse to me than my father when I was young. He did some terrible things . . . a really terrible thing when I was fifteen, so terrible that nothing was ever right afterwards until I met Jan, and he was so sweet and understanding and then, thank the Lord, it all came right . . .'

Believe it or not, there was the wet glint of a tear in one of her eyes. But it wasn't breaking my heart that her brother had messed about with her as a girl. I wanted to get out of this room alive. Wanted to – but how? One move from me and that thing in her hand would go off in my face, and that would be the end of me and Wilkins. I cursed myself then for not telling Olaf about the letter. At least he could have carried on. Thank God, she didn't know about Olaf or she would be leaving here to finish him off in his rum-sodden sleep at the hotel.

She stood up suddenly and stepped sideways to the window.

'I'm sorry,' she said contritely, and she stretched her right arm out, taking aim. If there had been bullets in the gun I would have taken a chance on her aiming badly and missing me as I jumped for her. But this stuff would spray wide, enveloping me as I moved.

Her lips firmed up, there was still the glint of a tear in her cornflower blue eyes, and she was all set to kill me. Vaguely, for there is no controlling the mind at such moments, I wondered who the other two had been, wondered why I hadn't paid more attention to Miggs once telling me that her husband had been as bent as a bedspring, and wondered why I'd been so dumb as to miss that J. could have stood for Jan.

Vaguely, too, I thought I ought to say something, something significant to haunt her for the rest of her life, some last, dying words; Anaxagoras, the old schoolmaster-philosopher saying, 'Give the boys a holiday'; Rabelais with his 'Let down the curtain, the farce is over.'

Well, the curtain had something to do with it. From high above her head at that moment came the faint jingle of brass curtain rings. I glanced up and saw, too, the faint movement of her head following mine. Lilith was up there still, from this morning, and finally bored with sulking. I saw the slow movement of her grey-silver coils and then she dropped in the lazy, clumsy Siamese cat way, aiming for the chair below.

She missed it, struck Gloriana on the shoulder, and knocked her back into the chair, the twelve-foot length of the python sprawling over her like a hose pipe. Gloriana screamed, then kicked and beat at the snake with her arms and legs. Suddenly Lilith wasn't sulking and bored; she was irritated, nervous, and angry at the treatment, and with smooth swiftness the coils went round an arm, the flat, axe-shaped head weaved upwards and, before I could do anything, the long length of her body was coiling and constricting around Gloriana's neck. If she had stayed still, fought down her panic, Lilith would have eased up, lost her fear at the threshing movement of Gloriana, and slid away.

I ran to the sideboard and picked up a bottle for a weapon and charged back to the sprawling mass of woman and snake in the chair, but Gloriana's right hand came up, holding the spray gun, and it was pointed at me. I backed off, and then saw that it had only momentarily been aimed at me. She was choking and breathing hard, trying to locate Lilith's head. She grabbed at it with her left hand and brought the right round but as she fired – a long, soft hiss of sound – the python's head jerked, forcing her hand aside and I saw the quick spread of vapour envelop the tousled red-gold hair and obscure her face.

They went, both of them, woman and snake, within three seconds, collapsing, both of them, into the chair, and perhaps for another five seconds there was a slow dying ripple of movement along the length of Lilith's coils, but no movement from Gloriana. She lay there with her blue eyes seeing nothing.

I got a taxi and went to Letta's club and met her. I took her back to my hotel and got a room for her. She wanted more explanations than I was prepared to give but in the end – knowing about Gloriana lying dead in her apartment – agreed not to go back until Manston got in touch with her at the hotel. Manston had people in Paris who would clear up the situation smoothly and without publicity.

TWELVE

Trio in a Flat

I told Olaf the full story on the plane – and then it took me an hour to convince him that the best way for him to help Wilkins was to stand by at Ibiza airport as a contact for Manston when he arrived.

His parting words to me were, 'You make a mess of this, Mr Carver, and I break your neck. Hilda is the world to me.'

I took a taxi from the airport to San Antonio. It was about a twenty-mile drive from the airport. It was hot with the promise of real baking summer days to come. Old ladies in black sat under the olive trees, knitting, and keeping an eye on their goats and sheep. The earth had that dry, reddish colour and was the kind that the wind breaks down to fine dust and spreads over everything. The hills were green with scrub and, here and there, a pair of buzzards circled high in some air current over the crests. I didn't look at the scenery much. I kept telling myself that what I was doing was right. I had to get more definite information. I wanted to have enough information to be sure that Manston would have to take action on it. Bill Dawson was going to be returned anyway. But I wanted Wilkins back.

San Antonio was spread around the shores of a wide lagoon on the north-west of the island. One side was packed with new hotels for the tourist trade, and the other side held the old town, sloping gently uphill from the waterfront, a maze of narrow alleys and streets. It was all pink and white and ochre, and fast being spoiled and modernized. Buildings were going up everywhere, and every other shop was a tourist trap – postcards, beach hats, sandals, sunglasses, pottery, and trashy jewellery. It was a miniature Brighton or Blackpool under a hot sun. Every holiday resort in Europe was getting to look more and more alike, a babel with a twenty-four-hour developing service, fish-and-chips and beefsteak and middle-aged mums wearing shorts or holiday outfits that they wouldn't have dared to sport at home. Well, good for them.

The taxi took me into the town, up the hillside through a maze of crowded little streets, and finally dropped me at the end of the Paseo Maritimo. It was a narrow passageway running parallel to the hillside. Number 7 was wedged in between a butcher's shop and a carpenter's workshop. An old man in faded blue shirt and trousers, barefooted, was sitting on the doorstep contemplating his dirty toes.

I said, '*Por favor, José Bonifaz?*' That practically exhausted my Spanish.

He jerked his thumb over his shoulder at the hallway and stairs behind him. I went into a gloom that smelled of frying fish and tobacco smoke. At the top of the first flight of stairs a small girl was sitting, cuddling a doll and crooning to it. I gave her a big smile and repeated my Spanish. She got up, still crooning, and went along the landing to one of three doors and knocked on it for me. I heard a voice say something inside and I went in.

José Bonifaz may have been a student but he certainly wasn't studying. The place, I realized now, was some sort of pension. This was a bed-sitting room. There was a table, crowded with books, under a small window, a chair with an opened can of peaches on it, a wardrobe with a cracked mirror front, and an iron bed with José Bonifaz on it. He was reading an English paperback with a lurid cover and, although it was long past midday, was still wearing pyjamas, the jacket open to show a thin chest as brown as a berry from the sun. His hair was as black as coal and needed cutting, his eyes were almost as dark and were the twitchy kind, never still for a moment in their sockets. He had a thin, birdy little face with a tiny tuft of baby beard right on the end of his chin. My first sight of him didn't warm me to him.

He rolled slowly off the bed to a sitting position and said, 'Señor?' Then before I could answer, he called something in Spanish to the small girl who was standing in the open door behind me. She answered. He put out his tongue and she retreated, leaving the door open. I shut the door with my foot and said, 'I'm from Mrs Stankowski.'

He didn't get it at first. He just looked at me puzzled.

'Mrs Stankowski,' I said. 'You wrote to her sending the letter you found in a beer bottle.' I put my hand in my pocket and brought out a pile of Spanish notes and tossed them to him. I'd got them at the airport exchange bureau.

He caught them and the dark eyes flickered with sudden interest and understanding. He sat there, staring at the notes as though they had just fallen out of the blue into his hands, which in a way they had, and I knew that he was having a struggle not to start counting them. Some lingering trace of Spanish courtesy made him decide against it.

He said slowly, 'But it is unbelievable. I think it all a joke.'

'It's no joke,' I said. 'Apart from the one for Mr Carver have you found any other letters like it since?'

He stood up. 'No, sir.' He looked at me and then at the notes in his hands and shook his head.

'You can count them later. Tell me, would you have any idea who had returned the beer bottles?'

'No, sir. I am not in the shop when they come in. Only the evenings I am working to wash them.'

It looked as though I wasn't going to get much from him.

I said, 'Is there a Bar Tristan in this town?'

He sat down on the bed, put the notes at his side and then looked at me, cocking his head like a thrush listening for a worm, and it was a good ten seconds before he said, 'Yes, sir.'

I thought it was a bit too long for such a simple answer.

'Where?'

'It is around the corner from the supermarket. I shall show you.'

He began to fish under the bed for his shoes. When he came up with them he said, 'You stay somewhere in this town, señor?'

I didn't like that. I was the one who had come to ask questions, and I didn't think he was just making polite conversation. José Bonifaz had something on his mind.

I said, 'We'll leave that for a bit. Tell me – have you mentioned this letter business to anyone else? Your mother or father, for instance.'

'No, sir. I live alone here. They are out in the country. A farm, you understand? I am here for my studies and to work.'

'What about your friends? You tell them?'

'No, sir.'

'Sure?'

'Yes, sir.' He stood up and wiggled his feet into his loose sandals. 'If you like I show you the Bar Tristan now.'

I moved a little nearer him, and I could see that he was nervous about something. His eyes were flicking as though they were full of grit.

I said, 'You usually walk around the town in your pyjamas?'

He looked down at his pyjama trousers and was genuinely surprised. Then he gave a nervous laugh and began to move towards the wardrobe.

I put a hand on his shoulder and stopped him.

'Tell me,' I said, 'who have you talked about it to?'

'But señor—'

'No buts, José – this is a serious matter. You have talked to someone, haven't you?'

He drew away from me. 'No, sir. Not me. I write to Mrs Stankowski and Mr Carver and I say nothing to anyone.'

For all I knew I could be on a wrong tack, but I had to take a chance on it. Something really was worrying José.

I said, 'You ever been in trouble with the police, José?'

'No, sir.' It was quite definite.

'You might be if you don't tell me the truth. This is a serious matter. After I've finished here I am going to the police. Once they know about it it won't be good for you if you haven't told the truth.'

I had him hooked and wriggling. Getting mixed up with the police had his black eyes blinking fast and his birdy head bobbing about with apprehension.

'You have talked to someone, haven't you?'

'No, sir. Not me. That is . . . well, someone talked to me.' Then cupidity came in with a rush. 'If I say, it is still mine, the pesetas?'

'If you say, you might get some more. As much, for instance, as anyone else has promised you.'

The relief on his face was like sunrise.

He ran the edge of his tongue round his lips and said, 'He say that I get five thousand pesetas.'

'Who did?'

'This man. He comes to the supermarket one evenings two-three days ago and ask me if I find anything in beer bottles. I tell him about the letters. I get five thousand pesetas if I let him know if anyone comes to talk about it. He was here again yesterday to see if I hear something.'

'Who was he? Did he give a name?'

I could see what had happened. Some time – wherever Wilkins was being held – Thérèse or Paulet had discovered one of her letters in a bottle. She would never have been content with writing two. It was common sense to run a check at the supermarket to see if any previous letters had got through. At the moment, now that they knew about the letters, they could be very worried – maybe even thinking of moving on. The Stankowski one they could discount, but not mine altogether.

'He is a young man called Mimo. Just Mimo. Five thousand pesetas he promised to let him know—'

'How were you to let him know?' My dislike for José was thickening. He worried too much about pesetas.

'At midday always he is in the Bar Tristan. But any other time, if anyone comes inquiring I let him know by going to his flat or phoning—'

'Where's the flat? Here, in San Antonio?'

'Yes. I shall show you, no?'

'No – just give me the address and tell me how to get there.'

He did, explaining that it was only a few minutes' walk away. I didn't think that Duchêne would risk holding Dawson and Wilkins in a town flat. They were probably out in the country somewhere. Mimo would be the anchor man at the town end. I couldn't wait to have a chat with Mimo and I was glad that I had the 9 mm Browning in my pocket.

José said, 'What about the pesetas, señor?'

'You'll get them – just so long as you keep your mouth shut. You haven't seen me. Is that clear?'

'Yes, sir. But you come back with the pesetas. This other man I don't like. His promises I don't trust. For that I tell you all this gladly.'

If it were just a question of money sense, the boy would go far. 'Somebody will be back,' I said.

I turned and went and he was counting the wad of notes before I reached the door.

The small girl was still crooning over her doll on the stairs. I gave her a friendly pat on the head, happy at the thought of seeing Mimo, hoping that this was the break I wanted to lead me to Dawson and Wilkins. The old man was still sitting on the doorstep, but he didn't get a pat. After the gloom of the house the sunlight hit me like a photo-flash and I damned nearly tripped over him.

I went up the street, blinking like an owl. Flat six, Casa Alcina, Mimo. For a while I wondered if I ought to go and get Olaf to help me. Then I decided against it. They might be pulling out fast, at this moment even. They must have had a bad moment when they found out about the letters. Suddenly the cold thought hit me that they might have done something about Wilkins there and then. I pushed it from my mind.

Casa Alcina was in a small square on the hill at the north end of the town. The square was like so many squares in booming Mediterranean towns, new apartment blocks were going up and old houses were coming down and the air was gritty with cement and plaster dust. Casa Alcina was an old block, probably due to come down soon. There were a couple of small vans parked outside. The hallway was bare of any furnishing, and there was an ancient self-service lift that creaked upwards, protest-ing. I got out on a small stone landing which had two doors. One was half open to show a collection of buckets and brooms. The other door was shut. The number '6' was painted on it in white. I took out the Browning and listened against the door. There was no sound from inside. It was getting on for three o'clock. Mimo would not be in the Bar Tristan. He might be having a quiet siesta; though I didn't see Mimo as the siesta type. I put my fingers on the door handle and tried it gently. The door was unlocked.

I went in quietly, slipping round the door, gun and shoulder first.

It was a big room, with wide windows on the far side that opened to a narrow, railed balcony. There was a big settee against one wall, a couple of armchairs, and a low table against another wall with glasses and bottles on it. An open door to the side of the table showed a small corridor with two doors opening off it, probably bedrooms. The air was thick with tobacco smoke and there was another smell, too, familiar to me, mixed up with it. And the reason for the other smell was clear before my eyes.

I just stood inside the door and stared. It wasn't the kind of scene you want to walk into more than once in your life. Pelegrina was lying on the settee in his shirt and trousers and his big head was lolling awkwardly towards me. There was a bullet wound just above his right temple. Never again in his life would he try and touch his daughter for money. On the floor, a little way from the settee, was Mimo. He was lying flat on his face and I couldn't see any mark on him. But blood had seeped on to the polished boards near his right shoulder and from the way he lay I knew that he would never whistle 'Winchester Cathedral' happily to himself again.

Sitting in an armchair by the low table was Freeman. He was wearing a grey linen suit. He had his legs crossed and was resting his arms on them and supporting his head in the pose of Rodin's 'The Thinker'. He was thinking too. So absorbed was he that he took no notice of me. A cigarette burned in the corner of his mouth and there was an ashtray full of stubs on the arm of the chair. On the floor at his feet lay an automatic pistol fitted with a silencer.

Keeping him covered I pushed the door shut behind me. The noise made him look round. He stared at me blankly. Then he frowned, ran his hand through his brown hair, and shook his head. All the colour had gone from his tanned face and he looked about ten years older.

I said, 'Just sit where you are.'

I crossed the room and picked up the automatic pistol from the floor. It was a .22 Star, made in Spain. Freeman made no move to stir from his chair. But his head followed me round, the brown eyes dull under their shaggy brows. I felt sorry for him, but I felt sorrier for poor old Pelegrina. From the thin black cord round his neck I saw his monocle dangling over the side of the settee. I found a bottle of gin, poured a fat slug into a glass, and took it to Freeman. He took it into his hands but didn't drink. Clearly he was in a state of shock and had been for some time. He was a dreamer all right, but this time he had dreamed himself into a nightmare. He and Pelegrina, a couple of ambitious incompetents, who between them had dreamed up a lot of trouble for a lot of people. When something went wrong, they went to pieces. Pelegrina had gone for good. I started to try and put Freeman together again.

'Is there anyone else in this flat?'

He shook his head. He raised the glass and drank, shivered against the raw spirit and then fetched a big sigh.

'When did it happen?' I asked.

I could see him pulling himself together. He wasn't alone now. He had company. Even sympathy. Perhaps a shoulder to cry on. In trouble, that's what his kind always needed.

'When?' I repeated.

'About an hour ago . . . that bastard . . .' he broke off, nodding at Mimo.

I began to take him along gently.

'Is this where you've been hiding up all the time?'

'Yes.'

'Where are the others, Dawson, and Wilkins?'

He straightened up, stubbed out his cigarette, and began to fiddle for another in a crumpled packet.

'I don't know. Somewhere out in the country. Mimo knew, but we didn't. God, this is a mess. What am I to do?'

Good form. He was coming back fast enough to start thinking about himself.

'We'll fix that later. What happened here?'

He looked at me. 'You think you can fix something?'

I held down my anger. Some people! Jose with his mind only on pesetas. And now Freeman full of pity for himself and wanting an out.

'Could be,' I said. 'But what happened?'

'It was all so bloody fast. Leon and I were sitting here. We haven't been out much . . . not together ever. We were waiting for Mimo to come back.'

'From the Bar Tristan?'

'No, no – from wherever they are. He's got a little van, takes supplies out. There'd been some talk of our moving on—'

'Just you and Pelegrina?'

'Yes.' He finished what was left of the gin. I went and sat on the edge of the other armchair. 'They were fixing us with passports and making all the final credit arrangements for the rest of our money. Then this swine walks in. Grinning, he was. The bastard, grinning. And he let Pelegrina have it without a word, and then he turned on me. I was sitting here. He just stood there and grinned. I couldn't move and he just grinned and took his time and then he fired. By some damned miracle he missed me. Right by my cheek and that made me jump. I went for him, full length for his legs, and I got the swine . . . I don't know what happened then. We were all over the place . . . I never did get the gun from him but I got my hand on it, over his, and then suddenly it went off and he flopped out . . . like he is now. Hell, what a mess! What a terrible mess!'

I said, 'You were both fools ever to think they'd let you off the hook on this kind of deal. The only reason they didn't finish you off at the Villa La Sunata was that it would have caused publicity and that they don't want. But now they're really worried and have to move fast. They don't want you around any longer.'

'But they paid me some money and let me write to Jane.'

'Of course they did. That was to keep you sweet, suspecting nothing until they were ready to deal with you. Do you think ten thousand pounds meant anything to them? How often did Mimo go out to that place?'

'Every other day. Look, what am I going to do? It's lucky no one heard the rumpus up here. Poor old Leon . . . God . . . But what am I going to do? I haven't got a passport or any money and I—'

'Can you walk?'

He looked at me blankly.

'What do you mean?'

'Find yourself a taxi and go to Ibiza airport. In the bar there you'll find a big Swede – Olaf. Tell him the score and then do exactly as he says. I'll be back there later. Is there a woman or anyone who comes in to clean this place?'

'No.'

'Then leave the door-key. Go on, get moving, the fresh air will do you good.'

He stood up, took a couple of weak steps as though he had been in bed for a month, and then stopped. 'You really think something can be fixed up for me?'

I was angry then. 'Look, you started all this. A lot of nasty things have happened. And a lot more could happen. Pelegrina's dead. You're breathing and standing. Just be bloody well content with that for the moment.'

He went and I didn't feel sorry for him, but I knew that if I could I would fix something up for him, but the fixing would depend on Sutcliffe and very much on what happened about Dawson and Wilkins. If Wilkins didn't come out of this walking, then I wouldn't be caring a damn about fixing anyone up, least of all Freeman.

I turned Mimo over and went through his clothes. He had nothing on him that helped me . . . just money, cigarettes, and a bunch of keys. I went through the three bedrooms. There was nothing there. Nothing anywhere.

I came back into the room and, although it was the wrong time of day, made myself a stiff drink and I sat in Freeman's chair and did a Rodin thinking act for myself. Mimo had a van outside, obviously one of the two which I had seen parked there. He made a trip every other day out into the country with supplies. Today he had come back with orders to polish off Freeman and Pelegrina and to abandon the flat. He wasn't going to go on living here with a couple of bodies. He would have turned the key on them and it might have been a week before they were discovered. It all might have worked, too, if he hadn't spent just a few seconds too long gloating over the pleasure of having Freeman at his mercy. Gloating had made his hand shake a little.

I wondered what other orders he had had. To return to the place in the country, or to take off on his own? Maybe even to run a final check on José Bonifaz to see whether anyone had turned up. They weren't going to risk that lead in to them not being covered. José had been given the promise of five thousand pesetas if the moment anyone turned up he got in touch with Mimo either at the Bar Tristan or the flat or . . . something cut into my thoughts sharply. I stared at the dead Mimo, frowning. What was it? Something was asking to be recognized. José had been told . . . José had to be able to get on to Mimo the moment anyone turned up, either at the Bar Tristan, or at the flat, or . . . what about if he were away on one of his supply visits? Freeman or Pelegrina at the flat would be no help. They probably hadn't known about the beer-bottle messages. If Mimo were away a lot of valuable time could be lost . . . Then it came. I saw José standing in front of me, restless dark eyes full of their peseta look . . . I stood up quickly. One should listen carefully to what people say. Certainly in my profession. A quick, impatient interruption could kill valuable information. I should have learned that lesson by now.

I went back and checked the bedrooms, the kitchen, the bathroom, and then the big room. I didn't find what I was looking for.

I went out, locked the flat door, and ran down the stairs. It was quicker than the creaking old lift. With me I had Mimo's bunch of keys. Only one van was standing outside now. It was a little grey Fiat, covered in dust. I slipped into the driving seat and tried Mimo's keys. The car ignition key on the ring fitted. I glanced in the back. It was empty. There was nothing in the dash pockets either.

I started the motor, fiddled with the gear, stalled the engine first time, and then got away. I was full of impatience and went down a one-way street against the traffic to a chorus of horns and shouts. A few minutes later I pulled up outside the butcher's shop in the Paseo Maritimo.

The old man was still sitting on the doorstep of No 7, but he had slid two feet to the right to catch the moving shade. The little girl had gone from the top of the stairs. I hoped that José had not gone from his room. Chasing José around San Antonio at this moment would send up my blood pressure.

José was still there, knees up, reading on the bed. The can of peaches, now empty, lay on its side by the bed. As I shut the door, he sat up quickly and gave me a big, hungry smile.

'You bring the other pesetas, sir?'

'They're coming,' I said, 'in a special gift wallet, red morocco leather with gold edges. Just repeat to me the instructions this man Mimo gave you.'

'But I tell you, señor, already.'

'Tell me again. The moment anyone came here about the letters, what were you to do?'

'I was to let this man know. Either to find him at midday in the Bar Tristan; or other time at his flat.'

'But you said something about telephoning. I'm sure you did.'

'Yes, sir. This he told me yesterday. If he's not at the flat I am to telephone.'

'Since there's no telephone in the flat, it must be somewhere else you had to telephone.'

He looked puzzled. 'Yes, I suppose so. I not think about it much. Just he gives me the number.'

'Fish it out.'

'Please?'

'Let's have it, the number.'

He stood up and went to the book-crowded table by the window and came back with a piece of paper. On it was written *San José* 21.

'Where's San José?'

'It's a little town, village . . . about six miles from here, sir.'

'José,' I said, 'you get dressed and come down to the Post Office with me. I want the address that belongs to that telephone number. It'll be a farm or a villa of some kind. You get that, and then show me on the map where it is and we'll make it five thousand five hundred pesetas.'

He was at the wardrobe for his clothes almost before I had finished speaking.

I waited impatiently. But at the same time I was dead against impatience. I had almost missed this vital piece of information in my earlier impatience to get to Mimo's telephoneless flat.

I must say that, with the firm promise of pesetas behind him, José was a quick worker. I dropped him at the Post Office, parked the car, and went for a beer in a café a few doors down. Before I had finished it he was back. But before he was back I had done some hard worrying about Mimo and the telephone number. He hadn't given it to José until yesterday. That could have meant that up till then it was a number which Duchêne would not have wanted José to have, but would want him to have to cover a minimum period of emergency. Once they knew the letters had gone off I was certain they would take no risks, certain that they would immediately set about changing their hiding place. It was my guess that now, with all arrangements poised for a move, with Mimo coming back this day to tidy up the Freeman-Pelegrina embarrassment, that the number had been given to José so that he could send a direct warning to them even while they were on the brink of a move. Wilkins getting the letters out had really put them in a spot. And now I was in a spot because the last thing I wanted was for them to move until I could get Manston and company on to them.

José came back, armed with a map of the island. San José 21 was the number of the Villa Las Vedras, listed under the name of Barja – that could have been a long-standing cover for Duchêne or the name of an owner that they had rented the place from. José knew the villa. It was in the south-west corner of the island, about half a mile from the sea. It was about eight miles from San José along a dirt road that ran through pine woods. Beyond the villa was a headland and just off shore from it a group of conical-shaped islands known as the Vedras, from which the villa took its name. I made him draw me a sketch map of the road out and also of the layout of the villa and the ground around it as far as he could remember these. By the time this was done I knew what

I was going to do. I got some notepaper from the café and wrote a letter to Olaf which José was to take to the airport. José was to tell Olaf all he had told me. In the letter I gave Olaf Sutcliffe's unlisted London number and told him to put a call through to him, if Manston hadn't arrived, and give him the facts. He was also to get in touch with the British Consul in Ibiza and pass him the code word Python and any information he asked for which he could give. He was also – though I didn't say anything about this to José – to keep José with him. It was just possible that José, peseta-lust in his heart, might take it into his head to phone the Villa Las Vedras and make a little extra for himself. For myself, I said I was going out to have a look at the villa and to keep an eye on things. At least if they did move while I was around, I might have a chance to follow them or even whip Wilkins, if not Dawson, away. All I knew was that I had to get out there. I had a feeling that time was running out fast. Wilkins' letter had helped me, but it had also, for certain, decided Duchêne upon a fast move.

It didn't take me long to get to San José. The road went inland, rising all the time until it reached the village that lay in a saddle between two hills. It was the usual affair, a church, a bar, a few shops, a tourist place for buying pottery and iron work, and a lot of old men sitting around watching time and the traffic pass.

I had José's sketch map on the seat alongside me. Just beyond the village I found the turning off to the right. A main sign read Cabo Llentrisca – that was the headland José had mentioned – and nailed under it were the name boards of the various houses and farms along the route. One of them read – Villa Las Vedras.

It was a dirt road, built on a switchback pattern and, although I had to go slowly, I raised a great trail of dust behind me. I wasn't pleased about that. Once I was in sight of the house it might attract attention. Duchêne wasn't the kind not to have someone watching the road up to the villa. At first the road was bordered with little patches of maize, tomatoes, red fields of olive and almond trees, with here and there a peasant's single-floored house. After about a couple of miles it began to rise slowly, through pine woods and hillside covered in tall, dark-green scrub. Now and again there would be a turning to left or right with a house sign on it. After a while the turnings grew less frequent until finally the only sign left on the direct road was that of the Villa Las Vedras. I stopped and consulted José's map. A mile before the villa was reached he had said there was a small cottage. Half a mile after the cottage I would find a gate across the road, which marked the beginning of the Las Vedras property. From just beyond the cottage I meant to make the rest of the journey on foot. Anyone who wanted to come out of the villa had three routes. Either along this road, or out along the headland and down to the sea – or by an airlift. To a man like Duchêne any of these could be arranged. He had behind him any facility he liked to call on.

I found the cottage. It stood up off the road, door shut, windows boarded up. Behind it ran the telephone wire for the villa, strung out on short poles through the pine trees. I went about four hundred yards past it and then, as the ground began to rise sharply, I pulled off the road and ran the van into the cover of some scrub.

As I got out the air was full of the crazy fiddling of cicadas and the whine of a jet making a half-circle overhead to go in to land at Ibiza airport twenty miles away. I set out through the trees, keeping away from the road, but following the line of telegraph poles. After fifteen minutes I was running with sweat and half-deafened by cicadas. Twenty minutes after that I came panting up a hillside and out on to the edge of a small bluff that gave me a view which would have sent a tourist reaching for his Instamatic.

Ahead of me the ground sloped down gently through scrub, umbrella pine, and low oaks to a long hollow into which snaked the dirt road to end at the Villa Las Vedras. It was a long, low white building with flat roofs that looked as though it might have been converted from an old farm or group of cottages. Beyond the villa the ground rose to the beginning of the Cabo Llentrisca, a great block of headland thrusting out to the sea. Beyond that was a wide sun-dazzle of sea with away to the right the sharp, green sugar-loaf shapes of the Vedras lying about a mile off shore. To the left, just a hazy outline on the horizon, was the island of Formentera. Farther left, almost lost in the haze, I could see the houses clustered on the Citadel hill in Ibiza itself. I gave the view little attention. The villa held all my interest.

I worked around the side of the bluff for a while, keeping in the cover of the trees, then sat down, lit a cigarette to parch up my throat more, and studied it. There was a courtyard in front of the house and what looked like a wellhead to one side. Near this stood a large black saloon car. At a guess I thought it might be a Mercedes. I wished I had provided myself with field glasses. I wished so even more a few moments later because two men – I couldn't identify them – came out of the house and got into the car. It swung round and came back along the dirt road. For a moment I panicked, wondering if Wilkins and Dawson (or just Dawson) were already in the car and this was the take off. The road was away to my right. I got up and raced through the trees and came out just above the road in time to see the dust cloud trailing behind the car as it came slowly up the climb towards me. I threw myself down behind a myrtle bush.

The car came by me and I had a clear view of the two men in it. There was no one else. One was Paulet and the other was Duchêne. They went by me and I lay there and let their dust settle on me. At that moment I didn't realize how true that comment was to be. You should never let anybody's dust settle on you.

THIRTEEN

The Door is Closed

Life is full of unpleasant surprises. Half of them, with a little concentrated thought and circumspection, need never arise. But some there is just no way of avoiding unless you are the absolute master of circumstance – which, unfortunately, no man is. Some people, of course, just ask for it because right from the start they are underequipped. Like Freeman and Pelegrina. It was all very well for Browning to preach that 'a man's reach should exceed his grasp, or what's a heaven for?' Most of us are short-armed and have weak fingers, and the minds to match. Some of us, to stir up the metaphors a bit, just see only the wood and not the trees. That was me.

But long before I came to give myself this homily, I had had another crisis of thought. Seeing Duchêne and Paulet motoring away down the road, chatting away and smoking, Duchêne still favouring his Swedish cigar jobs, gave the feeling that clearly they were not evacuating the villa . . . certainly not for some hours. Dawson, certainly, and, I prayed, Wilkins too, would be there. Well guarded. But I had a dirty feeling that Duchêne and Paulet might be on their way to San Antonio – maybe because they hadn't had any message from Mimo confirming he had wiped out Freeman and Pelegrina, or maybe alarmed because he had not returned. I had a lot of thoughts along these lines and none of them were very comforting. It all boiled down to what I should do. I could either go ahead to the villa and do a one-man rescuing job against whatever odds there were there, or I could go back and get Olaf and we could tackle it together, or I could go back and rely on Manston arriving before nightfall. He mightn't be able to get here himself but he would certainly have all the weight in the world to get Madrid on the phone and have the Spanish police in Ibiza and San Antonio under instructions in a very short time. In fact that was what he would have to do. Unless something went wrong between Sutcliffe and the Prime Minister and a change of policy was vetoed. My interest was Wilkins, then Dawson. What was the best thing to do? In the end I decided to go back, get Olaf and go to the Spanish police. If they hadn't received instructions I hoped that, with José as interpreter, and with a backing from the British Consul, I could get some action within the next six hours. I still think it was the right decision. In fact it was. But it didn't turn out like that. That's what I mean about life being full of unpleasant surprises. Seeing Paulet and Duchêne go by together, I should – Browning again – have been 'stung by the splendour of a sudden thought'. I was just stung.

I went back to the van, hidden in the scrub off the road, determined in my mind what to do. I got in, mopped my sweating face with my handkerchief, and then half-twisted to get my hand in my trouser pocket for Mimo's keys. The movement made me cock my head to one side so that I could see, sitting in the shadowed back of the van, François Paulet. He had a Colt .45 levelled at me, and he was smiling.

I said, 'Hell!'

He reached over with his free hand and took my Browning from the pocket of my jacket which I had slung over the back of the spare seat. At that moment I saw Duchêne coming down through the pines. He, too, was carrying a gun.

Sadness in his voice, but a twinkle in his eye, Paulet said, 'It is a pity that one cannot think of everything, no?'

'It's the climate,' I said. 'The brain goes soft with the heat.'

'The little cottage back along the road, *mon ami*, is not empty. Peter Brown is there, and he reports anything that passes by telephone to the villa. *Ca vous explique tout?*'

'We all make our mistakes. But just tell me, is Wilkins up there with Dawson?'

He nodded and grinned. 'She is. She has been a lot of trouble. *Quelle femme!* In our organization we could have made a great operator of her – once her brain had been washed clear of moral scruples.'

At the window Duchêne said, 'Get out, and behave yourself.'

I did as I was told. They marched me back through the trees to the cottage. The black saloon was there. It was a Mercedes. Peter Brown, in blue canvas trousers, a white shirt, and silk scarf at his neck, opened the back door for me.

'Mr Carver. Nice to see you again.'

'I wish you hadn't.'

'I'm sure you do.'

Duchêne said nothing. He got in alongside of me and Paulet drove. Within five minutes or so we were at the villa.

The front was covered with plumbago and bougainvillaea and there were large red earthenware urns full of geraniums and petunias, flourishing in a way that would have delighted my sister. I was greeted by Saraband Two. She stood on the low patio by the front door, wearing gardening gloves and holding a watering can. She had a wide-brimmed straw hat, a bit like the jobs they used to put on horses, a floppy blue dress, and rope-soled alpagatas. Her pleasant aunty face warmed at the sight of me and she didn't look as though she had a worry in the world except greenfly and drought.

'Mr Carver,' she said, 'how nice. We thought you were dead.'

'That was the official bulletin.'

'It just proves,' she said, standing aside for me to pass, 'that you can't believe everything you read in newspapers. But I mean the second time.'

'Your girl Gloriana made a mess of it.'

'Indeed.'

I couldn't tell whether she was surprised or not.

They took me through a cool, stone-flagged passage into a wide, long room with a wooden floor and a wooden ceiling. Clearly it had been an old farmhouse. The furniture was mostly cane stuff for coolness and there were gay green, gold, and red tiles let into the walls. Through the window, between a clump of cactus, I could see the beginning of the rise to the headland. I flopped into a chair. Duchêne shut the door. Paulet went to a sideboard and said, 'Beer?'

I nodded.

Aunt Saraband took off her gloves and her hat, patted her neat greyish hair tidy and then brought a cigarette box and offered it to me. I lit up and said nothing.

Paulet brought me a glass of beer. It was all very friendly and controlled and I wondered how the real business would be.

Aunt Saraband, who clearly outranked Duchêne, opened the proceedings.

'Would you like to tell the story freely or do we have to be unpleasant, Mr Carver?'

She said it with her back to me, as she fussed at a vase of some short-stemmed lily flowers on a table.

'I hate unpleasantness.'

'Good.'

'Monsieur Carvay is always reasonable,' said Paulet. Trust him to put in a good word for me.

Aunt Saraband turned and smiled. I was being a good nephew.

'I suppose it started with the beer bottles?'

'Yes.' I'd decided to stick to truth as far as I could. They could be told a lot of things which were no longer important.

She sat down, crossed her legs, and pulled her dress down. There was no need, it was already only a foot from the ground. 'Your Miss Wilkins is a very fine and determined character. Too much so.'

'She's an excellent secretary too – and is very much missed at the office.'

'We shall miss her too. She has kept everyone on their toes here. She has twice tried to escape. That was after we found out about the beer bottles.'

'When I gave her exercise one day,' said Paulet, without rancour, 'she hit me with a large stone and ran. You know she is a fast runner. *Mon Dieu*, we had trouble with her. Since then she has no exercise.'

'Perhaps', said Aunt Saraband, 'we should let Mr Carver get on with his story, step by step.'

Looking at the table with the flower vase, I said, 'Those are new to me, those flowers.'

'Sand lilies,' said Aunt Saraband. 'And don't change the subject. I presume you received the letter from José Bonifaz?'

'There's a lad who should go far. Show him a peseta—'

Paulet moved, with that swiftness some big men have, and the flat of his hand slammed across my face. I blinked and my eyes watered.

'Of course, there's nothing personal in that,' I said.

'No, *mon ami,*' he said, as he stood over me, and he slammed me again.

'Enough, François,' said Aunt Saraband. He went back to his chair. She looked speculatively at me for a moment or two and then said, 'Mr Carver, we haven't much time to bother about you or Miss Wilkins. I am sure you realize that we are not staying here. In fact we leave at six o'clock tomorrow morning. You, of course, and Miss Wilkins, will be left behind.'

'In no state to talk,' said Duchêne with his prim, irritable voice.

'I don't feel like talking now,' I said. 'But perhaps if you gave me a whisky' – I looked at my watch, it was half past six – 'I might open up a bit.'

To my surprise Aunt Saraband nodded at Paulet and he got up to do the necessary. I saw the bottle. It was a cheap Spanish whisky fake. Surprisingly it didn't taste too bad, if you didn't think of it as whisky.

'What happened to Mimo?' asked Duchêne.

'José gave me his flat address. I walked in on a pretty tableau. Mimo standing over two dead bodies. He tried to make mine the third. I had to shoot him.'

Not on any of the three faces watching me was there a flicker of doubt, surprise, or even disapproval. They just looked at me and showed nothing.

'I locked the door,' I said, 'and left them for the charlady to find sometime. I found this place, of course, from the telephone number that Mimo gave José. It cost me five thousand pesetas. I hope it's going to be worth it. And thinking it over, why the hell should I tell you anything? You're not going to do anything for me and Wilkins in return except put us out of circulation. I call that a no-deal.' I took a gulp of the whisky. It tasted worse the second time.

'We would make a deal gladly with you, Mr Carver,' said Duchêne, 'if you had anything to offer.'

'Haven't I?'

'What?' It was Aunt Saraband.

'You want to know how close on your heels Sutcliffe and his merry men are. For all you know he may be coming up the dirt track now – or he may know nothing.' I smiled, though it took a little effort with my sore cheek. 'You really are in a spot. You're going to have to worry through life until six o'clock tomorrow morning, nearly twelve hours. And don't try to tell me you could go now, because if you could you wouldn't be wasting time on me at this moment. You'd be packing. What are you doing – going over the cliffside at dawn to make a rendezvous at sea with some Baltic or Black Sea timber boat? Or perhaps a quick helicopter lift out to sea to meet the *Sveti* on her way back – detouring, of course – from Algiers? So, you've got twelve hours to pass, worrying. Either I've passed the word to Manston or I haven't. What am I offered to tell you the truth?'

I looked around them. They looked back at me. They didn't have a thing to offer and they knew it. They weren't going to let Wilkins go and they weren't going to let me go.

Aunt Saraband stood up. 'You're quite right, Mr Carver. There is no offer. There is no need of one.'

'I could get the truth out of him,' said Paulet.

'It would take some time,' I said, 'and you would still have no guarantee that it was the truth.'

'We don't need any guarantee, Mr Carver,' said Aunt Saraband. 'In a situation like this the obvious line to take is that you have passed all or some of your information back. And – there's no point in denying it – since we cannot leave here until tomorrow, we must take the obvious precautions.'

'To stop anyone coming to the house?'

'Quite. We can hold out here for more than twelve hours if necessary, particularly as most of that time it will be dark. At first light we shall be lifted out by helicopter.' She spoke calmly, but underneath she had to be worried. The helicopter lift was all laid on and they clearly had no way of communication that would bring it earlier than first light. But her biggest worry was that if things did go wrong the really big boys of her service would be handing out painful demerit marks.

She moved to the door, paused and looked back at me. It was the sad, hurt look of an aunt whose nephew, loved and spoiled, had wounded her by stealing from her purse.

'We entered', she said, 'into an honourable contract with your government. They have broken the contract. It could have very serious consequences, particularly for young Mr Dawson.'

'People', I said, 'are always letting other people down. I gave up crying about it long ago. Anyway, a contract is only as honourable as the people who make it. In my book you and Sutcliffe are non-starters.'

She smiled then. 'Considering your position, you are remarkably provocative.'

'You've only got to shoot me to make an end of it.'

But I knew she wouldn't. Not yet. If a posse of tricorn-hatted Spanish police came roaring up in the night she wanted to have hostages, a couple of good cards in her hand to play with until the helicopter came. I knew it, and she knew that I knew it. Aunt Saraband was no fool.

'Put him up with the others,' she said, and she went out. Paulet and Duchêne moved towards me and formed a prisoner's escort.

They were in a long upstairs room, directly over, I judged, the room in which I had been interviewed. It had two camp beds in it, discreetly screened from one another by a couple of sheets hung on a wire. There was a table and a few odd chairs, and some gay rugs on the bare wood plank floor. Against the far wall was an old-fashioned wash-hand stand. There was a small window, set low in the wall, but no light came through it because it had been boarded up outside, and there were bars – their ends set in the stone on the inside. The light in the room came from two oil lamps. The atmosphere was warm and thick.

Bill Dawson sat on the end of one bed. He was in shirt sleeves and trousers. He had a square, freckled face and a mouth that smiled easily, and he wore thick, horn-rimmed glasses. He might have been a first-class geologist, but it soon became clear that he was a young man who took people on trust too easily. He had to be to be where he was. The first thing he said, after the introductions was, 'Have you got a British cigarette on you?'

I tossed him my packet. He was easily satisfied. Wilkins less so. She stood by the table, rusty hair a little untidy, a cold glint in her blue eyes, and marked the silence between us with an occasional sniff.

'You've caught another cold,' I said sympathetically.

'It's the same one,' she said, and fished in the pocket of her cardigan for a handkerchief.

'Hilda's like me,' said Dawson. 'Once I get one it takes ages to go.'

I looked around. 'Do you think they'll bring another bed up for me?'

'It's the least of our problems,' said Wilkins. She sat down on a chair, and went on, 'I might have known that you would make a mess of things. We don't want you here. You're just another complication.'

'Nice welcome for a rescuing knight.'

'What Hilda means', said Dawson, 'is that there's a motor scooter in their garage. But it only takes two. One pillion.'

'You've got it all fixed?' I really was surprised.

'Hilda', said Dawson, 'has been wonderful.'

'She always is.' I turned to her and, believe me, I really was anxious to get back into her favour. 'Your beer-bottle message worked. But they got wise to it.'

'And naturally,' said Wilkins stiffly, 'you didn't go straight to a set of responsible people – but you had to come here on your own.'

'There were complications.'

'There always are with you.'

'You want to hear the form or just go on grumbling?'

'The form is all fixed,' said Dawson. 'By the way, what happened to old Freeman? They really killed him, did they? Such a nice chap.'

I said, 'Don't let's bother about Freeman. We have to think about us.'

'He was my friend,' said Dawson. 'We had some good times together.'

I made no comment.

Wilkins said, 'Where's Olaf?'

'At the airport. You're on Ibiza.'

'Does he know you're out here? I mean, does he know about this place?'

'By now, yes.'

She sighed. 'That means he'll come charging out and upset things more. You shouldn't have let him know. He might get hurt.'

I said, 'For two people in deep trouble, you're not exactly wild about being rescued, it seems.'

'We've got it all arranged,' said Dawson. 'We could have managed nicely on our own.'

'You've only got until six tomorrow morning – and then you'll be lifted out of here by helicopter. You will. Wilkins and I will stay.' I gave her a straight look. She sniffed. But she knew what I meant. She was too intelligent not to be way ahead of me all the time.

Dawson, taking a deep draw at his first British cigarette for days, said, 'We can get out of here the moment they go to bed.'

'They won't go to bed tonight. They're not sure whether they're going to have a police visit. They'll be on guard all night.'

'You see', said Wilkins, 'how you've messed things up. We were going tonight.'

I sat down on a chair by the boarded window. I don't often feel chastened but I was now. A man works his fingers to the bone trying to set something up and when he's finished, or failed, he gets no thanks or sympathy.

'Perhaps', I said, 'you would tell me how you propose to get out? I know I've got no standing, of course, but it would be nice to know that you might let me follow you and run along behind this motor scooter.'

'Just try and take this seriously,' said Wilkins primly.

'A wonderful girl,' said Dawson. 'She's been a tower of strength. This I say sincerely.'

'Reminds me of your old dad,' I said. 'But let's have the facts.'

'How is my father?' asked Dawson. 'How's he taking all this?'

A little exasperated now because there seemed no way of pinning these two down to a straight line of talk, I said, 'He's reacted as any father would, and also with true British phlegm. For your safe return, he's agreed – no publicity, mind you – to a highly one-sided exchange of political prisoners between London and Moscow.'

His eyes popped. 'You mean we're being held by the Russians? I thought it was just for money. Didn't you, Hilda?'

She shifted uncomfortably. 'No, I didn't,' she said. 'But I didn't see that there was any point in bothering you with my conclusions. You've had a bad enough time.'

Firmly, I said, 'Just tell me, for God's sake, how you propose to get out of here?'

'There is', said Wilkins, 'no need to blaspheme.'

'It was Hilda's idea,' said Dawson. 'You see, when we first came here, they used to take us separately for exercise in the courtyard. Hilda saw this motor scooter in the garage, and she saw one of them use it once. The cars were no good because we guessed that they'd never leave the ignition keys in at night. So, one morning, Hilda hit the big French chap with a stone and ran.'

'It wasn't a very big stone,' said Wilkins.

'They chased after her,' said Dawson, 'but she got into the garage and shut herself in. It took them a little while to break down the door and get her out. That was clever of her, wasn't it? You see, they smashed up the bolts so that the door can't now be shut up at night. That means we can always get at the scooter.'

'Clever,' I said. And it was. I should have taken over the secretarial work long ago and let Wilkins do my job. 'But what good is access to the scooter out there if you can't get out of here?'

'Two birds with one stone,' said Dawson, beaming at Wilkins. 'You tell him, Hilda.'

'While I was in the garage,' said Wilkins, 'I took a pair of pliers from the work bench and hid them on me. They didn't search me when they brought me back here.'

I didn't ask her where she had hidden them on her because I didn't want more trouble from her. Instead, I said, 'He's right. You are wonderful. But don't forget I've been saying it for years.'

Dawson stood up, and pulled back one of the floor rugs. 'These boards, you see, are in short lengths and they're nailed to the rafter of the ceiling below. We've been working with the pliers for three days taking out the nails. All we have to do now is to lift out three boards and we can drop through into the room below.' He beamed at Wilkins and then at me. 'She thought of it all,' he said, replacing the rug.

At that moment the door opened and Paulet, gun in hand, came into the room, standing aside to let a woman with a tray pass him. I didn't have to be told that it was Thérèse. She was a neat, trim, dark-haired number of about forty, in a linen frock. She put the tray on the table, gave us a smile all round, held it a bit longer for me as she studied me and then said, '*Bon appetit.*'

She went out. Paulet gave us a nod and followed. The door was locked and bolted from the outside. I looked at the tray. There was a plate of cold meats and some salad stuff. I suddenly remembered that I had not eaten since early that morning and, instinctively, I said, 'Lord, am I hungry.'

Wilkins gave me a disapproving look.

The first part was easy. We waited until about half past four in the morning. In another hour it would begin to be light. During the night there had been a lot of movement and voices from the room below us. But now everything had been quiet for over an hour.

We pulled the rug back and Dawson and I between us carefully and quietly lifted out the first board. In our room we had put out the lamps so that no light would shine through into the room below. I put my head into the board space and looked down. The room below was in darkness.

We lifted out three more boards and then I went through, hanging by my hands and then dropping little more than a couple of feet to the floor below. Wilkins came next. I reached up and got her by the waist and eased her gently to the ground. Dawson followed.

We all three stood there in the darkness, listening.

There was no need for talk because we knew exactly what we were going to do. It was too risky to go out through the front of the house towards the headland and come down to the back of the garage. There was a longish slope down the entrance road from the garage until it started to rise towards the bluff where I had hidden. Dawson was to ride the scooter, Wilkins on the back, and free wheel away down the slope, not starting the engine until he was almost at the bottom. Once they were away I was going to take off into the scrub and pine woods and make my way back, staying clear of the road. But first of all I was going to climb one of the short telegraph poles and cut the line so that the party in the house could not get in touch with Peter Brown if he were still in the cottage on watch. Simple, straightforward, and it should have worked. Would have done with most people, even with someone like Aunt Saraband – if it had not been for the beer-bottle episode. They had slipped up on that one. Aunt Saraband and Duchêne never made the same kind of mistake twice. From that moment they had upped Wilkins' IQ rating to a level which would have made her president of Mensa for life.

I went towards the window, Wilkins and Dawson following. I was still four feet from it when two torches came on, pinning us where we stood.

Aunt Saraband's voice said quietly, 'Please don't move.'

For a moment I was tempted to ignore this and rush the window. But another voice, Paulet's, said, 'If you do, *mon ami*, Miss Wilkins will get the first shot.'

We stayed where we were. There was movement at the far end of the room, a match was struck, and suddenly the oil lamp flared. I saw that it was Duchêne lighting it. He turned away from the lamp after adjusting the wick and made a motion with his hand to us. 'Just come back into the centre of the room.'

We moved back, controlled by his hand which had a gun in it, shepherded, too, by the automatics that Aunt Saraband and Paulet held.

Aunt Saraband shook her head sadly at Wilkins.

'If we could have had you ten years ago, Miss Wilkins, and you'd been willing, we could have made you a great operator.'

I began to reach for my cigarettes.

'No, Mr Carver,' she went on, 'just keep your hands where we can see them.'

Paulet winked an eye at me over his big de Gaulle nose. 'You had a treasure there, Monsieur Carvay. Not until yesterday did it strike us. A woman, an ordinary woman, hits a man with a rock and runs . . . just runs.'

'But Miss Wilkins ran into the garage,' said Aunt Saraband. 'Why?'

'The answer comes,' said Paulet, 'when there is wood dust on the table there each morning, fallen from the ceiling boards. Thérèse, you know, is good housewife and very observant. So.'

Duchêne, who had been standing by almost, I thought from his face, disapproving of this exchange, said sharply, 'I think I hear it.'

They were all silent, listening. Far away I thought I could hear the sound of an engine.

'If it is,' said Aunt Saraband, 'Peter will put on the car lights.'

The noise grew louder, and then unmistakable. The helicopter was coming, coming in at the first faint streak of morning light. Another day was beginning – badly. I looked at Wilkins. Her face was expressionless. I wondered what she was thinking about? Her father in Greenwich, the socks she would not darn any more? Olaf, wanting to marry her, and she reluctant to leave her father? I knew what I was thinking . . . not of a hundred lost opportunities, the small, but bright change of life . . . not of never again the amber circle of whisky in a glass and the comforting hiss of the first siphon squirt of the day . . . no, I was just wondering how the hell I could get something into my hands that I could sling at the oil lamp. How do you get something into your hands when you have to keep them still and in the open?

Outside the helicopter racket increased. It was overhead now, circling. Peter Brown would have the Mercedes' lights on to monitor the pilot down to the courtyard. There would be a fast take-off with Dawson and Aunt Saraband's party and Wilkins and I would be left. Either here, in this room, or in the courtyard. No formalities, no bandage round the eyes, no last requests.

Of course, I'd made a mistake about Wilkins. She might have been thinking about her father and Olaf, but she was also thinking way above them, had to in the circumstances because the instinct for survival runs strong in all of us at such times, and in Wilkins probably stronger than most because it was backed by a natural obstinacy of character. She was to one side of me and a little ahead, a wing of rusty hair untidy over one ear, sensible old cardigan creased, sensible tweed skirt drooping a little unevenly to one side. To survive, risks had to be taken. Her hand came down sharply into the front pocket of her skirt. She whipped out the pliers she carried there and threw them awkwardly at the lamp.

She missed by a foot, but she hit the vase of sand lilies and the whole lot went crashing to the ground. Outside, the helicopter was down. The engine note had changed. Aunt Saraband's face showed her anger.

'You really are a dangerous woman.'

Wilkins looked at me. 'I'm sorry,' she said.

'Never mind,' I said. 'You tried. It's a good thought to go out on.'

Dawson said, 'It's funny about women not being able to throw straight.' Then to Aunt Saraband he went on, 'Look – I know now you're not going to do anything to me. But do you really have to . . . well, do anything to these two? It doesn't serve any useful purpose and I'm sure they would keep the secret. Please . . . why do something so unnecessary?'

Duchêne said, 'It has been decided not by us. We have orders.'

Aunt Saraband said, 'François, you take him out. Duchêne and I will do what is necessary here.' She looked at Wilkins. 'I am sorry. Personally I consider it unnecessary. I would trust you both, but unfortunately my employers haven't the first-hand knowledge of you that I have. To them you are just two people who could talk loosely and ruin this thing by creating publicity . . . bad publicity, for both sides.'

It was then that the oil lamp was shattered. Olaf did it. Though it was some time before the thing was sorted out in my mind because I was too busy going into action on the heels of a miracle.

There was the sound of a shot, the window glass crashed, and the oil lamp exploded in a brief flare of flame and then there was a grey gloom in the room, and the sound of a window being kicked in, frame shattered, as Olaf, a dark mountainous bulk, burst through.

I didn't wait to congratulate him. The edge of my right hand was already hitting out for the spot where I took Aunt Saraband's wrist to be. I got her inner elbow and heard the gun go to the floor. I heard Dawson shout, heard Olaf bellow, 'Hilda, this way!'

For a moment or two the room was a grey tangle of movements, noisy, with chairs going over and the sound of two shots. One of them fanned my neck and then I heard Duchêne roar, 'Stop shooting!' He was right. It was dangerous for both sides.

'I've got him!'

It was Paulet and briefly I saw him hurl himself at Olaf. Paulet, big, competent, and dangerous. Not the kind of man I would want hurled on me. But he had met his match. Olaf stretched out his giant arms, embraced him, crushed him, spun him round, picked him up, and threw him. Paulet hit the wall and dropped to the floor with a crash that shook the house.

I saw Olaf spin round and grab Wilkins. I kicked out at Aunt Saraband who was coming at me like a Kilkenny cat who was going to knock the English stuffing out of a London tom. I got her legs and she went down.

I picked up a gun from the floor and the next moment I was at the window with Dawson. We went through after Olaf and Wilkins in another minor explosion of glass and wood. Dawson fell and rolled over on the hard-baked ground. I jerked him up and we ran. I heard him sobbing and cursing to himself and he pulled back from me. I grabbed harder and kept him going. In the fall he had ricked his left ankle. Ahead of us in the growing dawn I saw Olaf running, pulling Wilkins along, heading up a small path that led to the headland.

As we crested the rise to the top of the headland plateau the sun began to lip the eastern edge of the sea away to our left. It was a good sunrise, as sunrises go, a fancy affair of orange and tangerine flame, with a high wash of slowly fading pearliness in the upper sky, and we had time to admire it because Dawson really had done something to his ankle. He could only just limp along.

Olaf said, 'We've got a mile and over to the end of the headland. Then a path to the beach. I've got a motorboat standing off.' He looked at Dawson. 'I carry you?'

Dawson shook his head.

'We've got to do something,' I said. 'Here comes the helicopter.'

It came up the wind, rising, crabbed around in a circle and found us. It came down to about two hundred feet and hung above us, the racket deafening.

Olaf fired a shot at it.

I said, 'Don't waste your shots.'

We made about two hundred yards as fast as we could with Dawson, the helicopter hanging over us. I couldn't see who was in it, but it was a Westland Whirlwind.

Wilkins looked back and said, 'They're coming.'

I looked round. Topping the headland crest now were Duchêne and Paulet and Peter Brown, running hard along the scrub-lined path towards us.

The path ahead of us twisted into a wide patch of scrub oak and pines, the trunks of the trees hidden some way up by a thick undergrowth of heath and myrtle. We were fifty yards into the trees when Dawson fell, pulling away from Olaf's great hand that held him.

'I carry him,' said Olaf. 'You cover us.'

He picked Dawson up and slung him over his big shoulders in a fireman's lift. I was puffed and blown. At the side of the path was a big notice on a pole. The best thing for me to do, I thought, was to get behind it and cover the path. I couldn't hold them up for long.

Ahead Olaf was trotting along slowly with Dawson. Wilkins stayed with me. 'Get going,' I said.

Overhead the helicopter clattered away like a crazy washing machine. She looked at me, tight-mouthed, eyes bright with anger at the indignity of it all. She shook her head.

'Have you got any matches on you?' she asked.

'No. A lighter. Don't tell me you're taking up smoking? Now get moving.'

She shook her head. Two hundred yards away I could see Paulet lumbering along.

'Look at the notice,' she said.

I did. It was Spanish and not much help to me. Something about *Cigarillos . . . Cuidado . . .*

'Lighter,' she insisted.

I fished in my pocket and gave it to her. She turned and ran along the path after Olaf and Dawson.

I got behind the notice and let off a warning shot at Paulet. I couldn't hit him at the range but I could stop his headlong rush. I did. He went off the path and I saw Duchêne and Peter Brown do the same behind him.

I fired another shot in their direction and then left the notice and sprinted up the path. As I did so the first acrid breath of smoke came wafting down on the wind to me. Then there was a spurt of flame ahead and just off the path. I got it then; the notice had been a fire warning.

I found Wilkins moving through the trees at right angles to the path, scrabbling up bunches of dried grass and scrub and lighting them from my lighter.

I didn't stop to tell her what a treasure she was. I was in there, grabbing tufts of last year's bracken and grass and helping to spread the line of flame. For a few moments the whole thing sulked and then suddenly there was a small whoof and the fire went away, racing and crackling down through the trees towards our pursuers.

On the path in the middle of the trees I saw Paulet suddenly stop. Then a great coil of smoke obscured him. A small pine suddenly went up like a Roman candle.

I swung round and made for Wilkins who was still spreading the line of fire.

'Enough,' I shouted, and grabbed her. We turned and ran, and the noise of the spreading fire behind us was music. If you really want a good blaze there is nothing like a sun-baked, scrub-and-pine-and-heath-packed Mediterranean headland . . . a pyromaniac's dream. In a few minutes the whole headland behind us was ablaze, leaping flames and great clouds of smoke barring the way against pursuit. Two days later, I was told, it was still smouldering.

And that was that. Except for a few minor details.

Duchêne, Paulet, and Peter Brown couldn't face it. But Aunt Saraband had a go. She was in the helicopter. It came down to fifty feet above us, and she hung out, gun in hand. I knew that now, knowing there was nothing to be saved of the grand design, she had to be full of old-maidish spite. She just wanted to hurt someone because she knew that when she reported back to Mr Semichastny she was going to be hurt.

She would have hurt someone, too, if it had not been for Freeman, coming fast up over the top of the cliff from the beach, hunting rifle in hand. He stopped and took a couple of pot shots. However bad he was at other things, he could shoot. One of the shots must have got the helicopter in a non-vulnerable spot. But it was enough. The pilot suddenly opted for discretion. The machine lifted, wheeled, and circled away.

After that there was the beach path down to the sea, and waiting a few yards out a motorboat with José Bonifaz at the tiller.

There were a few high points after that. I remember particularly Manston's fury because he had arrived at the airport to find no one there. No Olaf, no Freeman, no José.

It was José's lust for pesetas, of course, linked with Olaf's rum-whipped impatience to come to grips with the people who were holding his precious Wilkins, that had left Manston and company high and dry, without a single shred of information to work on.

José's parents lived in a small fishing village called Purriog, up the coast from the airport. One could go by sea to the Villa Las Vedras and his father would gladly hire Olaf a motorboat, and, yes, a hunting rifle. Olaf didn't stop to count the cost. They were off, Freeman dragged with them.

'Charging in,' said Manston, 'like a bull in a china shop. They could have spoiled everything.'

'They didn't,' I said. 'Anyway, don't let's argue about the way it should or should not have been handled. A man in love can only do what at

the moment he thinks is the right thing. And don't forget Wilkins'
MBE or OBE or whatever it is.'

He didn't.

José, not caring what it had all been about, went happily back to
San Antonio, loaded with pesetas. Spain will be hearing from him,
I'm sure.

Freeman got a discreet pardon and was ordered to leave the country
for good. I heard later that Jane Judd had joined him. Some women are
gluttons for punishment.

There was never any publicity, of course.

But there was Sutcliffe in his London flat, mild-mannered but still
disapproving of me. He handed me a letter from the Prime Minister
which thanked me for my services, but didn't invite me down to Chequers
for the weekend. Sutcliffe took the letter back and destroyed it.

I said, 'There's still the cheque for my services.'

'You'll get it.'

He pressed a wall switch and one of his modern paintings slid aside
and on a twenty-one-inch screen I had a view of Paulet and Duchêne
in the waiting room, shivering on the camp bed and looking miserable.
They were the only two they had managed to pick up.

'No music?' I asked. 'No brass bands?'

'Wagner. They hate it. But the sound is switched off up here. I hate
it too.'

I said, 'It's a pity Perkins turned out not to be a traitor. I'd like to see
him down there.'

And then it was back to work – without Wilkins because she was
still off with Olaf catching up on her holiday.

Some days later, going back to my flat, after a hard day repeatedly
turning the basset hound off my desk chair, I found Mrs Meld hanging
over the gate enjoying the summer evening.

'Nice evening, Mr Carver.'

'Splendid, Mrs Meld.'

'You look a bit baggy under the eyes these days.'

'I have worries at the office.'

'You got one waiting for you up in the flat.'

I went up and into the flat. As I stood at the door, a voice shrieked, 'Shut that bloody door! Shut that bloody door!'

It was Alfred in his cage on the table, a note from Miggs pinned to it: 'This bastard is losing me business, so back to you. M.'

Alfred carolled, 'Bloody! Bloody!'

I ignored him and went into the bedroom. Letta was lying on the bed reading *Vogue*.

I said, 'I thought you were in Athens?'

She smiled and said, 'I was. But now I've got two free weeks. If I stay here, though, you'll have to choose between me and that bird.'

I said, 'Friend of mine keeps a pub round the corner. He'll love him.'

'Good.'

She sat up, her dark hair taking the evening sun through the window in a hundred burnished points.

I said, 'Isn't it a bit early in the evening only to be wearing a copy of *Vogue*?'

She dropped it to the floor.

Outside, Alfred cried, 'Shut that bloody door!'

I did.